DEATH
ON THE
BEACH

STEPH
BROADRIBB

THOMAS & MERCER

Published by Thomas & Mercer, Seattle

www.apub.com

Amazon, the Amazon logo, and Thomas & Mercer are trademarks of Amazon.com, Inc., or its affiliates.

ISBN-13: 9781542027533
eISBN: 9781542027540

Cover design by @blacksheep-uk.com
Cover image: © Anton Petrus / Getty Images

Printed in the United States of America

For Will, Rachael, Darcey and Sadie xx

PROLOGUE

It's almost perfect.

Jessie Beckton casts her gaze around the open-plan living space of the penthouse apartment, double-checking that the staging is working, and any real-estate agents, and the prospective buyers they've brought with them, will get the full impact of the view as soon as they step through the door.

The minimalist furniture is unobtrusive, and the layered neutral tones of the soft furnishings create a calming feel without attracting attention. Across the room, the double sliding doors are open on to the balcony, drawing the gaze in that direction and giving an uninterrupted line of sight from the entryway, through the living space, and out across to the white powdery sand beach and the ocean beyond.

That's the money shot.

Setting her purse down on the kitchen counter, Jessie moves quickly through the apartment, doing her final checks. In the master bedroom, she smooths out an imaginary crease from the bed linen, and fixes the angle of the cushion on the armchair. She switches the light on in the walk-in closet, and spritzes the master bathroom with a generous mist of Beach Vibe room fragrance. Setting the bottle back on the marble countertop of the double vanity, she checks her refection in the mirror and tucks a stray strand of her long platinum-blonde hair back into place. Then she checks the rest of the bedrooms and bathrooms are presented at their absolute best, before heading out to the balcony to set up the refreshments.

She positions the patio table between the slider and the eight-person hot tub, before covering the table with a white linen cloth and lighting the tealight candles that encircle the centrepiece arrangement of gardenia blooms. Then she sets out the champagne flutes, wiping them to make sure there are no smears on the glass, and then lining them up like toy soldiers on parade. Opening the cooler, she removes the canapes first, decanting them from the packaging the high-end deli, Rossetters, has wrapped them in, and then positioning them symmetrically on to the silver platters. Once they're in place, she takes the bottles of champagne from the cooler and sets them in the ice buckets, then opens one bottle and pours it into six glasses. She puts the empty bottle back into the cooler, out of the way, and decides she'll wait until people have started arriving before opening and pouring the rest of the bottles. People are often late, and there's nothing worse than lukewarm champagne.

Stepping back, Jessie looks at the table, pleased with what she's created. It looks classy, expensive. Her boss, Sindee, has very exacting standards, but Jessie thinks even she would appreciate the effort she's made.

Glancing at her watch, she checks the time – it's not much longer until the real-estate agents will be here – and takes a breath, trying to settle the fluttering feeling in her stomach. Tonight is the most important event of her career so far: it's the first time her boss has trusted her to host a broker's open in a penthouse apartment alone.

This is her opportunity to really impress the top brokers in the area and make an early sale before the property hits the MLS database tomorrow, alerting other realtors to the property. If she can pull this off, her boss has promised her the primary agent slot on the upper penthouses, here at the Surf-Sand Vista building at Shimmering Sands Resort, which are still under construction. Being the primary agent on such a high-end listing is exactly what she needs to elevate her career to the big time.

She really wants it.

Fanning out the stack of brochures beside the canapes, Jessie mentally runs through the listing details: new construction penthouse condo, three bedrooms and three bathrooms, just under three thousand square feet plus a spacious balcony. Hardwood floors throughout. Carrara marble kitchen counters and Calcutta Gold marble in the bathrooms. High-end finishes throughout and the best view in the building.

Perfect.

As the lights between the palm trees flicker on along the length of the beach, Jessie smiles to herself. The view really is spectacular and tonight, with the setting sun turning the sky a pinkie-orange colour, the lights twinkling along the boardwalk, and the soothing sound of waves lapping at the shore eight floors below, it's going to be awesome.

She jumps as she hears the click of the apartment door shutting in the distance behind her, and glances again at her watch. It's still ten minutes before showtime; someone must be really keen to have arrived this early. Quickly, she hides the cooler behind the hot tub, and flicks the switch to activate the hot tub's neon underwater lighting and sound system. Jessie waits until the first few bars of smooth jazz have played, then fixes her professional realtor smile in place, and turns to greet the early arrival.

'Get ready for a two-million-dollar view at a much lower price tag . . .' Jessie frowns, stopping mid-sentence as the person steps on to the balcony. 'Oh, it's you.'

Their eyes widen but they say nothing as they come closer, invading her personal space. There's a strange expression on their face, and a fish-gutting knife in their hand.

Jessie tries to take a step back, but there's no room. 'What's that? Why are you—?'

'You shouldn't be here,' they hiss.

Palms slam into her chest and she stumbles backwards, her spine smacking against the iron railing of the balcony with a crack. 'Stop. I don't—'

The knife clatters to the floor and she's yanked around to face the ocean. Pushed against the railing so hard it knocks the breath clean out of her lungs. She gasps for air. Can't get her words out.

Hands grip her waist. Jessie tries to smack them away, but they clasp her wrists together in one hand and pull at the waistband of her pant suit with the other, lifting her.

Oh no. Jeez. 'Stop,' she croaks, struggling beneath their grip. Trying to get free. 'Why are—?'

They don't stop.

They don't speak.

Next moment, Jessie's off her feet. Suspended over the balcony railing.

Unable to escape.

On the horizon the setting sun has reached the ocean. Burnt orange and blood-red streaks illuminate the darkening sky. Their reflection on the water makes it look as if the ocean is on fire.

That's the last thing Jessie Beckton sees before plunging to her death.

1

MOIRA

It was never going to go well.

Sitting in the third row of The Homestead Theatre, Moira has a clear view of the two people on stage. The current speaker, a red-faced, uncomfortable-looking forty-something man in a white shirt with damp patches under the armpits is Matthew J. Frye, the general manager of resident relations. The immaculately dressed thirty-something woman in a navy skirt suit, with the spotlights from the rig above the stage reflecting in the glossy shine of her bobbed brunette hair, hasn't given her name yet. The pair are polar opposites of each other in both style and demeanour: one tense, the other serene. Both are representatives of the management.

As Matthew J. Frye continues to drone on, Moira can sense the audience is getting restless. The residents of The Homestead, a luxury over-fifty-fives retirement resort community nestled in Florida's Lake County, have come to this meeting for answers. So far all they've had is management speak, platitudes and bullshit.

Beside her, her close friend, man mountain and ex-DEA agent, Rick, leans closer and whispers, 'This guy really needs to read the room.'

Moira agrees, but she fears it's already too late. The mood of the crowd is turning from impatient to angry. Things are going to turn bad pretty soon at this rate.

'So, I hope that's cleared up the . . .' Matthew J. Frye pauses to wipe the sweat beading across his forehead. 'The . . . erm . . . misunderstanding and—'

There's a heckle from the back of the auditorium. The words are too muffled for Moira to make out, but from the tone they're clearly not complimentary.

On stage, Matthew J. Frye falters again, becoming tongue-tied over his words, and again dabs a tissue across his forehead. Moira hopes he's taken the heckle as a hint that he's on borrowed time and has finished waffling. But, having tucked the tissue back into his suit trousers, he continues reading from his notes in his monotonous way.

She looks at Rick and grimaces. There are mutters from the audience. Heads are shaking. Fists are being clenched. Matthew J. Frye glances up briefly from his notes. An expression that looks a lot like terror flits across his face.

Moira's not surprised. Every seat is full for this morning's one-off performance: a presentation from The Homestead management following an article published by freelance journalist Jake Malone. An article that Moira had more than a little input into after she'd started looking into the strange 'bad news blackout' that seemed to be happening across the local media and social media channels – misreporting of crimes as accidents, deletion of negative comments or references to bad things happening from the community forums, and hints at possible interference in police investigations. When she'd been threatened and told to stop her investigation by a PR manager linked to The Homestead, Moira had handed over all her evidence to Jake Malone. The double-page spread in the *Florida Chronicle* last week had caused shockwaves through the community.

'And that brings me to . . . to the end of my presentation.' Increasingly red-faced and flustered, Matthew J. Frye seems relieved to have finally got to the end of his spiel. 'So, like I said at the start, we're in listening mode.' He glances at the serious-looking woman sitting at the table beside him. She nods, her shiny bob swinging as she does so. He clears his throat nervously, and continues. 'So I'll open the meeting up to questions.'

It's about time, thinks Moira. The meeting has dragged on for ages. Hands shoot up around the auditorium, many of the audience members keen to interrogate the management. In the row ahead of her, retired actor Olivia Hamilton Ziegler sits next to her friend Betty, who is dressed immaculately as usual in a peach twinset and her usual pearls. Betty is re-reading through some questions she's scribbled on the back of an envelope. On her other side, Alfred, flamboyant as ever in a fuchsia silk shirt and black pleather jeans, is whispering his thoughts to her. A few seats along the row to her right, the hippie twins, Mark and Jack, already have their hands raised, their multiple layered bracelets jangling as they try to attract attention from the stage.

'I've got a few.' Beside her, Jake gets to his feet, not bothering to raise his hand before speaking. 'I'm Jake Malone, journalist.'

Matthew J. Frye pales and looks at the woman sitting beside him. He looks incredibly nervous, as well he should. Word is that since Jake's exposé article was published a number of potential residents have pulled out of their house purchases, and the stock price of Homestead-Handley Holdings Inc. has dropped severely.

'Cue the fireworks,' says Rick, on her other side.

Moira nods, and looks back over at Jake.

'Do you admit you've had a bad news blackout in place?' says Jake, his Bostonian-accented voice loud enough for everyone in the auditorium to hear.

Matthew J. Frye swallows hard and glances towards the woman beside him, but she doesn't return his gaze. 'I . . . erm . . . well, the thing is we don't have a specific policy on that sort of thing.'

'Don't you?' says Philip, Moira's friend and British ex-detective chief inspector from the Thames Valley, who is looking smart in a navy polo shirt and cream trousers. He stands up from his seat next to Rick and runs his hand over his bald pate. 'Then how do you explain the fact a murder here at Manatee Park was reported as an accidental drowning in the media?'

'And why a member of your community, a resident here, received threatening messages when they started asking around about bad news blackouts?' adds Jake.

'Well, like I said, the management didn't have any specific knowledge . . .'

'It's bullshit,' says Moira to Rick. 'Of course they knew.'

Rick, and their friend Lizzie, British ex-CSI and wife of Philip, sitting across to their left, nod. There's muttering and tuts from the crowd. In the front row, Moira sees the hippie twins, Mark and Jack, raise their hands higher. She clears her throat, and says loudly, 'How are you planning to ensure more open communications?'

'Yes, yes,' mutters Philip, remaining standing. 'You absolutely can't continue to censor us. We're grown adults living in homes we've bought; we deserve to be treated as such.'

'I . . . we . . .' Matthew J. Frye gulps the air like a landed fish.

'And what will you be doing to improve security?' asks Peggy Leggerhorne, brushing her short, silver-blonde hair back off her face as she waves the newspaper she's clutching towards the stage. 'We thought we were safe here, but our home was burglarised and now, from this article, I learn that staff in the gatehouses don't even check all the vehicles entering the property as they should be doing.'

'We were told there was zero crime,' shouts Betty as Alfred and Olivia nod beside her. 'Seems that's a crock of shit.'

'And the CCTV system needs upgrading,' says Philip. 'Are you aware that several of the cameras don't work?'

'I'll . . . we'll look into that,' says Matthew J. Frye. 'We're fully committed to—'

'Don't spout more of your "fully committed" nonsense. This is not acceptable!' bellows Philip, slamming his fist on to the arm of his chair. 'You people lied to us, and withheld the truth from us and the media. Maybe even the police. And that . . . that's completely out of order, yes? The police should have free rein to investigate.'

'And they do,' says the woman who until this moment has been sitting silently beside Matthew J. Frye. Unlike her colleague she is calm; in control. 'We would never seek to influence or hinder the authorities in any way.'

Her voice is as smooth as liquid honey, and she gives Philip a reassuring smile, but there's a coldness to her eyes that makes Moira shudder. Her previous experience, of being an undercover detective and having to read people, makes her doubt that this woman has an ounce of compassion or empathy in her body.

'And who are you?' asks Philip, his stern tone and rigid posture indicating he's not taken in by her either. 'You've not even had the decency to introduce yourself.'

'Why, I'm Skylar Handley, honey,' says the woman, her smile becoming even more sickly sweet as she gestures around the room. 'I run this show.'

Rick leans closer to Moira and whispers, 'She's the daughter of the developer who built this place. Real tough cookie by all accounts. Ruthless with the staff, if the rumours are true.'

Moira nods. Ruthless sounds about right. It would explain why the PR company that had been hassling Moira were sacked the day after Jake's article came out, as were a couple of The Homestead's staff who'd spoken to Jake about some of the dodgy dealings going on behind the scenes.

'This has all been a terrible misunderstanding,' continues Skylar. Her smile looks as warm as the Florida sun, but her eyes remain ice cold. 'But as a gesture of good faith we'd like to set up a focus group with residents from across The Homestead community to explore in more depth how we can do better, and put in place a manifesto to ensure no further misunderstandings occur.'

There's a cough from somewhere at the back of the auditorium. Loud murmuring from a couple of ladies closer to the front. Betty shuffles the paper in her hand. The twins put their hands up again.

Skylar ignores them all, and looks meaningfully at Matthew J. Frye.

'Erm . . . yes, we sure do.' Matthew consults his notes, rifling through the pages until he finds what he's looking for. 'Anyone who'd like to be a part of the focus groups, please get in touch with us at community@TheHomestead.com and we'll get you signed up.'

'But, really, will it change anything?' says Philip, still looking aggrieved.

'It will,' replies Skylar, her smile and confident tone unfaltering. She presses her palms together, her long, crimson nails meeting, as if in prayer, and looks around the auditorium. 'The Homestead is your happy ever after, and we're totally committed to giving you the retirement of your dreams. Thank you all so very much for your time this morning.'

It's clear that the meeting is over. As disgruntled residents file slowly out of the auditorium, Moira hangs back with Rick, Philip and Lizzie, waiting for the queues to go down.

'It's nonsense,' says Philip, his voice trembling as his face and neck flush red. 'Those bastards are fobbing us off. Feeding us with nonsense and management tripe. Treating us as if we're past it, or idiots, or both. I won't stand for it. I really won't—'

'Then we need to sign up for the focus group,' says Lizzie, calmly, as she takes his arm and tries to steer him towards the exit. 'Remember what we learnt at the self-care retreat Jennifer took us to in Australia. *Be the change* and all that.'

'Nonsense,' says Philip, jabbing a finger towards the now empty stage. '*We* don't need to change, there's nothing wrong with us. They're the ones in the wrong.'

Moira agrees with Philip. Nothing will change as a result of the focus groups – the management are obviously in damage control mode and the focus groups are just lip service bullshit to make it look like they're taking things seriously. It worries her but after everything that's happened it doesn't surprise her. What both surprises and worries her is how pale and drawn Philip looks beneath his tan. He's lost weight since she last saw him, and she notices there's a slight tremor to his right hand before he shoves it into his pocket.

Something is very clearly wrong.

2

RICK

Back home, in the kitchen, Rick slides his arms around Moira and kisses her neck. He inhales the light coconut scent of the shampoo she always uses and smiles as she puts her arms around his waist and snuggles in close. 'Do you think we should tell them about us?'

Moira goes rigid in his arms. Shaking her head, she steps back, away from his embrace. 'It's too soon.'

Is it? Unknown to their friends, Philip and Lizzie, they've been dating in secret for the past three months. Hell, they've even stayed together most nights, over at Moira's place, given the dogs are happier in their own space rather than here at Rick's house. Even if it does make the bed a little cramped with all of them squeezed on to it. The timing feels good to him. He's fed up of the little white lies and sneaking around required to keep their feelings for each other a secret.

'You're okay with that, aren't you?' says Moira, looking worried. 'It's just that I don't want them to make it out to be a big deal, it's so new still.'

'Yeah, for sure,' says Rick, turning away and getting busy loading a new filter and a few scoops of coffee into the machine. He has no kind of poker face and he doesn't want her to see his hurt expression, or the truth of how he feels: that their relationship is already a big deal to him. Moira's the first woman he's felt strongly about since his beloved wife, Alisha, died of cancer five years ago.

'Are you going to join the focus group?' asks Moira, running her hand through her cropped black hair.

'Maybe,' says Rick as he sets the coffee machine going and turns to face her, trying not to stay hung up on her still wanting to keep their relationship a secret. 'You?'

She shakes her head. 'No point. Whatever we say isn't going to make any difference.'

Rick knows Moira's right, but not getting involved doesn't sit right with him. 'I'd still kind of like to know how things go down.'

'Then go along,' says Moira with a shrug. 'We should probably have someone there, and it can't be Philip because he'll lose his temper like he did earlier and I really don't think that'd be good for him. I thought he was looking a bit—'

On the granite counter, Rick's cell phone starts ringing and vibrating, cutting Moira off mid-sentence. He gestures towards it. 'I'll just . . .' Picking up the cell, he answers the call. 'This is Denver.'

'Rick Denver? Are you the retired detective guy who solves crimes in age-controlled communities?' asks a nasal-sounding guy with a strong New York accent.

Rick looks at Moira and raises his eyebrows. 'Erm, sure. There are four of us.'

'Good.' The man on the other end of the line exhales hard. 'Because our daughter is dead and we need your help.'

Rick says nothing for a couple of beats. Then he switches into work mode.

'I'm real sorry for your loss, sir. Let me put you on speaker.' Setting the cell down on the granite counter, Rick presses the speaker button on the screen. 'Okay, you're on with me and my colleague, Moira Flynn. Can you give me your name, sir?'

13

'I'm Jim Beckton, and my wife, Doreen, is here with me. I was given your name by Hank who works in the CCTV station at your place, The Homestead? He's an old buddy of mine from back in the day and he said you and your pals are good at solving mysteries.' He pauses. Swallows loudly, and when he continues speaking his New York accent is even more nasal. 'The cops around here didn't get the job done. We need your help to get justice for our daughter.'

'What's your daughter's name, Jim?' asks Rick, softly, looking at Moira.

Moira gives a sad shake of her head. He understands how she's feeling. Situations where people have died are awful for the deceased, but they're also real hard on the relatives left behind. Working with them, helping them navigate the grief and shock, can be one of the hardest parts of the job.

'Jessica . . . Jessie.' Jim Beckton's voice cracks as he says his daughter's name. 'She was . . . she . . .'

'Tell us what happened to her,' says Moira, her tone gentle.

'Someone killed her.' A woman's voice says in a rush: Doreen Beckton, Jim's wife, Rick assumes.

'And what is it that you'd like us to do?' Rick asks.

'We need you to find her killer. The police don't think it was murder but they're wrong. They won't listen but they're . . .' Doreen's voice tails off into sobbing.

It's very usual for relatives to be in denial about their loved one's death. The shock takes a long time to work through. Rick tries to put it as kindly as he can. 'If the evidence shows that—'

'No, she was murdered,' says Jim, his voice louder now, and shaking with emotion. 'We've got proof.'

Moira raises her eyebrows.

Rick holds her gaze for a moment, then nods. 'Okay, I hear you, Jim. Now whereabouts are you?'

14

Jim blows out hard. 'We live at Shimmering Sands resort, it's a new retirement community on the beach near Tampa.'

Tampa's less than a couple of hours' drive but too far to go without knowing the details first. He could get those details now, but Rick wants Philip and Lizzie in on the call too. They decide which cases they take on as a group – it's one of their rules: go all in, or all out. 'So, here's what we'll do, Jim. I'll get my crew together and then let's get on a video call in an hour's time. You can take us through the situation and we can see if we can help you.'

'We'd appreciate that,' says Doreen, sounding tearful.

'We sure would,' says Jim.

'No problem,' says Rick. 'We'll talk in an hour. And, again, I'm real sorry for your loss.'

'You think they actually have proof their daughter was killed?' says Moira as Rick ends the call.

'Maybe,' says Rick. 'But either way, I figured we should hear them out. They've clearly been through hell.'

'Agreed,' says Moira. 'If we're going to meet up with Philip and Lizzie I should nip back home and let the dogs out beforehand.'

'Okay,' says Rick, swallowing down the pang of loss he feels every time Moira leaves. 'Or you could just bring them over here, you know they're always welcome.'

'Yeah, I—'

The doorbell chimes, followed by four loud raps on the knocker.

Moira tilts her head. 'You expecting company?'

'Nope,' says Rick, shaking his head. 'Just ignore it, it's probably someone trying to sell me stuff I don't need. I'm going to get on to setting up the video call.'

'We never get cold callers around here,' Moira says. 'Don't worry, you set up the call and update Philip and Lizzie, I'll go get the door.'

As he taps out a message on the Retired Detectives Club WhatsApp chat, Rick is vaguely aware of Moira walking down the hall to the entryway and opening the front door. He hears her say hello, and there's something about her tone that makes him look up.

The door is open and Moira's standing to one side. Through the gap, Rick sees a young woman with a blonde ringlet-haired toddler balanced on her hip. Shock punches him in the throat. His mouth goes dry. Dropping his cell phone on to the countertop, he hurries towards the front door.

The woman in the doorway is scowling at Moira. 'Who the hell are you?'

'I . . . I'm . . .' Moira turns and looks at Rick, confused. 'Do you know this woman?'

'What the hell's going on?' says the young woman, her furious stare moving from Moira to Rick as she clutches the toddler closer to her body.

Rick looks at the child. The little girl must be around three years old and she looks so much like her mom, but there's no mistaking the resemblance to him either. *Jeez.* He can't believe this is happening. That she's here, at his home, after all this time. He looks back at her mother's scowling face.

The shock is clear in his voice as he says, 'Estelle?'

3

MOIRA

They're gathered around the kitchen table at Philip and Lizzie's place.

'Well, this is all very exciting, isn't it?' says Lizzie, as she places mugs of coffee and a plate stacked with oatmeal and raisin cookies in front of them. 'A potential new case, and over by the sea too.'

'Yes, yes,' says Philip, lifting a cookie from the plate and taking a bite. Using his napkin, he mops up a few tiny crumbs that he's made on the white quartz countertop. 'These cookies are delicious.'

Lizzie smiles, positively glowing. Her long white hair is twisted up into a messy bun and held in place with a paintbrush, and there's a dab of turquoise on one of her forearms, no doubt left over from an earlier painting session. 'I thought you'd like them.'

'Thanks, Lizzie,' says Moira, forcing a smile. She can't let her friends see how she's feeling; doesn't want them to ask why she's so tense. Although since they returned from their six-week trip to Australia visiting their youngest daughter, Jennifer, they've seemed to have eyes for no one but each other. It's unexpected, but she's happy for them after all the turmoil they've been through lately when Philip was kidnapped and beaten during their last investigation. 'It'll be good to have a new case to work.'

'For sure,' says Rick, who's busy setting up the laptop for the video call.

Moira glances at him. They haven't spoken since she left his house an hour ago. She'd felt oddly out of place when the young woman and her child had come inside, and it was clear from the woman's reaction when Moira opened the door that she was angry about her being there. So, she'd left Rick to it with his visitors, thinking he'd give her a call to explain what was going on as soon as he could; but he didn't.

Since then, she's taken the dogs for a run, and walked briskly over to Philip and Lizzie's place, but she still can't get rid of the adrenaline coursing through her veins. Watching Rick calmly open the video calling app on the laptop and sign in, Moira clasps her fingers together in her lap. She wishes she could ask him right now who the hell the young woman is who just turned up on his doorstep. From the way they'd looked at each other, it's clear they know each other well. Moira shivers. She's trying not to jump to conclusions, but is jumping to them anyway. Are the pair of them lovers? Is the child Rick's?

She closes her eyes and takes a breath, but it doesn't help. The woman was younger than she is, a lot younger. And the way she'd looked at Moira – it was as if she hated her. She must have had a reason to act so possessively over Rick. Yet if Rick is seeing other people, why was he so keen to tell their friends that the two of them are together? It makes no sense.

'Don't you think, Moira?' asks Philip.

She flinches, Philip's question pulling her from her runaway thoughts. 'Sorry, what was that?'

'I was just saying that if we take this case we'll probably need to spend a few days staying over in Tampa,' says Philip. 'It's a bit of a way to drive back and forth, yes?'

'I guess,' says Moira, as she considers the logistics. 'I'll have to find somewhere for the dogs though, I can't leave them home alone.'

'Yes, yes, of course,' says Philip.

'I hear the Dog-N-Pup Home-from-Home over on Seahorse Drive is getting great reviews,' says Lizzie, smiling brightly. 'Darla Henshaw left Pixie there when she went on that Caribbean cruise recently. She said the little princess didn't want to leave.'

'Great,' says Moira. The last thing she feels like doing is leaving her dogs with someone else, but another case would be good. She needs something to take her mind off whatever the hell is going on with Rick and the mystery woman.

'Okay, we're all good, it's connected,' says Rick, sitting back in his seat and taking a mouthful of coffee. 'I'm calling the Becktons now.'

There's a beeping tone as the call rings before connecting. Moments later two people appear on the laptop screen. A gaunt-looking sixty-something man with thinning brown hair and wire-framed glasses, and a round-faced but drawn-looking woman with dark circles under her eyes and a mass of greying, curly hair.

'Jim and Doreen?' says Rick, raising his hand in greeting. 'Hi there, I'm Rick Denver, we spoke earlier, and these are my fellow retired detective friends – Moira, Philip and Lizzie.'

'Thanks for taking a meeting with us,' says Jim, his nasal, New York-accented voice sounding thin and nervous.

'We really appreciate it,' adds Doreen, her own voice equally shaky. 'We just want justice for our baby.'

'For sure,' says Rick, gently. 'Now, can you tell us what happened?'

Doreen looks at Jim. Jim clears his throat. 'Jessie was at work, setting up for a broker's open house at a new penthouse apartment in the Surf-Sand Vista building at Shimmering Sands retirement community. She'd gotten a job as a realtor here in Tampa about six months back. You see, we retired here from New York about a year ago, and she said she missed us, and fancied herself some year-round sunshine, so she relocated too.'

'We'd seen her just an hour earlier,' says Doreen, her eyes watery as she tries to hold back tears. 'She was super excited about the broker's open – it was the first time she'd run one for a penthouse property.'

'But when the brokers arrived, they couldn't get inside. The penthouse was locked and their knocks on the door went unanswered. They tried calling Jessie's cell phone but it went straight to voicemail.' Jim pauses, swallowing hard. 'The reason she wasn't answering is she was already dead.'

'The police detective told us she'd jumped from the eighth-floor balcony,' says Doreen, emotion making her voice sound reedy and thin. 'By the time those brokers knocked on the door she . . . she was . . .'

Jim puts his arm around Doreen. 'Jessie was already outside. Some people on the way to the beach found her on the walkway from the building to the sand. They called an ambulance but . . .' He takes a couple of breaths before continuing. 'It was too late.'

'We're sorry for your loss,' says Philip. 'Did anyone see her fall?'

Jim shakes his head. 'No. The balcony was to the side of the apartment building, facing out across the gardens.'

'When did his happen?' says Rick.

Jim glances at his wife, then back to Rick. 'It was a few months ago.'

'I see,' says Rick, looking thoughtful. 'And what's the status of the police investigation?'

'They went and closed it,' blurts out Doreen, angrily.

'They said there was no evidence to indicate foul play,' says Jim. 'The CCTV showed Jessie as the only person who accessed the penthouse apartment up until the time the other brokers arrived.

And they said she was found with the only key to the penthouse in her pocket.'

'And the apartment door was locked when the brokers arrived?' asks Philip.

'It was,' says Jim.

Moira leans forward towards the screen. 'On the call earlier this morning you told us you had evidence that your daughter was murdered. Can you talk us through it?'

Neither of the Becktons speak. Jim glances at his wife, who bites her lip and gives a little nod.

Jim exhales hard. 'When we saw Jessie that afternoon she told us about a trip she'd booked for the three of us. It was at the end of the month, for my birthday; a three-day cruise. If she was planning on taking her own life before then, why would she make the booking?'

Moira doesn't say it, but Jessie having paid for a trip a few weeks ahead isn't evidence that she was murdered. She looks at Rick, Philip and Lizzie and can see from the expressions on their faces that they're thinking the same.

'Jim, Doreen, as Philip said, we are all real sorry for your loss,' says Rick. 'But from what you've told us I'm not getting the sense that we'd find anything different to the cops. I don't think—'

'*Please* help us,' says Doreen, the tears she's been holding at bay now cascading down her face. 'You're our last hope at finding the truth about what happened.'

Rick keeps his voice gentle. 'Ma'am, I just—'

'Don't turn your back on my little girl,' says Jim, the emotion heavy in his voice. 'We want answers. We need to know who did this to her and . . .' His voice gives way and he swallows hard again. 'We want to know why.'

'If we come and investigate, you need to be prepared that we might draw the same conclusion as the police,' says Moira.

21

Beside her, Rick turns to look at her, surprised. He'd been about to tell the Becktons that they couldn't help, she knows that, but these people are grieving and even if the cops are right, and Jessie Beckton died by suicide, at least having a second opinion might make it easier for them to accept. As a DCI in the Metropolitan Police Moira hadn't had the time to work with victims or relatives of victims for very long, but now, as a retiree, she can make her own rules. And her gut instinct tells her these people need helping. Usually that would've been Rick's stance too. Moira wonders if his unexpected visitor this morning is a factor in his reluctance to take the case.

On her other side, Lizzie nods. 'But we'll pledge to look at all the evidence, to leave no stone unturned, before we come to a conclusion.'

Philip is nodding at Lizzie. 'Yes, yes, we can do that.' He looks back at the Becktons on-screen. 'If something happened to one of our daughters, I'd want the same. We'll give your daughter's case the utmost care and attention.'

'Well, okay then,' says Rick, clearly realising he's outnumbered. 'We'll take the case, and investigate Jessie's death on your behalf. We'll need to come to Shimmering Sands and learn more about Jessie and her life, and talk to people who knew her, especially those who saw her on that last day.'

'We understand,' says Jim, nodding. 'You can stay at Surf-Sand Vista – it's a mix of vacation rentals for seniors, hotel rooms and retirement condos. And we'll email you the notes we took at the inquest into Jessie's death, and a copy of the coroner's report.'

'Great,' says Rick, although his voice doesn't have its usual enthusiasm. 'We'll make some reservations and all being well we'll be with you later today.'

As they say goodbye to the Becktons, and Rick disconnects the call, Moira's pleasure that they've taken the case starts to be replaced with other emotions. She isn't keen on staying in the building where Jessie Beckton died, but, even more than that, she's not so sure that she wants to be stuck away from home, and in such close proximity with Rick. She might not have wanted to tell Philip and Lizzie about their relationship yet, but that wasn't because she doesn't have feelings for Rick.

Quite the opposite in fact.

She's worried that she's fallen for him far too fast.

4

LIZZIE

Philip has always taken far longer than she does to pack. Lizzie's small pink wheelie case is already sitting beside the front door ready to go, but when she pops her head into his room Philip looks as if he's barely started. There are neatly stacked piles of clothes on the bed but nothing seems to be in his overnight bag. She can't see Philip, but she can hear him in the ensuite, clattering around.

'Hey,' calls Lizzie. 'How are you getting on?'

Philip appears in the doorway between the ensuite and his bedroom, clutching a blue and white striped washbag. 'Good, good. Just gathering a few essentials together.'

'Great,' says Lizzie, smiling. 'We should really get going in the next half an hour.'

'Of course, of course. I won't be long,' says Philip, walking across to his bed and setting the wash bag down on the navy duvet. He smiles, ruefully. 'We shouldn't have unpacked after we got back from seeing Jennifer.'

They've only been back a week from their Australia trip: six weeks seeing the sights and spending time with their youngest daughter. They'd all become tearful when it was time to fly home, and promised that they wouldn't leave it so long next time. Lizzie is determined that they won't. She wants to see all her children every year from now on. She's done with relying on just video calls. 'Maybe we need permanently packed travel bags.'

'Perhaps we do,' says Philip.

Lizzie smiles. Until now, Philip has been resistant to travelling out of Florida, but his recent near-death experience during their last investigation seems to have given him a new perspective on life, and for that she is grateful. After all, there's only so much yoga, golf and painting you can do; sometimes you have to be a little more adventurous.

Her phone pings, notifying her of a new email. It's from Rick and is a forwarded email from the Becktons with their notes from the inquest and the coroner's report that they'd mentioned on the call earlier.

'Rick's sent across the information from the Becktons,' says Lizzie, looking up at Philip. 'I'll have a look while you finish up in here.'

'Yes, yes, good plan,' says Philip, as he folds each pair of under-pants neatly before placing them into his overnight bag.

Leaving him to it, Lizzie heads back to the kitchen and sits down at the table. Opening the email, she starts to read. A few lines in and she's not in holiday mode any longer. Medical reports and inquests are tough-going at the best of times, but Jessie Beckton was just twenty-three years old – the same age as Jennifer. All that life, gone so soon. So suddenly. Lizzie feels sadness wash over her. She feels something else too: a strengthened desire to help the Becktons get the closure they need, or as near to closure as it's possible to get when you lose a child.

As she reads through the notes, Lizzie checks off the details that they'd discussed in the video call earlier – that the CCTV only recorded Jessie travelling to the penthouse until the group of realtors arrived for the broker's open event, that the door to the apartment was locked, and that Jessie had no obvious defensive wounds. The verdict is recorded as death by suicide.

Moving on to the coroner's report, Lizzie finds nothing in Jessie's previous medical history that jumps out as unusual, and the injuries listed at the time of death all seem consistent with a fall from a high building. But when she reads the probable cause section, Lizzie frowns. She re-reads the section again, and as she does her heart starts to pound faster.

There's a red flag. An inconsistency with the rest of the information.

'Philip, we need to get going,' she calls, the urgency clear in her voice.

'Yes, yes. With you in a sec,' says Philip, above the sound of a case being zipped up.

Hurry up, thinks Lizzie, glancing back at her phone and the coroner's report. Again, she reads the description and the details of the location where Jessie Beckton lost her life.

She's not imagining it. Something doesn't add up.

Lizzie needs to see the exact spot for herself.

5

MOIRA

This is awkward.

She'd rather have walked home, to be honest, but when Rick offered her a lift back to her place from Philip and Lizzie's house, she'd thought that he wanted to talk; to explain. Only that isn't what's happening.

Neither of them has spoken. Their usual easy chatter snuffed out by the appearance of the mystery young woman and her child. As Rick steers the jeep along the streets towards her house, Moira feels the tension between them ratcheting up. Her hands are clenched tightly together in her lap. There's a muscle pulsing in Rick's jaw.

It's ridiculous. They're two grown adults; they should be able to talk about it. She's had enough of the silence.

'Who was she?' Moira's voice sounds unusually loud.

Rick glances across at her, looking startled. 'I . . . she . . .'

Moira frowns. The start of a headache throbs at her temples. Rick's usually so open and forthcoming; it's one of the things she loves about him. Whatever's going on, it has to be serious. 'It's not a difficult question. You obviously knew each other.'

'Her name's Estelle,' says Rick, his eyes not moving from the road ahead.

'Yes, I got that at the time.' Moira turns in her seat to face him. 'But who *is* she?'

Saying nothing, Rick indicates and manoeuvres the jeep to a stop outside Moira's house. He exhales hard. Gives a single shake of his head.

Moira feels a sickly combination of frustration and fear flip inside her stomach. 'Come on, Rick. She turns up on your doorstep with a child and treats me like I'm the one in the wrong place. Don't I deserve an explanation?'

'Yes,' says Rick, turning to face her. 'You do.'

'Well?' Moira holds his gaze, fearing the worst. If he's going to tell her bad news, she wishes he'd get the hell on with it.

Rick's voice is quieter than usual. 'Estelle is my daughter.'

'You never said you had a daughter,' says Moira, confused. 'I know you were married, but you've not mentioned kids. Why did—'

'We've been estranged since Alisha died.'

'For five years?' Moira can't keep the surprise from her voice.

Rick looks sad, embarrassed almost. 'I tried a bunch of times to make contact but Estelle . . .' He shakes his head. 'Today was the first time I got to meet my granddaughter.'

Moira can see how hard it is for him to talk about Estelle. She takes his hand and gives it a squeeze. 'But why? What happened?'

Rick looks away, avoiding her gaze. 'The thing is, I wasn't a great dad.'

6

PHILIP

'This is it,' says Philip, as he pulls off the street and steers the Toyota steadily along the driveway towards the Surf-Sand Vista building. It's an ultra-modern glass and white stucco tower, the chrome window surrounds glinting in the bright Florida sun. It's flanked by palm trees and ornamental fountains that are dwarfed by the tallness of the building. As they get closer, he sees a large covered carport – big enough for five or six vehicles – directly outside the building entrance. Philip's impressed for a moment. Then he sees a three-sided booth, and the uniformed attendants standing beside it, and his heart sinks. It's valet parking. Dammit.

Glancing at Lizzie, he rolls his eyes.

Laughing, she pats his thigh. 'When in Rome . . .'

'I suppose so,' Philip says, gruffly, as he halts the car next to the attendants' cabin. Sure enough, he's barely got the car into park before a red-waistcoated attendant strides over to them.

'Good morning, sir. Can I assist you?' says the young man, a red peaked cap perched at a jaunty angle on his strawberry-blond hair, and a broad grin on his face.

Philip would like to say no, but he knows that's not the done thing, so he hands over the keys to the Toyota with the parking fee plus a five-dollar tip. 'Can you park her for us?'

'No problem, sir. Thanks so much,' says the attendant, handing him a ticket stub and attaching the corresponding stub to Philip's keys. 'You have a great day now.'

'Will do,' says Philip, forcing a smile, before turning back to the car and removing their luggage from the boot. It's not that he begrudges these fellows making a living; he admires a strong work ethic. It's more that he's perfectly capable of parking his own vehicle for free, and so he'd rather do it himself. He hates all this tipping nonsense.

Carrying the bags, he heads up the steps to the entrance with Lizzie alongside him. The bags feel a lot heavier now than they did when he was lifting them into the car at home. He'd rather tip someone for carrying them than parking the car. When they reach the top of the steps the automatic doors to the building glide open, but Lizzie stops.

'You okay?' asks Philip, putting the bags down for a brief rest.

'It's a long way down, isn't it,' she says, looking up at the nine-storey building.

'Yes, yes, very much so,' says Philip, his tone sombre. He handled more than a few jumper cases in his time as a DCI in the Thames Valley Police back in England, and he found each of them incredibly sad. As an officer of the law you try to harden yourself to the sights you see day in, day out, but really you're just fooling yourself; it's impossible not to dwell on the victims, especially those you're unable to get some sort of justice for.

They walk through the doorway into the chilled air of the hotel atrium. On the wall to their right, beside the huge, human-height flower arrangement, is a large map of the Shimmering Sands Resort Community. Striding over to it, Philip puts the bags down again. Shaking his arms to relieve the pins and needles spreading along his forearms, he studies the map. 'Looks like the hotel rooms are all in this building – the first two floors are bars, restaurants and the fitness and spa centre, the next two are the hotel, and the top five are apartments. It's much smaller than The Homestead, isn't it?'

'Much,' says Lizzie, joining him at the map. She traces her finger across the pathway from the Surf-Sand Vista building that they're currently in, past the outdoor pool and grill area, a beach restaurant and along an oceanfront boardwalk that leads to some individual villas. 'It says here there are twenty beach villas in addition to this building.'

Philip has no idea why someone would want to live at the beach – all that sand getting into places it shouldn't be. It'd be impossible to keep a place tidy, especially if you had carpets, and he does like a bit of carpet in the bedroom. 'Well, thankfully, our reservation must be in this building.'

'It's a shame they don't rent out the villas,' says Lizzie, wistfully. 'I do love the feeling of the sand between my toes.'

Philip shudders. Ignoring Lizzie's raised eyebrow, he picks up the bags and heads towards the reception desk. He's never pretended to be a beach lover.

'Hello, sir, how can I assist you?' asks the uniformed young man with black-rimmed glasses and a welcoming smile behind the desk. The brass name-badge pinned to the pocket of his blazer says 'Justin'.

'Good afternoon, Justin. Sweetman, party of two, checking in,' says Philip. He thinks about the long drop from the top level of the building to the ground. Leaning closer, he drops the volume of his voice a few notches. 'We'd appreciate a low floor if that's possible.'

'I'm sure that will be absolutely no problem,' says Justin, tapping his keyboard. 'I have your reservation here and I can get you fixed up with one of our superior oceanfront rooms on level three.'

'Yes, yes, that sounds just fine,' says Philip.

'Perfect,' says Justin, tapping his keyboard a few more times before printing out a sheet of paper and passing it across the desk to Philip. 'If you can just check the details and sign, I'll get your key-cards all ready for you.'

Philip does as he's asked and passes the booking confirmation back to Justin in exchange for the key-cards. 'Thanks.'

'You're very welcome, Mr Sweetman. Now, if you head across the atrium here and take a left, you'll see the elevators directly ahead of you. Take any of the first three elevators up to the third floor, the fourth elevator is penthouse level only, and then follow the signs for 303.'

'Can you let me know if our friends have arrived?' asks Lizzie. 'Moira Flynn and Rick Denver.'

'No problem,' says Justin, tapping his keyboard a couple more times. He looks back at Lizzie. 'I'm sorry, they haven't checked in at this time.'

'Thanks anyway,' says Lizzie. She looks at Philip. 'Shall we go and get unpacked?'

'Good thinking,' says Philip.

As they walk across to the elevators, Philip's glad he won't have to carry the blasted bags much further. His arms are feeling weird, the pins and needles having morphed into a dull ache. Out through the huge glass windows over at the other end of the reception space he can see a large patio area with tables and chairs, and a pool. He can see a few people sitting out there with food and drinks. His tummy growls. 'We could grab a spot of lunch after, while we're waiting for Rick and Moira.'

'Sounds good,' says Lizzie. 'She said she'd be later than us as it'd take a while to settle the dogs into the Dog-N-Pup Home-from-Home.'

'Yes, yes, and it was good of Rick to offer Moira a lift out here,' says Philip. 'Saves on petrol.'

Lizzie looks at him, a strange expression on her face that he finds hard to read.

'Don't you think?' says Philip, not sure why Lizzie's looking at him in that odd way.

'Petrol saving . . . oh, yes, I'm sure that's it,' Lizzie says, a sly smile on her face.

Philip frowns, feeling rather stupid. He's always prided himself on having a good nose for investigation, but he must be missing something.

He has no idea what Lizzie's implying.

7

LIZZIE

After a lunch of lobster roll, fries and lemonade at the poolside restaurant, Lizzie is keen to get on with the investigation. Rather than join Philip for an afternoon nap in their room, she decides to make a start on her own. Taking her phone from her handbag, she opens her email with the information sent over earlier by the Becktons, and re-reads the coroner's report.

She's barely to the end of the first paragraph before a group of seniors in brightly coloured swimwear march purposefully across the patio to the pool. They ease themselves down into the water. Moments later, the thumping, rhythmic beat of a dance track starts, and a twenty-something fitness trainer dressed in a bright yellow crop top and flared skirt bounces over to the pool and starts shouting instructions at the people in the water.

Lizzie's never tried aqua aerobics but it looks like a lot of fun. Unfortunately, though, it's not a useful activity to have going on just feet away from her while she's trying to concentrate. Finishing the last of her lemonade, she pays the bill and heads away from the pool area towards the beach and takes a seat on an unoccupied deckchair.

There are a few people lying on sun loungers, a couple walking along the sand with their two yappy sausage dogs galloping around them, and a small group of grey-haired surfers practising their moves, but aside from that the beach is pretty quiet. It's idyllic really with perfect white sand, a shimmering turquoise ocean and the occasional palm tree dotted along the dunes. It's hard to believe anything bad could happen here.

But as Lizzie reads through the coroner's report again, it's clear something awful did.

Having read through it twice, she looks back towards the Surf-Sand Vista building, and uses the description in the report to pin-point the rough location of the penthouse apartment Jessie Beckton had been setting up for an open house.

Getting up, Lizzie walks along the boardwalk until she finds another of the large community maps. She double-checks the location on the map, and then steps off the boardwalk and strides purposefully along a paved pathway towards the place Jessie Beckton's body was found.

It takes her less than five minutes to find the spot. It's around the side of the building – in sight of the beach, but shielded by the palm trees that line the boardwalk, and facing out more towards the lush community gardens packed with tropical plants in a rainbow of vibrant colours.

A little way across the lawn, Lizzie can see a group of older guys, all dressed in board shorts, Hawaiian shirts and sandals, prac-tising their putting on a three-hole putting green. In the distance she can hear the beat of the aqua aerobics music still audible over the crashing of the waves. There's a stand on the boardwalk selling maple-roasted pecans, and the sweet aroma is enticing. The place feels more like a holiday resort than a year-round retirement com-munity for seniors, but then she supposes that's the idea.

She looks at the ground. There's nothing to show that this is the place a young woman lost her life, although Lizzie hadn't expected there to be. Crime scene clean-up is highly advanced these days and, especially in a place like this with its idyllic retirement vibe, they'd have wanted to scrub away any trace of trauma fast. The paving is a bright

35

white, the same as the rest of the pathway, and the grass on either side of it is trimmed neatly to the same uniform height of the lawns.

Lizzie looks up and pinpoints the balcony of the eighth-floor penthouse. She shudders. It's a very long way to fall. She steps across the pathway to the exact place described in the coroner's report and looks up again, frowning.

Just as she thought, something is wrong.

Lizzie has worked enough crime scenes to know the difference between a person falling or jumping. If a person jumps from a balcony or railing, the act of pushing away from that structure sends them out into the air before gravity takes hold. It's all done in a tiny fraction of a second, but it happens none the less.

But it didn't happen here.

The eighth-floor balcony is almost directly above her. Jessie is described as having been found lying with her upper body on the white stone pathway and her lower body on the grass. Lizzie studies the area from all angles. For Jessie to land in the spot described in the coroner's report, she would have had to have fallen directly downwards from the edge of the balcony. There's a line in the report that refers to her as having 'fallen forwards' and the autopsy concludes that given the significant head trauma, Jessie would have fallen, and landed, head first.

And that would be incredibly difficult to do.

In Lizzie's experience, falling vertically, head first, indicates one specific thing – that the person was dropped rather than having been pushed or having jumped. She shudders again, imagining being suspended over the balcony railing head first, and then the person letting go. The terror that poor young woman must have felt in her last moments hardly bears thinking about.

Between what the coroner's report has detailed, and what the location is telling her, Lizzie has no doubt in her mind about what happened here.

Jessie Beckton *was* murdered.

36

8

MOIRA

Moira wishes she'd declined Rick's offer to drive and brought her own car. Rick clearly doesn't want to go into any more detail about his relationship with his estranged daughter, and Moira has always hated small talk. The result has been deafening silence and maximum awkwardness for the one hour forty minutes that it's taken to drive from The Homestead to Shimmering Sands. As they draw up to the main entrance, get out of the jeep and Rick hands the keys to the parking attendant, Moira can't help but exhale in relief.

'We're meeting the Becktons on the terrace,' says Rick, checking the time on his watch. 'They're expecting us now so we'd better check in when we're done.'

'Sounds a good plan,' says Moira, hoisting her overnight bag over her shoulder and falling in step with Rick as they go up the steps into the building and across the foyer towards the outdoor terrace. 'Are Philip and Lizzie joining us?'

'They should be,' says Rick. 'I think it's important the Becktons meet the whole team.'

'Agreed,' says Moira.

Rick's tone is all business, and she's okay with that for now. They need to focus on getting as much information about Jessie Beckton from her parents as they can. With the case having been closed by the local cops, and the inquest already held, it's essentially a cold case they're reopening. The more time that's passed, the harder it is to generate good leads, and they're going to need to generate new avenues of enquiry if they're to find anything the cops might have possibly missed. And that's assuming a crime did actually happen here. That's something they need to establish fast.

They step through the patio doors and out on to the poolside terrace. Moira scans the people sitting at tables, looking for the Becktons. She spots them over on the far side of the terrace. Philip and Lizzie are already there and all four look as if they're in deep conversation.

'Over this way,' she says, glancing at Rick and gesturing towards their friends and the Becktons.

Silently, Rick follows her across the terrace. Moira takes a breath and hopes he's going to lighten up once they reach the table. Jim and Doreen need their full attention and support, so Rick needs to get his head in the game no matter whatever else he's got going on back at home.

Moira smiles as she reaches the Becktons' table. 'Hi, I'm Moira and this is Rick. It's good to meet you in person.'

'Jim,' says Mr Beckton, rising to his feet and gesturing for them to take a seat.

'Thank you for coming out here to help us,' says Doreen, her smile genuine but still unable to disguise her grief.

'It's no problem,' says Rick, first pulling out Moira's chair for her to sit down beside Lizzie, and then taking a seat to her right.

'Yes, yes, well, now that we're all here, it would be very helpful if you could tell us more about your daughter,' says Philip, picking up his pen and hovering it, ready to write, above his notepad. 'Don't leave anything out. The more we know about her as a person and her daily life the better.'

38

'Sure,' says Jim, taking his wife's hand and holding it tightly. 'Jessie, Jessica Maye, is . . . was . . .' He swallows hard. 'She was twenty-three years old. Like we said earlier, she'd moved out here around six months ago and started working for a local real-estate firm.'

'Can you tell us the name of the company?' asks Moira.

'Beachseekers,' says Jim. 'They're one of the top brokerages here and she was so excited to be offered the job.'

'She'd been doing really good,' says Doreen Beckton. 'She paid for the cruise we mentioned earlier with one of her commission cheques. She loved the work, and she was determined to become a premier agent, that's why running the penthouse broker's open was such a big deal for her – lots of other agents had more experience but she was the one her boss asked to host it.'

'Was there bad blood between her and any other agents because of that?' asks Rick.

The Becktons are silent for a moment, then Jim says, 'Not that she mentioned. I mean, it's a competitive business so rivalry is commonplace between co-workers, but she didn't tell us about anything that worried her.'

'Did she ever mention her co-workers by name?' asks Rick.

'Not often, just her boss – Sindee McGillis.' Doreen thinks for a moment, then says, 'She mentioned an Elton, I think, who she'd been for drinks with a few times.'

They pause the conversation as the server comes over to take their order. As he heads off to fetch their drinks, they continue.

'That's very helpful, thank you,' says Philip, jotting down the names on his notepad. 'Was she in a romantic relationship, with this Elton perhaps?'

'No, definitely not,' says Doreen. 'Elton had a husband and, anyways, Jessie had recently come out of a relationship, she wasn't interested in getting into another right away – she was focusing on her career.'

Moira catches Rick's eye and she can tell from his expression that he's thinking along the same lines as her. 'Did the relationship end on good terms?'

'It did not. That asshole . . .' Jim blows out, unable to continue.

'What my husband is trying to say, is that Jessie's boyfriend was bad news,' says Doreen. 'We were very relieved when she ended things between them.'

'Can you describe why you thought he was bad news?' asks Moira, leaning to her left to allow the server to put her drink – an iced coffee – on to the table.

Doreen waits for the server to finish with the drinks and move away before she answers. 'He was always trying to control what she did. He didn't like her going out without him, and he hated it when she moved out here from New York – he was always trying to guilt her into moving back and then raising hell when she refused.'

Lizzie leans forward in her chair. 'Did he ever get violent?'

Doreen Beckton thinks for a moment, then says, 'I don't think so, but maybe he did and Jessie didn't tell us. He certainly had a temper on him.'

'I never liked him,' says Jim, the anger barely contained in his voice. 'The way he'd speak to my little girl sometimes – ordering her to go get him a beer or a sandwich, and never paying her a compliment or encouraging her career. He actually tried to ban her from coming to see us after he and I had a difference of opinion over a football game. It was ridiculous.'

Moira understands why Jim didn't get on with the guy. He sounds like bad news. 'We'll need to speak with him. Do you have his contact details?'

'His name's Josh Stratton.'

'And he's in New York, right?' says Rick.

'Not any more,' says Jim, grimacing. 'He moved out this way around four months ago. Got a transfer to a car dealership about ten miles away so he could be with Jessie. That's probably one of the reasons he got so pissed when she ended things a week later.'

'How long was this before she died?' asks Moira, raising her voice slightly so she can be heard above the tuneless rendition of 'Happy Birthday' being sung on a neighbouring table.

Doreen Beckton bites her lip, looking tearful.

'About ten days,' says Jim. 'We told the police all of this, but they obviously didn't think it was relevant.'

'Well, we'll be sure to check it out real thorough,' says Rick. 'Be assured on that.'

'Did Jessie keep a diary?' asks Moira. 'If she did it could give us some more insight into her relationship with Josh Stratton.'

'No, sorry, we didn't find one in her apartment,' says Doreen. 'But you could ask her room-mate, Bethany.'

'We'll do that, thanks,' says Moira.

'Do you have her mobile . . . erm, cell phone?' asks Lizzie. 'One of my girls uses the notes app as a diary, maybe Jessie did the same.'

'Maybe she did,' says Doreen. 'But we don't have her cell. It wasn't with her purse and the other personal items that the police returned to us, and it wasn't in her home or at her office.'

'Did she own a cell phone?' asks Moira.

'For sure,' says Doreen. 'We just don't know where it's at.'

Moira frowns. In her experience, people these days, especially people under thirty, take their phones everywhere with them. If Jessie's wasn't with her or at any of the places she'd usually have kept it, that's a big question mark. They need to find the phone.

'Aside from her romantic relationship and work, what else was she involved in?' asks Philip, tapping his pen against the table. 'Any hobbies or side hustles?'

'She was very sporty,' says Jim.

'And real community minded,' adds Doreen, a tremble in her voice. 'She helped out as a junior coach at SSC Sports, teaching martial arts and general sports classes. Jessie loved working with those kids.'

'She was a blue belt herself. An undefeated champion,' says Jim, the pride clear from his words. 'She trained five times a week over at the Girls Club.'

Interesting, thinks Moira. If Jessie was a blue belt in martial arts she knew how to fight. If someone had attacked her up in the penthouse, she wouldn't have been easy to throw off the balcony. 'Did the cops know that?'

'We told them everything,' says Jim. 'It was Detective Durcell from the local PD who led the enquiry. I can give you his number.'

'That'd be great,' says Moira. She looks at the others. Philip's still scribbling notes, but Lizzie and Rick give her a little nod, obviously thinking as she does that the Becktons have probably given them enough for now. 'I think we've got all we need. Thank you so much for talking with us, we really appreciate—'

'There's something else you should know,' says Jim, glancing at his wife.

'The cops seemed to think this was of critical importance,' says Doreen, her eyes becoming even more tearful.

'Jessie sent us an SMS message. From the timing of when she was found and the estimated time of her death it must have been just before it happened,' says Jim, his voice breaking as he says the word 'death'.

'What did she say?' asks Moira, feeling her heart rate accelerating.

Jim looks anguished. 'It . . . she said . . . "I'm sorry".'

'But we didn't understand it,' says Doreen. 'She had nothing to be sorry about.'

9

RICK

'"*I'm sorry*" does sound like a suicide note in text message form,' says Philip, solemnly. 'My money is on the cops taking it as such and then using any evidence they found to reinforce the theory.'

Rick agrees with Philip. Since the Becktons told them about the SMS they'd received from Jessie around the time she died he's even more convinced than he was earlier that their daughter died by suicide. It's real tragic, but however hard they investigate the circumstances they won't be able to change that fact. Although the others are keen to investigate anyways, Rick thinks it'd be kinder to tell them straight up, and not take the case. He was outvoted during the discussion with the Becktons, but now it seems like maybe Philip is having second thoughts.

Having finished their meeting with the Becktons, the four of them have regrouped in Rick's hotel room, and are gathered around a makeshift murder board made from pieces of paper that he's tacked on to the long wall to the right of the queen-sized bed. At the top, they have a photo of Jessie Beckton that was given to them by her parents. She's smiling confidently at the camera; her long, platinum-blonde hair is pulled back into a sleek ponytail, her make-up is natural-looking, and she's looking real smart in a blue shift dress with sky-high red heels and a matching purse. She sure looks like a successful realtor to Rick.

Beneath the photo he's written the key facts they know so far – twenty-three years old; moved here six months ago; works for Beachseekers; recently come out of a toxic relationship. He's noted the places and persons of interest they need to pursue as lines of enquiry, but before they go any further they have to do a reality check and make a call on whether to proceed, given the information they've just gotten from Jim and Doreen Beckton.

'Philip's right,' says Rick. 'That SMS has me thinking the cops called it right.'

Sitting on the bed beside Lizzie, Philip's expression is sombre. 'Exactly.'

'I guess you could be right,' says Moira, thoughtfully, from her position leaning against the closet doors. 'What with that, and the fact the door was still locked when the brokers arrived for the open house, and the CCTV only showed Jessie going up to the eighth floor until that time, it does seem less likely foul play was involved.' She exhales hard. 'I just really wanted to help the Becktons. They seem like good people and losing a child must be unbearable.'

'For sure,' says Rick, meeting Moira's gaze.

She looks away quickly and he feels heat flush his face. He's messed up: not telling her about Estelle already, and then handling this morning the way he did. He feels such a damn idiot.

Plus, Estelle wasn't real pleased when he told her he had to go away for a few days on a case. From the disappointed look she gave him, to the tone of her voice, he could tell she thought he wasn't prioritising her, again. He'd tried to explain that the case had been on the cards before she'd arrived, but she told him not to bother; she didn't want to hear it. It feels as if he's managed to screw things up with Moira, and at having a second chance with Estelle, in the space of a single day.

'They didn't lose her,' says Lizzie, her voice cutting into his thoughts. It's the first thing she's said since they started discussing the case. 'Jessie Beckton was murdered.'

'Says what evidence?' asks Philip, running his hand over his bald pate. 'We can't just decide that on the basis of her having just booked a three-day cruise for the end of the month and because her parents are nice.'

'I never said we could,' says Lizzie, firmly. 'I have evidence.'

'Okay,' says Rick, surprised. Surely there hadn't been time to look into the facts of the case since they'd gotten here? But Lizzie has that look she gets – confidence and determination – so he figures she must have already gotten to work. 'Care to talk us through it?'

'Of course,' says Lizzie. 'I used the coroner's report to work out the precise location Jessie's body was found and then cross-referenced the information with the autopsy details. From the description of her injuries, it's clear she landed head first, which in itself is very unusual in a jumper, but that isn't all. In order for her to have landed in the exact spot described, she would have had to have fallen vertically down from the balcony rail. The majority of times when someone jumps, or is pushed, they push, or are pushed, forward, away from the building, and so the place they land is a foot or more further out from the place of origin. That isn't true with Jessie. From the information in the reports, and having seen the balcony and the ground location she was found, my conclusion is that she didn't jump but she was suspended from the balcony head first and then dropped.'

Sweet Jesus, thinks Rick. Jessie Beckton was only twenty-three; virtually still a child.

They all stay silent for a moment.

Philip mutters under his breath, 'That poor girl.'

The revelation is unexpected, but that's why they're here: to focus on the evidence and find anything that might have been missed before. Rick looks back at Lizzie. She's the CSI expert; if anyone knows how to read the forensic evidence it's her. 'How sure are you?'

'About ninety-eight per cent,' says Lizzie. 'Errors are always possible, but I'd say the evidence is pretty conclusive.'

'Then why was it ruled a suicide?' says Moira. 'Surely the inquest should have reached the same conclusion as you?'

Lizzie shrugs. 'I don't know. I think they should have, but obviously that didn't happen. It could be they felt the circumstantial evidence – the locked door, and the text message to her parents, et cetera – outweighed the trajectory issue and so they put it down to a fluke.'

'Doesn't sound very thorough,' says Rick, pulling the wooden chair out from beneath the desk and taking a seat. He hates the idea of local law enforcement doing a sub-standard job, but recently they seem to be finding more and more examples of that.

'Another thing is her phone. The Becktons said it hasn't been located,' says Moira. 'That's a big red flag in my book.'

'Yeah, true,' says Rick. 'So are we talking ourselves back around to continuing with the case?'

'I'm continuing,' says Lizzie, determinedly. 'A young woman has been murdered and her parents want us to help them get justice. There's no way I'm walking away from this.'

'Me too,' says Moira. 'If there's a chance she was murdered then I have to stick with it. I can't let a killer walk away free.'

'Yes, yes, count me in,' says Philip.

'Okay then,' says Rick. He's outnumbered again, but it doesn't matter. He's changed his mind. They need to investigate Jessie Beckton's death; with what Lizzie's talked them through, there's enough now to indicate the real possibility of it being a homicide. 'Then let's plan our next move.'

'We need to get inside the penthouse as a priority,' says Lizzie. 'Like I said, I'm almost a hundred per cent sure Jessie was dropped from the balcony, but I'd like to see the layout in the apartment and double-check the angles from the balcony railings to be certain.'

'Good plan,' says Rick. 'I think it's better if we view the apartment in pairs, posing as potential buyers without telling the realtor what we're doing. I doubt they get many groups of four looking at property together here. Word's sure to get around about what we're doing at some point, but the longer we fly under the radar the better.'

'Agreed,' says Moira. 'We don't want people hiding things from us.'

Rick nods, hoping that's not a dig at him. There's no malice in Moira's tone, but her expression is hard to read and she's still not making eye contact with him. 'For sure. So Lizzie and Philip, why don't you go ahead and set up a viewing appointment for yourselves as soon as, then Moira and me can then set an appointment up for a little later – so we've both seen the crime scene and can compare notes.'

'Yes, yes, good plan,' says Philip. Standing, he picks up the pen from the desk and jots down what they've agreed on the makeshift murder board. He consults his notepad. 'We've got a long list of people we need to speak to: Jessie's boss and this friend, Elton, at Beachseekers; the parents mentioned rivalry and jealously between the realtors – we need to know how bad it was, and whether there was anyone specifically out to get Jessie. Then there's her flatmate, Bethany, and the controlling ex-boyfriend, Josh Stratton. And we should find out more about her life outside work from her martial arts mentor at Girls Club, and the head coach over at SSC Sports. The Becktons might not have been aware of any issues in either of those places, but we need to make sure.'

'I think the flatmate, Bethany, needs to be spoken to as a priority,' says Lizzie. 'She might be able to give us more on the relationship between Jessie and the ex-boyfriend.'

'And we need to see if she has any idea where Jessie's phone might be,' adds Moira. 'And whether she kept a diary or anything.'

47

'Good call,' says Rick; he looks at Moira. 'You up for doing that together?'

Moira nods, her expression still unreadable. 'Okay.'

'Excellent,' says Philip, writing the actions they've agreed on the murder board. 'And if there's time, perhaps you could pay the ex-boyfriend a visit – it'd be good to get an early read on him.'

'Agreed, he's our number one person of interest right now,' says Moira. 'Then let's regroup here this evening. We've got a load more people to speak with, but let's decide the order once we've finished these initial conversations.'

'Yep,' says Rick, glancing at his watch. It's almost two o'clock, so they'll need to get moving. One thing they're missing so far is an insider view on the local police department investigation. He wonders if his friend and ex-co-worker law enforcement buddy has contacts in this area. Thinks it's worth a call. 'I'll see if Hawk can get us any inside intel on the original investigation.'

'That seems enough to keep us busy this afternoon,' says Philip, noting down the last of the actions on the murder board and handing the pen back to Rick.

'It sure does,' says Rick. 'Let's get to it.'

As the others go back to their rooms to freshen up before they head out on the investigation, Rick stands in front of the make-do murder board. He looks again at the picture of Jessie Beckton, and sighs. A pretty and ambitious young woman, recently out of what seems to have been a controlling, coercive relationship, now dead at twenty-three.

He shudders as he thinks about Jim and Doreen Beckton being told that their daughter is gone. Getting that knock on the door, it's something he's feared for the past five years, but now it's gone. Estelle is safe. He's gotten his daughter back.

Now he just has to figure out how to make things right.

10

MOIRA

The apartment Jessie lived in is in a smart low-rise cream stucco building with distinctive green doors and balcony railings, a couple of blocks from the beach. The walk-up apartment is on the third and top floor, and Moira is feeling the full effect of the Florida humidity by the time they reach the apartment door. She glances at Rick before pressing the buzzer. He's sweating too.

'Go ahead,' he says, removing a tissue from his pocket and wiping his brow.

Moira rings the buzzer and waits, acutely aware of how close she's standing to Rick, and yet how far apart they feel. Their conversation in the car on the way over here focused on preparing for this meeting; she was reluctant to take focus from the case and ask him anything more about Estelle and the reason he's been estranged from his daughter for so long. She glances sideways at him, and realises he's looking at her. She forces a smile. 'You ready?'

'Always am,' Rick says, his smile looking equally strained.

The door opens a couple of inches, stopping when it reaches the end of the security chain. A woman's voice says, 'Hello?'

'Bethany Thompson?' says Moira, stepping closer to the emerald-green front door. 'My name is Moira Flynn, and this is my colleague, Rick Denver. We're working on behalf of Jim and Doreen Beckton. We spoke on the phone earlier?'

'Yeah, sure,' says Bethany. There's a clunk as she disengages the security chain, then opens the door wider. 'Please, come in.'

The woman standing in front of them is about five feet tall and wearing a flowing orange-flowered maxi dress. Her long, strawberry-blonde hair frames her face in a mass of ringlets, and her emerald-green toenail polish matches the front door. Jessie's parents had given them Bethany's personal details, and Moira thinks she looks a lot younger than her twenty-four years.

'Thanks,' says Moira as they step inside and follow Bethany into a large open-plan living area. There's a white kitchen at one end with the gas hob on the island which faces out into a lounge space. There's a big L-shaped sofa and one of the largest televisions Moira's ever seen mounted above a modern pebble and flame gas fireplace. Pretty much everything is white or off-white: kitchen, countertops, sofa, curtains, the whole lot. Even the floor is pale, white-washed wood, and the walls are painted white. The place seems sterile; more like a showhouse or an art gallery than a home.

'Go ahead and sit down,' says Bethany. 'Can I get you something, a soda or coffee?'

'I'm fine, thanks,' says Moira, sitting gingerly on the sofa, and hoping she doesn't put any dirt on it.

'Same here,' says Rick, as he takes a seat beside her. 'We've just got a few questions about Jessie we think you might be able to help us with.'

'Okay,' says Bethany, sitting down on the other side of the sofa's L-shape. 'But I thought the inquest was final. Why are you . . . ?'

'Jim and Doreen, Jessie's parents, asked us to take a look at their daughter's case,' says Rick. 'As a second opinion.'

Bethany looks troubled. 'I know they don't believe Jessie hurt herself. I mean, it does seem impossible that she would . . . she was always the life and soul of everything, you know what I mean? That she'd deliberately throw herself . . .' She exhales hard. 'Look, I'm happy to answer your questions, but I'm not sure I'll be any help.'

'Thank you,' says Moira, her tone reassuring. 'Anything you tell us will help us build up a picture of Jessie – her life and the people in it, as well as what happened on the day of her death.'

'Okay,' Bethany says, clasping her hands together. 'What do you want to know?'

'Why don't you start by telling us about how you met Jessie,' says Moira.

'About six months ago I saw an ad for an apartment share. I was looking for a place closer to the beach, and so I got in touch. Jessie had literally moved in a few days earlier.'

'So Jessie rented the apartment in her name?' says Moira, wondering, if that was the case, how Bethany is still able to live here.

Bethany shakes her head. 'She owned it. She'd been working in real estate in New York before she moved out here and had made decent money. As far as I know she bought the place for cash.'

Moira glances at Rick. An apartment like this must be three to four hundred thousand dollars. That's a lot of cash for a rookie realtor to have available. 'And what happened after she died?'

'The apartment went to her parents,' says Bethany. 'They are such kind, sweet people. They've said I can keep living here as long as I want to for the same rent I was paying Jessie. Their only condition is that I leave her room just as it was when she was alive.'

Moira feels a wave of sadness for the Becktons. She guesses them wanting their daughter's room to stay untouched is a coping mechanism – a way of being able to feel like she's still here if they visit. 'And how would you describe your relationship with Jessie?'

'We were friends, good friends. Sure, it started off as a transactional thing with me renting a room and all, but Jessie didn't need the money – she had me here because she didn't like living alone. In fact, if I'm honest, I think she didn't feel safe alone.'

'You got any idea why?' asks Rick.

Bethany frowns. 'Yeah, I have. That asshole boyfriend, ex-boyfriend, of hers for sure.'

'Josh Stratton?' says Moira.

'That's him.' Bethany clasps her hands together tighter. 'He was a real son-of-a-bitch, always hassling Jessie about something, saying she wasn't giving him enough attention, complaining she wasn't replying to his messages fast enough, and getting jealous when other men talked to or even just smiled at her.'

Rick grimaces. 'Had he always been like that, or had things gotten worse?'

'From what Jessie told me, I think he'd always been possessive, but it got a whole lot worse when she moved here and he was back in New York. She wasn't super keen when he relocated here a few months after her – I'd kind of got the impression she'd hoped things would fizzle out, y'know? But it seemed to have the opposite effect. Then she'd hoped he might chill, being closer and all. He'd been her first serious boyfriend and she kept trying to see the good in him.' Bethany shakes her head. 'But he became even more of an asshole.'

'What made her finally end it?' asks Moira.

'He got physical one evening. I wasn't here, but Jessie said he didn't actually hit her, but it was a real close thing. They were arguing about something stupid like her not having messaged him back quickly enough when she was at work and he'd got her backed up against the wall over there.' Bethany gestures to the wall over by the fireplace. 'He got all up in her face, and when she refused to apologise and told him to cool it he punched the wall to the side of her head. They'd been having problems for a while, but that was the last straw for Jessie. She threw him out and ended the relationship right then.'

Moira nods. She can understand that. Hitting something close to a person can be the last step before hitting the person themselves. Jessie was right to end it. 'How did he take the break up?'

'Real bad.' Bethany unclasps her hands and starts to fiddle with the charm bracelet on her wrist. 'He'd call and message her at all times of the day and night. Sometimes he'd be angry and shout at her, saying she'd made a big mistake and she'll be sorry, then the next time he'd be tearful and begging her to take him back. She blocked him in the end. That's when he started turning up at her office, or the sports centre, or here. There was this one time he came here, he was pounding on our door, and yelling awful things . . .'

'What sort of things?' asks Moira.

'That Jessie was a whore, and that she deserved to die for treating him the way she had.' Bethany meets Moira's gaze and shudders. 'That he'd make her regret making a fool of him.'

'Did you tell the cops this?' says Moira, glancing at Rick. His expression is serious.

'Sure,' says Bethany. 'But they already knew. Jessie had called them that time and he was arrested for disturbing the peace. She got a restraining order after that, and it worked, he didn't hassle her again.'

'When was this?' asks Rick.

Bethany's lower lip trembles. She looks down at her hands. 'About a week before she died. She didn't tell her parents as she knew they'd be worried.'

'I know this must be tough to talk about,' says Moira, her tone gentle. 'We do really appreciate you going through it with us. Can I ask, are you sure he didn't attempt to contact Jessie in that last week? And that she didn't relent?'

'I'm totally sure, she was much happier in that last week than she'd been in months. Like I told the cops, that last day, when I saw her before she went to work that morning, she was excited and

53

full of plans for the future,' says Bethany, getting up and walking over to the fireplace. Removing a framed watercolour of the beach from the wall, she gestures to the hole in the plasterboard it had been covering. 'She left this here as a reminder of why she'd ended it, in case she was ever tempted to let him back into her life. As far as Jessie was concerned, they were a hundred per cent done.'

'Can you tell us about the other people in her life – co-workers and friends?' asks Rick.

'Sure,' says Bethany, looking relieved to be moving on from talking about Josh Stratton. 'She knew a hell of a lot of people, but she wasn't especially close to anyone. There was a guy at her office – Elton – who she had drinks with a couple of times, but I think that was more to bitch about their boss than a genuine friendship. She'd socialise with people from her martial arts gym sometimes too, her trainer was Phoenix Salford-Keynes but I don't know the names of the others, sorry.'

'No problem,' says Rick. 'You mentioned her boss, was there some sort of issue there?'

'Nothing major, I don't think,' says Bethany, looking thoughtful. 'More that she was a real boss bitch, a hard ass, y'know? Jessie worked super-long hours and got very little praise – it kind of grated at times is all.'

'Was she bullied by her boss?' asks Moira.

'I don't think so, from what she said it sounded like her boss was tough on everyone. If anything, Jessie got off lightly, she said once that the bitch boss referred to her as her "mini me".'

Rick runs his hand across his jaw. 'And she didn't have any trouble with any other co-workers?'

'Not that she told me,' says Bethany. 'But she was kind of a private person, so there might have been issues she didn't tell me about.'

'Thinking on that,' says Rick. 'Are you aware of her keeping a diary or anything?'

'The cops asked me that, but I never saw one,' says Bethany.

'And her cell phone wasn't found. Have you any idea where it could be?' asks Moira.

'None,' says Bethany. 'Jessie was glued to her iPhone, it's real weird they didn't find it in her hand or her purse.'

Indeed, thinks Moira. *It is weird.*

Bethany looks thoughtful. 'Well, she did have that trouble on Instagram.'

'What trouble?' asks Rick, leaning forward in his seat and glancing at Moira.

'Jessie got trolled really bad. It happened a few weeks before she died – a bunch of keyboard warriors leaving bad comments on her posts. She was really upset. In the end she deleted her account.'

Moira leans forward too, mirroring Rick; still in sync despite the tension between them. This new information could bring a different avenue to explore. 'What sort of things did they say?'

'The usual mean shit,' says Bethany. 'Horrid things about how Jessie looked, which was ridiculous given she was a total babe. And some other stuff about her being a homewrecker. At one point I wondered if Josh was behind it, but I figured probably not – there was so much of it, it would have taken forever to set up all the accounts and post all the comments.'

Moira wonders. Josh Stratton does sound like the type of guy petty enough to troll an ex online. 'Did she tell anyone about it, or find out who was doing it?'

'No, but . . .' Bethany thinks for a moment. 'She did mention something about the sports club and a disagreement of some sort, but she didn't want to go into details and I didn't push it. She deleted her account and that was the end of it.'

The mean comments might have stopped, but that doesn't mean the troll's anger had gone away, thinks Moira. It could have been some randoms targeting a pretty woman with a good job, or it could be someone closer to home. They'd need to look into it to be sure.

'Okay, thanks,' says Moira, glancing at Rick. 'I think that's all the questions we have, but do you mind if I use your bathroom quickly before we go?'

'Sure, no problem, it's just down the hallway to the right,' says Bethany.

As Moira heads towards the bathroom, she hears Rick asking Bethany what she does for work. Confident he'll keep her chatting for a while, Moira tries the handle of the first door she comes to and peeps inside. The bedroom is a riot of clashing colours: purple curtains, a fluffy pink rug, a bed covered with a patchwork quilt, a silver blanket and a mess of jewel-coloured cushions scattered on top. Above the purple velvet headboard, a pink neon sign spells the name 'Bethany'. Moira smiles. If this is Bethany's bedroom then it's clear that the minimalist, white style must have belonged to Jessie.

Closing the door behind her, Moira continues on along the hallway. She passes the bathroom, continuing on to the door at the far end of the hall. It's closed, but given it's the only room she's not seen yet, she's pretty sure it must be Jessie's.

Pausing for a moment to listen, Moira makes sure she can still hear Bethany talking, then slowly eases down the handle and opens the door. The bedroom is white. Everything in it is white. Correction, everything apart from a strip of photographs that have been stuck around the large mirror on the dressing table.

Quickly, Moira pads across the fluffy white rug to the dressing table. Across to her left she sees the ensuite bathroom is, again, entirely white aside from the chrome fixtures. Yes, the neutral palette was definitely Jessie's choice.

The dressing table is neatly ordered with make-up in a white rectangular box with a pot containing brushes alongside, a white hairbrush and another white box, this one filled with skincare creams. The photos show Jessie in various poses with a very attractive man; the pair are laughing and pulling comedy faces at the camera. It looks like they were taken in a photo booth. Moira wonders who the man is – they haven't seen a picture of Josh Stratton yet, and maybe this could be him, but it must have been taken long before he started getting so controlling as the pair in the photos look completely happy and carefree.

Moira snaps a picture of the photos on her phone. Whoever this man is, they're going to need to talk to him. Putting her phone back into her pocket, she tries the drawers of the dressing table, but they're locked. Moira wonders where the key is. Glancing around the rest of the room, she sees no sign of it. Jessie's PJs are folded on her bed, and there's a half-drunk glass of water on the bedside table. The place looks as if she's due to return home at any moment. Moira feels a pang of sadness that she never will.

She's still wondering about the missing key and what might be in the locked drawers when Rick's voice from down the hallway makes her jump. *Dammit.* She's taken too long. Hurrying back across the room, she slips through the door and closes it behind her. There's no sign of Rick or Bethany, but their voices are louder so they must be moving this way.

Heart thumping, Moira rushes along the hallway to the bathroom. She flushes the loo, and washes her hands, and then strides back into the main living area. Rick and Bethany are standing in the kitchen. Moira smiles at Bethany. 'Thanks so much.'

'No problem,' says Bethany.

As they head towards the door, Moira stops and turns back to Bethany. She can't ask her directly about the man in the photos without admitting she'd been looking around Jessie's room, but she needs to find out who he is. 'Just one more thing, do you have a picture of Josh Stratton?'

'No, sorry,' says Bethany. 'Jessie trashed all the pictures she had of him. But if you go online and search Josh Stratton at KMP Auto Outlet, there's a big picture of him on their website.'

'Great, we'll do that,' says Moira, as she follows Rick out of the apartment. 'And if you think of anything else that could help us, anything at all, please just call.'

As they take the stairs back down to the parking lot, Rick glances across at Moira. 'Find anything good?'

'Maybe,' says Moira, giving him a small smile for guessing why she'd really asked to use the bathroom. 'But the first thing we need to do is talk to Josh Stratton.'

'For sure,' says Rick. 'A violent, threatening ex-boyfriend has to be our number one suspect.'

Moira nods. There's a lot to look into: the violent ex-boyfriend, a missing phone, an unknown man with Jessie in the photos attached to her mirror, and a load of anonymous hatred from Instagram keyboard warriors, plus the issue that all the police evidence indicates Jessie was alone in the penthouse. The facts of this case just don't add up right.

That makes her even more determined to find the truth.

11

LIZZIE

Lizzie and Philip meet the real-estate agent in the atrium of the Surf-Sand Vista building. He introduces himself as Elton Bruce from Beachseekers, and leads them to the closest elevator to go up to the penthouse apartment.

As they travel the eight storeys in the large, mirror-walled lift, Elton asks them what brings them to the Tampa area and Philip launches into a monologue about them being retired and how much better the weather is here in Florida than it is in England. Lizzie doesn't mind though. She's happy for Philip to chat away – it gives her the chance to study Elton a little more. The Becktons mentioned Jessie had gone out for drinks with him a few times. It must be weird for him to have to show them the place where his friend died.

He really is very handsome, with a perfectly trimmed beard, not a hair out of place in his black quiff, neatly manicured eyebrows and lashes that could possibly have a little touch of mascara helping them to look even longer than they already are. Elton might live here at the beach, but Lizzie still can't understand how he's able to wear a navy three-piece suit in this weather; it's absolutely sweltering.

'And what about you, Mrs Sweetman?' asks Elton, a broad, genuine smile on his face.

Lizzie blinks. She hadn't been following the conversation and she has no idea what Elton is referring to. 'I . . .'

'Lizzie loves to paint,' says Philip, taking her hand in his and giving it a squeeze. 'She's very artistic.'

'Well, perfect,' says Elton, his smile widening. 'There's a fantastic artists' community here, and with the beach views you get from the balcony you won't help but feel inspired to do your best work.'

Lizzie returns his smile. His enthusiasm is rather infectious. 'That sounds great.'

'Oh my God, I just love your accent so much,' says Elton, pressing his palms together in a brief prayer position. 'I visited London with friends for my thirtieth birthday a few years back and I totally loved it. London's near where you lived, right?'

'Quite close,' says Lizzie, thinking that, in relative terms, everywhere is close in England compared to the vastness of America. 'So, what can you tell us about the apartment?'

'It's a total dream,' says Elton, as the lift stops and the door opens to reveal a hallway with far fewer doors off it than the lower floor that their hotel room is on. He steps out and gestures for them to follow. 'There are only eight penthouse units on this level, so you get a lot of square footage and, like I said, premium views. But, as there are two penthouse levels, the upper – ninth floor – penthouses are nearing completion but not on the market yet – you're not paying the highest price for the view, but you're getting it just the same.'

Philip tuts. 'Another level of penthouses, did you say? Surely a penthouse can only be at the very top floor of a building?'

'That's an often held misconception,' says Elton, leading them along the cream-carpeted hallway. The walls are painted a soft ivory, and the pictures on them seem to blend in with the rest of the subtle but expensive-looking decor. 'But many buildings have two levels of penthouses. In a place like this, where the views are so stunning, and in a seniors' community with all the amenities Shimmering Sands has, you're always going to attract more clients than you have penthouses, so two levels with the highest-end finishes are the way to go. Beachfront retirement is very popular here, and Shimmering Sands is one of the best communities, seamlessly pairing the comforts of home with the luxury of a five-star holiday resort – you've got your water sports, tennis, pickleball, sunset yoga, spa and gym, along with multiple pools. Here, your life can literally be one long holiday.'

'I see,' says Philip, patting his crown. 'Well, that all sounds very nice, but you say the higher-level penthouses aren't ready yet?'

'No, sir, but they'll be open for viewings by the end of next month,' says Elton, his smile faltering. 'Are you still interested in seeing this one, or was it a top-floor property you were especially after, because I've got another listing in the Sunshine View building along the street that we could go—'

'We want to see this one,' says Lizzie, hurriedly.

'Well, great,' says Elton, turning on a megawatt smile and stopping beside an oak door. 'Because here we are.'

He opens the door and gestures for Lizzie and Philip to enter first. The entryway opens up into a spacious open-plan living space with the kitchen, dining and sitting areas impeccably furnished in soft, neutral tones. Lizzie can see the ocean through the big sliding doors at the end of the space; she can imagine that a sunset viewing would be spectacular.

'Welcome home,' says Elton theatrically, opening his arms out wide. 'So here you have three bedrooms and three bathrooms, in all the apartment is just under three thousand square feet plus you've got a fabulous balcony giving you plenty of additional outdoor space. There are hardwood floors throughout. High-end kitchen appliances and the counters are Carrara marble. The bathrooms have remote-controlled showers, and dual vanities with Calcutta Gold marble counters.'

'It's lovely,' says Lizzie, running her hand along the cool smoothness of the marble kitchen counter.

'Yes, yes,' says Philip. 'Good-sized space here. What about the bedrooms?'

'They're just through here,' says Elton, ushering them through a door off the main living space into a short corridor. 'Here you have the two guest bedrooms, each with their own ensuite, and then along here is the master.'

Lizzie looks into the two guest rooms and then follows Elton and Philip into the master. The room has high ceilings and lots of natural light flooding in through the floor-to-ceiling windows along one side. Again, the furnishings have been done in stylish, neutral tones. 'This is huge, and this bed, is it a king?'

'Absolutely,' says Elton, smiling. 'Like I said, these penthouses have very generous square footage. And of course,' he says, moving through to the open-plan living space and sliding the glass doors on to the balcony open. 'You have one of the best views in Tampa.'

'Outstanding,' says Philip. 'This ocean view is quite something.'

'It is,' says Lizzie, stepping out on to the balcony. It must be three or four yards wide and runs the length of the apartment. Walking to the edge she takes in the view of the white sand beach, the lush tropical gardens and the gulls circling overhead. Then, she presses her palms against the black iron railing and looks down. As she'd anticipated, the section of pathway that she had looked at earlier is directly below the balcony. If Jessie had stood on these railings and jumped she'd have landed at least a metre further away from the building, and on the grass. And if she'd climbed over the railings and done more of a dive from the building, she'd still have landed too far out to hit the path. It's a long way down, and Lizzie shudders at the thought of Jessie Beckton's last moments. As she'd suspected, the only way for Jessie to have landed head first in the position that she did is if she was dropped over the railings.

'Don't worry,' says Elton. 'It's high but it's all perfectly safe.'

'Is it?' says Lizzie, turning to face him.

Elton's smile droops slightly. 'Well, yes, of course.'

Philip frowns. 'It's just we heard someone died here.'

Lizzie's glad Philip kept the phrasing vague. 'Someone died' is better, softer, than saying 'was killed' or 'jumped'. Especially given they've been led to believe that Elton was Jessie's friend.

'They . . .' Elton's smile has gone and there's a tightness around his eyes now. 'It was a tragic accident.'

'Do you know what happened?' asks Philip. 'I mean, if we're going to buy the place then we should know the details really, so we can make an informed decision, you understand.'

'Sure, yes, totally,' says Elton. He's clearly shaken, although he's trying to keep his tone upbeat. 'One of my colleagues fell from the balcony when she was setting up for an open house. But everything's been checked and there are no safety issues or code violations you need to be worried about. I was in the building at the time showing an apartment on one of the lower floors. I rushed outside when I heard but the police had cordoned the area off and . . .' He shakes his head, sadly.

Lizzie nods sympathetically. 'Losing your colleague like that must have been a real shock.'

Elton's eyes become watery. 'I . . . it was . . .'

'Were you close?' asks Lizzie, her tone gentle.

Elton holds her gaze for a moment, then says, 'Yes. We were friends.'

'That must have been very hard for you,' says Lizzie. She puts her hand on Elton's arm and gives it a squeeze. 'I know how tough it is when you lose someone close.'

Beside her, Philip bows his head solemnly and nods in agreement. For a moment no one speaks. Far below them, over on the beach, the waves crash rhythmically against the sand.

Elton looks from one of them to the other. He dabs at his eyes with the pocket square from his jacket, and then fixes a smile back in place, but it's shakier than before. 'So what do y'all think of the apartment?'

'It's very nice,' says Philip, putting his hands in his pockets and leaning against the glass doors. 'But we'd rather talk with you about Jessie Beckton.'

Elton's rather brittle smile disappears, but he says nothing. Lizzie knows they're going off script here and taking a gamble; they'd agreed with Rick and Moira to keep the investigation under the radar at the viewing, but given Elton was Jessie's friend this is an opportunity they can't miss. She keeps her eyes on him, and her expression kind. This is the moment they'll either get him to talk or he'll clam up and eject them from the property. It needs to be played delicately. She keeps her tone soft. 'We know Jessie was your friend, Elton, because her parents Jim and Doreen told us. They said you'd been on nights out together and she spoke well of you.'

Elton's lower lip trembles and he looks away, towards the ocean.

'Can I trust you, Elton, if I share something with you?' asks Lizzie.

'Yes,' says Elton, his voice quieter, reedier, than before.

Lizzie glances at Philip and he gives a small nod. 'Okay then. You see, the Becktons aren't happy with the verdict given at the inquest. They don't believe Jessie would have harmed herself, and they've asked us to look into what really happened to her.'

'But I don't . . .' Elton looks from Lizzie to Philip and back again. 'You're retired seniors, not police detectives?'

'We're retired law enforcement officers,' says Philip, pulling himself up to his full height and pushing out his chest. 'And we like to help out other retirees.'

Elton looks uncertain, his gaze flitting back and forth between them. 'Jessie was a good friend. We hadn't known each other very long, but we just clicked, y'know? She wasn't like most of my other co-workers.'

Lizzie nods, but stays silent, waiting for him to continue.

'We used to grab drinks after work when our schedules allowed.' Elton smiles at the memory. 'She was fun to be around and she loved to dance. We had fun.'

'You said she wasn't like most of your other co-workers,' says Philip. 'What did you mean by that?'

'Real estate is a competitive business. We try to get along in the office, but there's always a bunch of jealous bitching if people do well.' Elton shakes his head. 'Jessie wasn't like that. It was refreshing.'

'And how did she get along with the team?' asks Lizzie. 'Did everyone like her?'

'Most people.' He frowns. 'I mean, she had her share of challenges, like we all do, and Jessie maybe had to deal with more bitchiness than others, because she sold a lot of real estate, and I mean *a lot*, so that got people's back up.' He lowers his voice. 'Plus, our boss, she's a real hard ass. A total bitch sometimes. But Jessie probably got on with her the best of any of us.'

'Were you aware of anyone she didn't get on with?' asks Philip.

'Aside from her loser ex-boyfriend? No.' Elton rolls his eyes. 'Jeez, that man! He looked like a total angel but he was really all devil. He tried to ban her from seeing me, the fool, but she wasn't having any of that shit. He didn't take it well though.'

'Were you aware of him ever being violent with Jessie?' says Lizzie.

'She never mentioned anything but . . .' Elton's eyes widen. 'Wait, you don't think he killed her, do you?'

'Do you?' asks Philip.

Elton looks thoughtful. 'He had a lot of anger for sure, but I don't see how he could have gotten to her. She was alone – the CCTV proved it. No one else came up here before she died.'

Having said goodbye to Elton after swearing him to secrecy, Philip and Lizzie take a walk along the boardwalk. The heat from the sun is scorching, and Lizzie is grateful for the light breeze that gusts off the ocean and for the wide-brimmed sunhat she'd remembered to bring. Over on the beach, a group of seniors are playing a vigorous game of volleyball. The women are in swimwear, the men are bare-chested with shorts; they all look hot and sweaty from their efforts, but from their shouts and cheers they're clearly enjoying the game.

She glances at Philip. He looks sweatier and more red-faced than the volleyball players. She takes his hand. 'Are you okay?'

'Fine, fine,' says Philip, flapping his hand at his face like a makeshift fan. 'I'm just not well suited to beach weather.'

'Come on, let's cool off by having a paddle,' says Lizzie, kicking off her sandals and leading Philip off the boardwalk and on to the sand. Reluctantly, Philip follows, although from his expression it's obvious that he's not keen. Lizzie looks down at his feet, still clad in trainers and socks. 'Aren't you going to take them off?'

Philip grimaces. 'I'd rather not.'

'Okay,' she says, letting go of his hand and setting off towards the water.

'What did you think about that chap, Elton?' says Philip, puffing a little as he trots to catch up with her.

'He seemed genuine,' says Lizzie. 'And he clearly misses his friend, but aside from confirming the ex-boyfriend wasn't nice and giving us a sense of the internal politics and culture at Beachseekers, I don't think we learnt anything new.'

'Yes, yes. It's interesting though.'

'What is?' asks Lizzie, turning to face Philip.

'Although he was surprised that Jessie's parents had hired us, he didn't argue against the theory that she was murdered.'

Reaching the ocean, Lizzie wades in until the water passes her ankles. 'I guess so, but he also said that he didn't think it was possible.'

Philip stays a couple of steps back from the water, looking serious. 'If you're sure that Jessie was dropped from that balcony rather than jumping then it must have been.'

Lizzie thinks about the path below the balcony and the trajectory Jessie would have taken to reach it. 'I'm ninety-nine per cent certain.'

Philip raises an eyebrow. 'That's more than earlier, and it's good enough for me. She was murdered, and so we need to find out who did it, why they did it, and how they got into the penthouse unseen.'

As the water laps around her ankles, Lizzie wiggles her toes and looks back across the white sand beach towards the buildings. The eighth-floor balcony of the Surf-Sand Vista is just visible through the palm trees. It strikes her as odd that there were no witnesses to what happened, although she supposes there would have been less light just before sunset, so perhaps that was a factor.

She's still thinking about it when movement along the beach, towards a white wooden pergola, catches her eye. A bride, dressed in a long, ivory A-line dress with a long veil in her hair and a bouquet of blue and pink flowers, is walking across the sand towards the pergola. Waiting for her, standing between two large flower arrangements on the steps, is a blond man wearing a cream linen suit. Lizzie smiles and points towards them. 'Look, a wedding.'

Philip turns to look. His expression softens. 'Lovely.'

'Isn't it?' says Lizzie, an idea forming in her mind. Their time away in Australia had been fantastic. It had helped them reconnect as a couple, and work through the issues that had almost seen them split up just a few months ago. Now things are better than they've ever been. 'You know we talked about renewing our vows sometime, why don't we do it on a beach?'

'Here?' says Philip, looking horrified. 'At the scene of a murder?'

'Not specifically at *this* beach, but *a* beach here in Florida. Maybe St Pete beach, we do love that place.'

'Do we?' says Philip, not looking very enthusiastic. 'I'm fond of the harbour, perhaps.'

'Well then,' says Lizzie, looking at him expectantly. 'Don't you think it's a great idea? St Pete beach would be wonderful.'

'It's jolly hot out on the beach, and the sand would get everywhere and—'

'It adds to the fun of it, though, doesn't it,' says Lizzie. Excitement fizzes through her. She can see it now: Philip, handsome in a linen suit, her in a long maxi dress with a garland of flowers in her hair. Hopefully the kids would fly out to join them for the ceremony, and they'd invite Rick and Moira, maybe have them as best man and maid of honour, and all their friends from The Homestead could come. It would be one hell of a celebration. 'I think it would be perfect.'

Philip says nothing for a long moment. Then he takes Lizzie's hands, his expression turning serious again. 'If you say so, dear girl. But before we plan anything, we need to solve this murder.'

Lizzie nods. He's absolutely right. They do.

12

RICK

'Josh Stratton isn't the guy in the photos,' says Moira, turning her cell phone towards Rick so he can see the screen. It shows a page from KMP Auto Outlet's website with a picture of a blond, classically handsome man grinning, his white teeth looking extra bright against his deep tan. The caption is 'Meet our salesperson of the month: Josh Stratton'.

'You were right then,' says Rick. It doesn't surprise him; Moira has a sixth sense for these things and she'd been sure that the guy in the pictures pinned to Jessie's mirror hadn't been Josh. It was something about the way the two of them were so happy together, she said; she'd doubted Jessie would look that relaxed with Stratton, given how controlling and violent he'd become. Rick glances across the parking lot to the KMP Auto Outlet building. 'So how do you want to play this?'

'Good cop, bad cop?' says Moira, her tone all business as she takes off her seatbelt and opens the door of the jeep. 'You can play the good guy.'

'Sure,' says Rick. He holds Moira's gaze for a beat longer than usual. He wants to tell her he's sorry for keeping the fact he had a daughter from her, that he'd been embarrassed to say that they were estranged for so many years, but he can't get the words out. Moira gives a slight shake of her head, and then climbs out of the jeep.

Play the good guy, yeah that's about right, thinks Rick. *I'm not the good guy. Not after what went down this morning, anyways.*

They walk across the lot, past the rows of gleaming cars with signs across their windshields each claiming that particular vehicle is the deal of the century. The KMP Auto Outlet building is a modern glass and chrome structure. The glass doors slide open as they approach.

As they step inside, they're hit with a blast of sub-zero air conditioning, and a smart, pant-suit-wearing woman with neat, flame-red bobbed hair and a clipboard rushes over to greet them. 'Hi there, welcome to KMP Auto Outlet, will you let us help you find the car of your dreams?'

'Good afternoon, ma'am,' says Rick. 'We're looking for Josh Stratton.'

'Great choice of salesperson,' says the flame-haired woman, her smile staying in place as she speaks. She gestures across the showroom, where there's a group of six desks. A blond man in a grey suit is sitting at the desk furthest away. 'Please, go right over. Josh is one of our very best, you'll be in great hands.'

Rick thanks the greeter, and he and Moira stride across the showroom, past a super-shiny silver 4x4 that's parked with its doors and trunk open ready for viewing, and on towards the desks.

Josh's grin widens as they approach. 'Welcome, please take a seat. Can I get you a coffee and doughnut while we talk over your requirements?'

Rick and Moira stop in front of his desk. They don't sit. And they don't say anything. Oftentimes silence is the best way to put a suspect on edge; it keeps them guessing what's about to be asked, and how much is already known.

The smile on Josh's face loses a little of its brilliance. He narrows his eyes; clearly becoming suspicious given that they're not behaving like typical car buyers.

'Can we have a word?' says Moira, her tone serious. 'It's about the investigation into the death of Jessica Beckton.'

'Really? You're coming to my place of work?' says Josh, standing up and moving around the desk towards them. He's big and broad-shouldered, and looks the type who would've played football in high school and have gotten a real kick out of bashing into the little guys. 'I thought we were done with this shit.'

What a charmer, thinks Rick. Josh has clearly gotten them pegged as cops, but he doesn't want to dissuade him from that theory right now. Keeping his tone amicable he says, 'We just have a few questions.'

Josh scowls. 'What's wrong with you people? I told you everything I knew. Why don't you just leave me—'

'We want you to be honest about what happened with Jessica Beckton,' says Moira, her gaze flinty and her tone granite-hard. 'You used to hit her, right?'

Jeez, thinks Rick. Moira's not pulling any punches. She's not keeping her voice low either.

Josh looks round real fast, checking his co-workers aren't within earshot. 'Not in here.'

Interesting that he didn't deny it, thinks Rick. Maybe Bethany was wrong and the asshole did do more than hit the wall after all. Straightening up, Rick still has a good couple of inches on Stratton. He crosses his arms, forgetting for a moment that he's supposed to be the good cop. 'We're not leaving. We need to talk and I suggest real strongly you don't make us do this the hard way.'

'Okay, okay,' says Josh, some of his bravado leaving him. He takes a half step back and holds up his hands. 'I'm due to go on break. Let's do this outside.'

'Okay,' says Moira.

They follow Josh out of the door and around the building to a small, covered area with a couple of benches. Rather than sitting, Josh leans against the back of one of the benches. He looks from Rick to Moira. 'Okay, what do you wanna know?'

'Tell us about your relationship with Jessica Beckton,' says Rick.

Josh blows out hard. 'I've already been through this. I don't get why—'

'Just answer the damn question,' says Moira.

'Yeah, fine, whatever. We had a thing, and then we didn't.' He looks from Moira to Rick. 'Are we done?'

'We're done when I say we're done,' says Moira, looking at Josh like he's something unpleasant she's just stepped in. 'So how about you tell us the whole story.'

'I don't—'

'Look, Josh,' says Rick, his tone conversational, almost gentle compared to Moira's pointiness. 'Don't bullshit us. We know she ended things with you after you'd moved out here to be with her and we know that you took that news real bad.'

'We know about the hole you punched in her apartment wall and the restraining order she took out against you,' says Moira, nodding. 'We know you threatened her. That you implied you wanted her dead.'

'It wasn't . . . I didn't . . .' Josh pales. 'It wasn't like that.'

Rick wonders why the guy seems so thrown by the fact that they're bringing this stuff up. Surely the cops would have questioned him about these things as a matter of routine? 'What was it like, Josh?'

Josh gives a smug grin. 'Jess was crazy about me. I was the one who should have gotten myself a restraining order. She was like a bitch on heat, always trying to rip my clothes off and getting all kinds of jealous if I so much as looked at another girl.' He shakes his head. 'I told her I had more than enough Josh to go around, but she wanted me all to herself. I never hit her or anything, I'm a lover not a fighter.'

Stratton is clearly deluded, thinks Rick, struggling to keep his expression neutral.

'I wasn't upset that we ended.' He raises his eyebrows at Moira, and makes a show of looking her up and down. 'Makes it easier to have a good time.'

'Drop the act. Your bullshit story isn't fooling anyone,' says Moira, looking at Stratton like he's worse than a cockroach covered in crap. 'We know you were the clingy one in the relationship. In fact, we heard you begged Jessica to take you back, just before you threatened her life and she had to take out the restraining order.'

Josh says nothing but a muscle starts pulsing in his forehead. Taking a soft pack of cigarettes from his pants pocket, he taps one out and lights up. He inhales deeply, before he looks over at Rick. There's venom in his voice when he speaks. 'It was that bitch, Bethany, who told you I hurt Jess, am I right?'

'Why'd you think that?' asks Rick, pushing down the disgust he feels for this macho asshole in order to keep him talking and hopefully get what they need.

'Because she hated me.' Josh sucks on his cigarette a few more times before tossing it on to the ground and grinding it out under his heel. 'Me and Jess were good before she moved here and that bitch came into her life. But Bethany, she just hated me coming over. Hell, I'd have been the one living in that damn apartment if it wasn't for her. Instead, she kept on feeding Jess with poison about how I was bad news until Jess believed it and ended things.'

Moira narrows her gaze. 'The way we heard it, you got violent and Jessica dumped you.'

Josh clenches his fists and steps fast towards Moira, hissing, 'That's not true. Don't you say that. I never hit her.'

Moira doesn't flinch and doesn't step back. She keeps her gaze focused on Josh. 'But you wanted to, didn't you? Just like you want to hit me right now?'

Rick is in awe of her grit. It's one of the things he admires about her; one of the many things. But it's a dangerous game, baiting this guy. It's clear Stratton has a hell of a temper, and it sure doesn't look like it'd take much to set him off.

Moira and Josh keep their eyes locked on each other.

'I didn't do it,' says Josh, his voice filled with menace. 'I punched a wall, yeah. I threw some plates, sure. But murder, no, not that. I didn't kill her.'

'I don't believe you,' says Moira, her tone firm, unwavering. 'Prove it.'

'I . . .' A wave of anguish passes across Stratton's face and for a brief moment Rick thinks the man is going to drop the macho act and come clean. Then Stratton laughs. 'Because I didn't need her, I'd already moved on. I mean, the bitch took out a restraining order on me. Me! We were done right then in that moment. I didn't care about her.'

'Nice alternative storyline,' says Moira, shaking her head. 'Too bad it's fiction.'

'It's the truth,' says Stratton, his face flushing red, and his voice increasing in volume. 'I *never* killed the bitch. At the time she was dying I was partying in Starfish, the new cocktail bar on the beach.'

'Stand down.' Rick puts his hand on Stratton's shoulder. 'Don't do something stupid that you're going to regret.'

Stratton takes a couple of steps back, and smooths out an imaginary crease in the front of his jacket. He shakes his head. 'I'm done talking. You come and harass me at my place of work again, I'm going to be calling my lawyer.'

◆ ◆ ◆

They walk across the lot, back towards the jeep. The sun is starting to sink lower in the cloudless sky. It's been a beautiful day, but Rick can't help but feel on edge. Maybe it's the business with Estelle showing up, or having to leave her home alone at his place so soon, or meeting a granddaughter he never even knew about for the first time, or not knowing how to talk to Moira about it all when usually he can speak to her about anything. Or perhaps it's this case: the tragedy of a young life gone too soon, and the seething brutality of a son-of-a-bitch like Josh Stratton.

'Guys like that make me sick,' says Moira, as if reading his mind. 'All that arrogant bravado.'

'Yeah,' says Rick, climbing into the jeep. Not trusting himself enough to say more.

'He didn't do it though,' says Moira, fastening her seatbelt. 'There's a lot of pent-up anger in him, sure, and he's a grade-A asshole, but I believed him when he said he didn't kill Jessie.'

'Maybe,' says Rick, his tone non-committal. 'But he's the type that can get real violent real fast. And if someone threw Jessie off the balcony it could have been a spur-of-the-moment thing, a warped crime of passion. He's strong enough to easily lift her over the railing, and his violence with her was clearly escalating.'

'True,' says Moira, as they climb back into the jeep. 'So, he'd better stay on our suspects list until we've cleared his alibi.'

'Yep.'

Starting up the jeep, Rick grimaces as unwelcome memories flood his mind's eye. Stratton reminded him of Estelle's husband, Mark: slick, macho and a real show-off. Stratton and Mark have the same disingenuous smile, undercurrent of violence, and entitled outlook on life and about women.

Those were some of the reasons why he'd hated the man.

75

13

MOIRA

They meet up for dinner in Philip and Lizzie's room. Rather than using the makeshift paper murder board tacked to the wall in Rick's room, Philip has bought a large freestanding whiteboard and markers from the local Target. Before Moira arrived, he'd cleared everything off the desk and positioned it on top, propped up against the wall. According to Lizzie he's spent the last hour transferring everything from the paper they'd been using in Rick's room on to the board here. Moira has no idea why it's taking him so long, but, apparently, he's almost done.

While they wait for him to finish, Moira messages the Dog-N-Pup Home-from-Home, asking how Marigold, Pip and Wolfie are doing. She hates staying away from them overnight. Seconds later her phone vibrates. The message says all three dogs have settled well and eaten their dinner. There's a photo – the three of them stretched out on a large dog sofa looking chilled. Moira smiles and feels less anxious, thankful that they look like they're having a good time.

'There,' says Philip, standing back from the whiteboard. 'All done, I think.'

'Great,' says Lizzie, staring pointedly at the silver trolley over by the door. 'Can we eat now? It'll be getting cold.'

'Yes, yes, of course,' says Philip, putting the cap back on his marker pen and setting it down on the desk. 'You didn't need to wait for me.'

Moira tries not to roll her eyes; Philip likes everything to revolve around him, so she's pretty sure he'd have kicked up a fuss if they'd started without him. *Mind you, he does seem a bit more mellow since he and Lizzie returned from their Australia trip, so maybe he genuinely means it.*

She joins Lizzie and Rick, who are over at the trolley. Rick passes her a plate and she smiles in thanks. He looks away quickly, and Moira feels her stomach lurch. They still haven't had a proper talk, and it's awkward. She wishes things could go back to how they were, but she doesn't know how. She'd trusted Rick, and she thought he'd trusted her; so why didn't he tell her he had a daughter, even if they'd not been in contact for a while?

'Caesar salad?' asks Lizzie, pulling Moira from her thoughts.

'Great, thanks,' she says, holding out her plate for Lizzie to serve her, and then adding a portion of fries before heading back across the room and sitting down in the armchair.

Lizzie carries her and Philip's dinner across to the bed and sits down next to her husband, handing him his plate. He smiles affectionately at Lizzie as he takes it. That's when Moira notices that Philip's hand, and now the plate, are shaking. She wonders what's going on with Philip. He seems to sense her gaze on him and he looks over at her, the colour draining from his face as he realises she had been staring at his hand. He doesn't speak, but his expression says it all: *please don't tell her.*

Moira looks from Philip to Lizzie. She doesn't seem to have noticed anything is wrong. Lizzie is her friend, and Moira doesn't like to keep secrets, but until she's managed to find out from Philip what's going on she won't say anything. Looking back at Philip, Moira gives a quick nod. He smiles gratefully in return.

They all eat, aside from Rick. He remains standing, holding his plate in one hand and a fork in the other, but not taking a mouthful. After a couple of minutes he says, 'So shall we start with the debrief?'

'Yes, yes,' says Philip. 'Do you want to tell us about the flatmate first?'

'Sure,' says Rick, setting down his plate on the desk and picking up a marker pen. 'Bethany Thompson had lived with Jessie for just over five months.' He makes notes on the whiteboard as he updates Philip and Lizzie with the information they got from Bethany: that Jessie owned the apartment, that her boyfriend had been violent and she'd taken out a restraining order against him. Then on to how Jessie had been trolled online – being called a homewrecker – until she deleted her Instagram account, and that, according to Bethany, Jessie knew lots of people but had few close friends. 'So that's about it, but we are left with a few questions.'

'Like what?' asks Lizzie, finishing the last of her salad.

'Well, for starters how does a twenty-three-year-old afford to buy a beachfront condo with cash?' says Moira, balancing her now empty plate on the arm of the chair. 'Bethany also mentioned a disagreement at the sports club where Jessie volunteered, she didn't know any details but the social media trolling happened afterwards so it's possible there's a connection.'

Rick's nodding. 'Bethany also said that Jessie was always on her cell phone and never left it behind. It's real strange it hasn't been found, especially given the SMS sent to her parents just before she died. It must have been with her at the penthouse.'

'It's really odd,' says Moira. 'The simplest explanation is that Jessie's killer took the phone, but, just in case, I did a quick, covert search of Jessie's room. The drawers to her dressing table were locked, so it's possible there could be a phone or diary in them, but I'd assume the police searched them already so it's doubtful.'

'Interesting,' says Philip, dabbing at his mouth with his napkin. 'Anything else?'

'Yeah, Moira found some pictures taped to the mirror in Jessie's room,' says Rick, turning and noting this down on the whiteboard. 'We don't know who he is, but he isn't her ex-boyfriend.'

'I've got a picture on my phone,' says Moira, pulling out her mobile and getting the picture of the photos on to the screen. She passes it to Lizzie and Philip to look at. 'This is the guy.'

'Oh, that's Elton who showed us around the penthouse this afternoon,' says Lizzie. 'He worked with Jessie at Beachseekers. They were friends.'

'Do you want to tell us what you guys found out?' says Rick.

'Yes, of course,' says Philip, his voice taking on the grating air of self-importance it usually has when he's debriefing on a part of an investigation he's done. But, unlike usual, this time he looks at Lizzie and says, 'Go ahead.'

Nodding, Lizzie smiles at him, and gives his hand a squeeze. 'Elton Bruce confirmed he was pretty close with Jessie. He's obviously still upset about her dying, but he hadn't suspected foul play. Still, when we got him talking, he told us that her ex-boyfriend was, and I quote, a "devil". And that their boss was very demanding, but that Jessie seemed to get on with her better than most of the team.'

'I think we should talk to the boss,' says Philip. 'The main reason Elton didn't suspect murder is because there was no sign of anyone aside from Jessie on the CCTV. I think we need to look at the footage though. We didn't see a camera in the lift, but I assume there is one. There were a few visible in the eighth-floor corridor, but none that I saw in the penthouse itself.'

Lizzie is nodding. 'I checked the trajectory from the penthouse balcony. If Jessie had jumped of her own accord she'd have landed in a different spot. I'm ninety-nine per cent certain that she was murdered.'

Rick writes 'interview boss' and 'check CCTV' on the murder board actions list. 'Anything else?'

Philip shakes his head. 'Did you manage to speak to the ex-boyfriend?'

'Yeah,' says Rick, his disapproval of Josh Stratton clear in his tone.

'He's quite a piece of work,' says Moira. 'Obvious issues with women and massive anger issues. He didn't like it when I pushed him about getting violent with Jessie.'

'Stratton is a grade-A asshole,' says Rick. 'I think he has to be our top suspect.'

'I disagree,' says Moira. 'He's an asshole, yes, but I don't think he killed her.'

'He almost hit you,' says Rick, frowning. 'A guy like that—'

'He's got an alibi.' Moira looks at Lizzie and Philip. 'He says he was drinking at Starfish on the beach at the time of Jessie's death.'

Rick shakes his head. 'It's probably false.'

Moira frowns. Usually, she and Rick have similar takes on people; this is the first time they haven't seen eye to eye. She wonders what Rick is seeing that she's missing. 'Look, like I said earlier, let's keep him on the suspect list until we've cleared his alibi, but not focus exclusively on him. We need to keep an open mind.'

Rick makes a note on the murder board. 'For sure.'

'It sounds like we've made a good start,' says Philip, scanning Rick's notes on the murder board. His eyes are bright but he sounds weary. 'But we've got a lot more ground to cover tomorrow.'

'Agreed,' says Moira. She checks her watch; it's almost ten o'clock. No wonder Philip's looking a bit tired. It's been a long day – a lot has happened since they met the Becktons earlier. 'Shall we allocate tomorrow's tasks and then get some rest?'

'Good idea,' says Philip, looking relieved. 'Thoughts?'

'I think Moira and I should view the penthouse,' says Rick. 'We can also try and combine it with talking to Jessie's boss and finding out more about the CCTV in use.'

Moira nods. 'Okay. And I'd like to speak with Jessie's martial arts coach and the manager of the sports club where she volunteered.'

'Good plan, I need to get hold of Hawk, and see what he can find out for us about the police investigation,' says Rick. He glances at Moira. 'And check out Josh Stratton's alibi at Starfish.'

'And I think Philip and I should try and get some intel on Jessie's rivals in the real-estate business,' says Lizzie. 'If it's as cutthroat as Elton says, there could be jealousy issues there, and maybe a motive.'

'Yes, yes,' says Philip, stifling a yawn. 'I agree. And let's speak with the Becktons again, and see if they have a key to the dressing table drawers that Moira found locked.'

'For sure, I can do that,' says Rick, noting down the plan on the murder board. He puts the cap back on the marker pen and sets it down on the desk. 'Okay, let's call it a night, and get to it in the morning.'

Moira stands and moves towards the door. She looks at Philip and Lizzie. 'See you in the morning.'

'Breakfast at seven?' asks Lizzie.

Moira nods in agreement and opens the door. 'See you then.'

Out in the corridor, Rick and Moira walk in step towards their rooms at the far end of the hallway to Philip and Lizzie's. Their rooms are opposite each other. Stopping as they reach them, they turn to look at each other. The silence is uncomfortable. Moira hates it. Things have never felt like this with Rick before.

He clears his throat, awkwardly. Gives her a small smile. 'Fancy staying at mine?'

Moira looks up at him. He's still just as handsome as always, and the softness in his expression makes her stomach flip. She wants to join him, really she does. But they still haven't spoken properly about Estelle and the fact that Rick hasn't mentioned her once in all the time Moira's known him.

It's late now, and that's too heavy a conversation to start at this time of night. So, Moira shakes her head. 'Sorry, but I don't think that's a good idea.'

14

RICK

He has the dream again. Wakes with his heart punching at his ribs and his whole body drenched in sweat. Blinking his eyes open, Rick takes a gulp of water from the glass on the nightstand and tries to forget. But he can't. The dream lingers in his mind's eye like a movie on repeat that he can't find the off switch for. That last year of Alisha's life, playing on fast-forward.

The surgery. The chemo. The day the doc told them there was nothing more they could do. Alisha getting thinner, more tired; sicker.

The constant feeling of helplessness. The hopelessness. Of him feeling useless; unable to help his wife, and make things better.

He clenches his fists. Tries to force the memories away.

The denial.

How he couldn't bear to think about what was coming. How it was easier to throw himself into work; to double-down on the hours and the travelling. To pretend that everything was going to be fine.

But it wasn't. And he was a fool for trying to kid himself.

He scrunches his eyes tight shut. Doesn't want to see the rest, ashamed.

It's late and he's just arriving home from work. Alisha is already asleep. He goes into what used to be the dining room that they've now gotten made up with a hospital bed, and watches her sleep. She's so skinny now. There are dark circles beneath her eyes and her skin has a yellowish pallor. But she's still beautiful. Still his amazing, talented, generous wife.

Rick stands there watching her sleep. And, as he listens to the shallow rise and fall of her breath, he lets the tears flow.

'Where the hell have you been?' whispers Estelle, her voice full of anger.

Rick quickly wipes his eyes on the back of his hand before turning to face her. She's nineteen now, but in her cotton PJs and make-up free, Estelle still looks like a kid. He feels so sick that his daughter is having to go through this heartbreak he can barely get a word out. 'I was working.'

'You always are! Mom was asking for you earlier. She's dying. You should be here *with her, not out there chasing criminals. She needs you,' says Estelle. Shaking her head, she steps away from the doorway and back into the kitchen.*

After kissing his wife on the forehead, Rick follows Estelle out of the room and closes the door behind him. This is when the shouting starts, every time. He knows Estelle is angry: at fate for giving her mother cancer, at the hospital for not being able to do more, and at him for the way he's handling it. And if it helps his daughter to yell at him, so be it.

He doesn't blame her. He's angry too.

Rick feels the emotion like a lead weight on his chest. Sitting up, he checks the time on the alarm clock; it's just after 4 a.m. There's no way he'll be able to sleep again now and, even if he does manage to doze, the dream will come back.

Getting out of bed he goes to the bathroom and splashes water on his face, then takes his workout clothes out of his carryall, gets dressed, and heads out of his room to the gym.

Ninety minutes later, and no matter how much weight he lifts, it isn't helping. After a third set of a hundred reps he drops the kettle-bells on to the rubber matting, and shakes the ache from his arms. It's no good. Whatever he does, the memory is determined to play in his mind's eye, and he's too dog-tired now to fight it.

The wake is over. Used glasses, half-eaten plates of food, and a buffet table spread that looks as if it's been attacked by locusts are all that's left. Rick exhales. The house feels too quiet, too still. He glances through the double doors into the dining room. Alisha's hospital bed has been taken back by the medical company along with all the medical equipment they'd loaned her. He'd gotten so used to this room being her bedroom that it seems real strange and kind of empty, without the bed. Without her.

Grief builds in his chest and tightens around his throat.

He hears footsteps behind him and swallows down the emotion as he turns around. His daughter stops a few yards away. There's a carryall slung over her shoulder.

'Estelle?'

'I'm leaving, Dad.' Her voice has that hard edge to it that it always has when she talks to him these days. 'I can't stay here.'

'I know it's hard, honey, but—'

'I'm leaving because of you, not Mom.'

Rick doesn't understand. He moves closer to her, reaching out. 'You're angry, I get that, I'm—'

'I'm angry at you, for all the things you didn't do,' Estelle shouts, flinching away from him. 'For being more focused on your damn job than Mom.'

Her words slam into him like a volley of punches. He'd taken a leave of absence from work in Alisha's last few weeks so he could nurse her 24/7, but he knows he should have done it sooner. 'I did everything I—'

'Shut up. Don't even . . .' Estelle holds up her hands. 'Cancer might have killed Mom, but you never being around broke her heart. I can never . . . never forgive you for that.'

Emotion floods through him and he gasps out loud as pain throbs in his chest. Sitting down on to the lifting bench, he picks up his towel with shaking hands and wipes the sweat off his face. He wishes he could wipe away the memory of that day just as easily.

He hadn't been able to persuade Estelle to stay. Whatever he'd said, she'd gotten angrier and more determined. He'd thought that once she'd had a few days' space she'd realise he wasn't the enemy and come back home. He'd hoped that she'd forgive him.

But it didn't happen.

Three days later, Estelle had married Mark, her on-again-off-again boyfriend of two years. Rick hadn't been invited. He'd tried calling her, but it always went to voicemail and she never called him back. He'd tried sending SMS messages, but she didn't reply. He sent a wedding gift to the address he had for Mark's apartment, and Estelle had posted the gift back to him saying she wanted nothing from him.

He'd called her cell phone and the landline at Mark's apartment every hour. Eventually Mark picked up. He'd told Rick not to call again – that Estelle didn't want to speak.

Rick left it two days; that was all he could manage. He needed to make things right, just couldn't leave things the way they were, so he wrote Estelle a letter. He tried to tell her why he'd acted the way he had – even though, in the depths of grief, he barely understood it himself. He apologised, and made promises, and said he didn't want to lose his only child as well as the love of his life.

The letter was returned to sender with 'Not Known At This Address' stamped on the front. That was how Rick found out Estelle and Mark had moved. He tried calling their cell phones but they were no longer in service.

It took him almost three months of using law enforcement privileges he shouldn't have had, and calling in a few favours, to find them. By then he'd already submitted his papers for retirement and was working out his notice, so he took a few personal days and took a trip to Galveston, Texas – the beach town where Estelle and Mark were living.

On the front porch of their pretty blue and white beach bungalow, Mark told him that Estelle wouldn't see him – couldn't even bear the thought of looking at him – and that if Rick ever went back there they would call the cops and take out a restraining order against him. There wasn't a dot of compassion in the man's behaviour, and the way he looked at Rick – with his disgust and irritation real clear – made Rick feel like a piece-of-shit nothing, or a cockroach, or worse than a cockroach.

So, even though he felt as if his heart was breaking all over again, Rick left.

Since that day he's honoured Estelle's wishes – he hasn't gone back and he hasn't tried to call in the five years that have passed. But every month he's written her a postcard, telling her what he's been doing, sharing memories of her mom and of her when she was little, and say-ing how sorry he is. He doesn't know if she's even read them, but Estelle has never written back.

Taking his cell phone from his pocket, Rick opens the messaging app. He'd sent Estelle a bunch of messages last night; explaining where things were in the house and the places nearby that her and little Bibi might enjoy visiting. All he'd gotten in return was one word: *yep.*

As he stares at Estelle's answer, he worries that he's repeating the same mistake – running off here to Shimmering Sands on a case rather than staying home and finding out what's going on with his daughter. He hopes not. But he's never been able to leave a case unfinished, a murder unsolved. He has to find the truth and help the Becktons get justice.

He needs to make things right with Moira too, but she's been pushing him away. He wants their relationship to work, and he knows to do that he's going to have to tell her everything. And that terrifies him.

15

MOIRA

After a quick breakfast in the hotel, they split up to follow three different avenues of enquiry. Posing as a condo-hunting couple, Lizzie and Philip have an appointment with a rival realtor at the nearby Golden Wave over-fifty-fives beach retirement resort, and are hoping to get more information about Jessie and her work colleagues. Moira is heading to the sports club Jessie volunteered at, and Rick had been due to come with her, but there's been a change of plan and he's meeting his law enforcement contact, Hawk, at some beach bar instead.

Moira eases the jeep to a stop at the lights and sighs. It was good of Rick to let her take his vehicle, but he seemed even more remote this morning than he was yesterday. It's as if there's some invisible barrier between them that makes him impossible to reach.

The lights change and Moira accelerates forward, looking for the turn to the club. She hates having the situation with Rick unresolved. He's not just been a lover to her, he's been a friend. Rick is the first person that Moira's trusted, well, trusted the most, in a long while; and certainly since everything that happened after her last failed police operation in London.

Now it feels as if she's losing her best friend and she doesn't know how to fix it.

She spots a sign for SSC Sports and turns off the highway into the car park of a large, industrial-looking gym building. It takes a while to find a space, so she figures the place must be popular if they're already this busy before nine o'clock in the morning on a Saturday.

Stepping into the reception area, Moira's thankful for the chilled air that's blasting out of the air conditioning. She looks at the array of signs, each directing her to a different studio, and has no idea which one she needs.

'What are you here for, sweetheart?' asks the older lady in the SSC Sports polo shirt behind the counter. She's got a deep, leathered-looking tan, bright blonde hair and ruby lipstick. 'Cheer squad, tumbling, dance – tap, modern, ballet or jazz, gymnastics or taekwondo?'

Moira hadn't anticipated there would be so many different classes running at the same place. The Becktons had said Jessie did martial arts, so she goes with that. 'I'd like to chat to the person in charge of taekwondo coaching.'

'That'd be the club manager, Mr Donaldson,' says the lady. 'He's teaching a class right now but he's got a small gap in his schedule when it finishes in thirty minutes. He's always happy to speak to parents before they sign up.'

'Can I wait?' asks Moira, not correcting the lady's assumption that she's the parent of a potential new recruit to the club, and glancing towards a small seating area by the window.

'Sure, sweetheart, you knock yourself out,' says the older lady, smiling. 'I'll take you out back to see Mr Donaldson once the class is finished.'

'Thanks,' says Moira, walking over to the seating area and sitting down on the closest bench.

Moira waits. She learns that the older lady at the counter is called Norma, that she's worked at the club for over forty years, firstly for Mr Donaldson and his wife, Cherri, and then, since Cherri passed eighteen months ago, just for Mr Donaldson. She also learns that Mr Donaldson would like his daughter to take over the running of the club, but she's a fancy lawyer and refuses. Norma says that like Mr Donaldson, she'd like to retire, but she won't until he's found someone else to take over the running of the place. Moira has also realised that the songs played through the rather tinny speakers in the reception are all instrumental versions of eighties soft-rock hits, played on a ten-minute loop. She has no idea how the repetition doesn't send Norma crazy.

Just before 9.30 a.m. the reception starts to fill up. First a little girl of no more than four or five, wearing ballet slippers, a tutu and a leotard all in the same shade of pale pink, comes into the reception with her mum. They're followed by three boys in athletic wear, a gaggle of tweens in tap shoes, and more tiny kids in pink ballet outfits. Moira stays out of the way on her bench while Norma expertly directs the children to the correct studios, and fields questions from the parents. The rush has only just subsided when there's a mass exodus of kids from the studios – teenage ballerinas, younger kids in athletic wear, and a flood of children of all ages wearing white doboks.

When the reception is empty again, Norma waves Moira over. 'Things should be calm for a little while now. Let me take you to see Mr Donaldson.'

After locking the front door, Norma leads Moira through the double doors towards studios 2, 5, 6 and 8, and along a corridor whose walls are lined with photos of champion-winning teams and individuals.

They reach the door at the farthest end. The sign on the wall beside it reads 'Studio 8'. Norma opens the door and steps inside. 'Knock, knock.'

'Here.' The voice comes from a small, slender man wearing a white dobok with a black belt. He's standing over by the full-length wall mirror, scrubbing at the glass with a tissue. 'Gerry did a bad job again. There are smudges all over this thing. I didn't get time to clean it during class – there are too many kids in that group, Norma. We need to find another assistant coach, I can't—'

'Mr Donaldson, there's someone here to talk with you about classes,' says Norma, gesturing for Moira to go over to him.

'Ah, hello then.' He smiles, holding his hand out towards Moira. 'I'm Brett, Brett Donaldson.'

She gives his hand a brief shake. 'Moira Flynn.'

'Sorry if you've had to wait, we usually have an assistant coach on Saturdays which makes it easier for me to talk to parents, but they . . .' He looks uncomfortable. 'Well, they're not able to do Saturdays any more so it's just me.'

'Are you talking about Jessica Beckton?' asks Moira, opting to go for the direct approach.

'Erm, yes,' says Brett, looking more uncomfortable and glancing back at the smudges on the mirror. 'How do you . . .'

'I've been hired by her parents to look into the circumstances of her death. They don't believe she took her own life, they think she was murdered. I'd like to ask you a few questions, as background on her life, if that's okay?'

'Jessie . . . murdered? Who would want to do such an awful . . . ?' He rubs his hand across his face. 'So you're not a parent then?'

'No,' says Moira, giving him a moment longer for the weight of what she's just said about Jessie to sink in.

He looks anguished, and mutters something to himself that Moira doesn't hear properly. Then he takes a deep breath, pushes the tissue back into his pocket and says, 'Okay, fire away. I'll tell you whatever I can.'

'Thank you, I appreciate that,' says Moira. 'How long did you know Jessie for?'

'Not long, I think maybe a little under two months. I was looking for a volunteer assistant coach and she was recommended to me by Phoenix Salford-Keynes.'

Moira's heard that name before. 'Jessie's taekwondo coach?'

'That's correct.' Brett smiles. 'I trained Phoenix back in the day, and she's always had a good eye for potential. She said Jessie had the right attributes to make a coach herself one day, and I have to say I'd agree.'

'So you hired her.'

'I did. Jessie volunteered every Saturday morning, that's when I have the biggest martial arts classes. She did a great job – worked well with the kids and was always on time.'

'I understand there was some trouble recently?' says Moira.

Brett looks rather pained. 'Well . . . there was a little issue, but that was cleared up and things were fine.'

'Can you tell me about it?'

He says nothing at first, then shakes his head. 'It was just a misunderstanding.'

'About?' asks Moira, not willing to let him fob her off with vagueness.

'Do you think it's relevant?' says Brett.

'It could be.'

Brett exhales hard. 'One of the junior students, Wilma Fossway, used to be brought to class by her father, Carl. This one time, Wilma arrived late for class and when I had a word with her mom, who'd brought her on that occasion, highlighting the importance of time-keeping, the woman got very . . . agitated.'

'What did she say?' asks Moira.

'She told me her husband, Carl, had been having an affair with Jessie Beckton and she was most insistent that I fire Jessie.' He blushes. 'She showed me some SMS messages that had been sent to her husband that morning. They were . . . explicit.'

'And they were definitely from Jessie?'

'I don't know,' mumbles Brett, looking away.

Moira stays silent. Waiting for him to say more.

Brett looks embarrassed. 'They were pictures of a young lady, but not their face, if you know what I mean.'

Moira can imagine the type of images. 'Was Jessie's cell phone number on the pictures?'

'I didn't look at them long enough to see, I'm sorry.'

'It's okay,' says Moira, even though it's frustrating not to know for sure if the pictures were sent by Jessie. 'Were you aware of Jessie getting hate messages on social media?'

Brett looks shocked. 'No, she never mentioned anything like that.'

Moira can tell from his tone that there's something he's not telling her. 'But?'

'Well, there was another altercation. It was out in the parking lot, after Saturday classes had finished a few weeks later, I can't remember the exact date.' He shakes his head again. 'Wilma's mom attacked Jessie. She was yelling and pulling Jessie's hair. It was very unpleasant.'

'How did it end?' says Moira.

'Jessie was a blue belt, she knew how to defend her space, and so she did. Wilma's mom didn't like that one bit. I had to threaten to call the cops; it was the only way to stop her shouting. She left the parking lot with her ego bruised and still yelling at Jessie.'

'When was this?'

He exhales hard. 'Less than a week before Jessie died.'

'Did you tell the cops investigating her death?'

'They never spoke to me,' says Brett.

Moira purses her lips. It sounds like the local PD wrote Jessie's death off as non-suspicious right from the get-go. They don't seem to have bothered with even a bare bones investigation. It's not right. Surely the forensic evidence, as Lizzie had discovered, should have led them to at least consider the possibility of foul play? She feels a rush of anger that the cops didn't do enough. 'Do you know how I can get in touch with Carl and his wife?'

'Well, here's the thing, they pulled Wilma out of the lessons and I never saw them again. We'd have their records in the files but I can't let you see them due to confidentiality.'

Moira looks serious. She needs that address, and Brett seems like a guy who cared about Jessie. She tries to play on his emotions. 'Not even if they could be connected to Jessie's death? I really do need to include them in my investigation.'

Brett looks conflicted. 'You think they might have had something to do with Jessie's death? That's . . . well . . . I don't want to stop you speaking with them.'

'It could be really important,' says Moira.

Brett blows out hard. He leans closer to Moira, his voice hushed as he ushers her out of the studio and back along the corridor. 'Okay, I'll show you, for Jessie – she was a good kid, had a lot of potential. If someone killed her then . . . the files are through here.'

It doesn't take long for her to find Wilma Fossway's record. As Moira makes a note of the address from the file, she resolves to get to the truth of what happened to Jessie Beckton. No matter what happened between her, Carl Fossway and his wife, Belinda, she didn't deserve to die.

She deserves justice.

And Moira's going to make sure that happens.

16

PHILIP

'Welcome to unit fifteen eleven here at Golden Wave.'

Philip takes a dislike to the real-estate agent from the moment he opens his mouth. No, from the moment he sees him. It's hard to say why; after all, the fellow is neatly dressed in a lightweight grey suit with cufflinks, and a pale green shirt, but he has a haughtiness about him that puts Philip on his guard. It's a gut instinct thing. And over the years, Philip's learnt it's important to always pay attention to his instincts when it comes to people.

Puffing out his chest, Philip draws himself up to his full height, and puts out his hand. 'Philip Sweetman, and this is my wife, Lizzie.'

'Sure, good to see you guys,' says the realtor, taking Philip's hand and giving it a firm shake. 'Lucas B. Francis, senior agent at Ocean Nest. I'm here for all your real-estate needs.'

'Good, good,' says Philip, the instant familiarity of the chap making him dislike him even more. 'Tell us more about this place.'

'So, this community is over-fifty-fives only, with all the amenities you'd expect in a luxury seniors' resort – tennis courts, indoor and outdoor pools, spa, pickleball, and a bunch of water sports options if that's your thing. You can even get yourselves a deeded slip out on the Golden Wave jetty at the marina as an optional extra.'

'Lovely,' says Lizzie, nodding.

'It is, for sure,' says Lucas, smiling brightly. 'And this ground floor unit is a real bargain at the price. It's oceanfront, as you can see, and comes fully furnished and is totally turnkey.'

Philip frowns. The kitchen is small, with pale oak cabinets and a sandy-coloured granite counter. There's a bistro table with two chairs, and a flowery three-seater sofa and one armchair closer to the patio doors. The pool is just feet away from the apartment's terrace area. 'Not very private, is it? Lots of noise from the pool, I'd expect, and people staring in at you when you're watching the telly.'

'But such easy access to the pool. Just open the gate and you're poolside in seconds,' says Lucas, his smile not faltering once. 'Plus, it's just a short walk until you've got your toes in the sand at the beach. And if you don't fancy walking, the resort is golf-cart friendly, so you can drive pretty much any place you want. Very convenient.'

'I suppose,' says Philip, unconvinced. It feels too warm in the apartment, as if the air conditioning isn't switched on. He can feel the sweat running down his back under his shirt. It's making him feel a bit queasy.

'Anyways, why don't y'all take a look around, and I'll be right here to answer any questions once you're done,' says Lucas, giving them another overly bright smile.

'Thanks,' says Lizzie, taking Philip firmly by the hand and leading him through the open kitchen/lounge space and into the master bedroom. It's a fairly big room but, like the rest of the place, rather nondescript: beige walls, beige carpet, furniture all perfectly functional but not especially exciting.

'Don't you think this is nice?' says Lizzie. Her expression and tone telling Philip to buck up and play his part as an interested buyer a bit better.

'I suppose so,' says Philip, loo0king around the room. It's okay, but after the luxury of the eighth-floor penthouse at the Surf-Sand

Vista, this place looks very basic. He'd rather just quiz this Lucas chap about Beachseekers and Jessie Beckton now and get out of here, but supposes they should at least pretend to be interested in the apartment before starting to ask questions. 'What's the ensuite like?'

'Nice,' says Lizzie, loud enough for Lucas to hear out in the open-living space. 'I love this tile.'

Philip looks at the bathroom. White sanitary wear, white flooring, and white subway tiles in the shower; neat, but standard. 'It's fine.'

Lizzie steps closer to Philip. She gestures back towards where they left Lucas and whispers, 'We need to find out whether he knew Jessie, or has any inside knowledge on what happened to her.'

'Yes, yes,' says Philip. 'I'm trying to soften him up; waiting for the right time to ask.'

'You're *not* trying,' scolds Lizzie. 'But if you stop acting like a grumpy child, you might be more successful in getting him to open up a bit more.'

'Noted,' says Philip, curtly. He doesn't appreciate being told how to do his job, even by Lizzie. Then he sees her frown, and he feels bad. He shouldn't have done that, but he's feeling a bit rough and that makes him oversensitive. It's not her fault. Reaching out, he gives her hand a squeeze. 'I'll get the intel we need.'

Lizzie nods, and they walk back through to join the realtor in the open-plan area.

'What did you think?' asks Lucas. 'Great, huh?'

'It's . . .' Philip glances at Lizzie and knows he can't be honest. 'It's very nice.'

'I knew you'd just love it,' says Lucas. 'So where else have y'all been looking?'

Philip smiles to himself. Lizzie will be proud; this topic of conversation is their way of moving into talking about Jessie. 'Shimmering Sands.'

'Interesting,' says Lucas, rubbing his designer-stubbled chin. 'You do know about what happened there, right?'

Lizzie widens her eyes, acting the innocent. 'What do you mean?'

'A realtor there fell off one of the top-level balconies.'

Lizzie gasps. Philip hides a smile, admiring her play-acting ability.

'I mean, I'm not saying there's a serious safety issue or anything,' continues Lucas. 'But really, they do need to get those balconies properly checked.'

'They told us everything was up to code,' says Philip.

Lucas gives him a condescending smile. 'Well, of *course* they did. That doesn't mean it's true though, right?'

Philip says nothing. He hates this type of salesperson: rubbishing their rivals in order to win a sale. It's not very sportsmanlike in his book. But he needs to get this fellow to talk, so he keeps his feelings to himself. 'Did you know the person who died?'

'Sure, a little,' says Lucas.

'That must have been hard,' says Lizzie, kindly.

'It's a shame she died, I guess,' says Lucas, not sounding at all like he thought it was a shame. 'But if you live by the sword you have to be prepared to die by it, yeah?'

'What do you mean?' asks Philip.

'Well . . .' Lucas lowers his voice. 'From what I hear she was in with a bad crowd, you know?'

'Not particularly,' says Philip, gruffly.

Lizzie gives him one of her looks and he knows she's thinking he should be more friendly. He's not a copper any more; he can't use his rank to get the truth out of people, so he should be more charming, and coax the details out of them with kindness and encouragement. And that's all very well, but he's feeling a bit queasier now. The heat is getting to him, and he's feeling slightly breathless even though he's just standing still. The combination makes him feel irritable rather than charming.

'What sort of bad crowd?' asks Lizzie, her tone rather conspiratorial.

'Okay, so you didn't hear this from me, yeah?' says Lucas, in a stage whisper. 'But apparently, she was into drugs. I'm not saying she was a user herself, but from what I've heard one of the reasons her and some of the others in the team over at Beachseekers get so many deals is that they like to party with their clients, and they're the ones who bring the gear.'

Lizzie raises her eyebrows. 'She was a drug dealer?'

Lucas shakes his head. 'Not, like, a dealer, but a facilitator for her clients, for sure.'

Lizzie meets Philip's gaze and he gives her a little nod. They're both thinking it: this is new information. It could be important.

'Do you think her death was connected to the drugs?' asks Lizzie, stepping closer to Lucas. 'Was she killed?'

He shrugs, and gives Lizzie a conspiratorial wink. 'Look, I don't know for sure, but it sounds like there was *a lot* of drama over it all. Trust me, you'd be better to have me handle all your real-estate needs.' He lowers his voice again. 'You know, the rumour is she had a totally massive fight with her boss, and they told her if the drugs didn't stop immediately, she'd end up dead. Well, so far as I know the drugs didn't stop.' He pauses, looking from Lizzie to Philip, then back to Lizzie. His eyes widen as he delivers the punchline he's obviously been working up to. 'That woman was dead within the week.'

17

RICK

At four minutes before ten, Rick's sitting in the corner booth at Coco's Beach Bar, facing the door. He orders a Coke, then pulls out his cell phone and looks at the screen. There's still no reply from Estelle, even though he messaged her over an hour ago to check in.

Pressing call, he puts the handset to his ear, and takes a deep breath.

'Hello?' Estelle doesn't sound especially happy.

'I . . . I wanted to check you've got everything you need?' says Rick. 'That you're both okay.'

'We're fine,' says Estelle, the irritation still clear in her voice. 'When are you coming back?'

'I'm not sure yet.' Rick smiles a thank you to the waitress as she puts his Coke down on the table in front of him. 'It looks like this should've been a homicide investigation. We'll get as much evidence as we can and then we'll need to—'

'Yeah, whatever,' says Estelle, her tone hardening. 'I would've thought you'd have wanted to be here and spend time with us. We need to talk.'

'I want that too, honey.' Rick feels the guilt gnawing deep in his belly. He fiddles with the napkin on the table beside his Coke, folding it this way and that. 'But I promised the young victim's parents I'd find the truth, I can't—'

'Yeah, I know. The case comes first, it always has.'

'I'll be back as soon as I can, but if you need anything at all I'm here for you, honey,' says Rick, hating the pleading tone in his voice. 'Just call, okay?'

Estelle sighs. The call disconnects.

'Honey? Estelle, are you there?' Rick looks at the handset – she's gone. He cusses under his breath. He wants to go home and reconnect with her, even though he's not sure how to do that after all this time and all the anger she still obviously feels towards him, but he can't leave the case. He promised the Becktons that he'd find out what really happened to their daughter, and he never goes back on his word. Dropping his cell phone on to the table, he puts his head in his hands.

'Bad time?' asks a familiar voice.

He looks up as Hawk slides on to the bench opposite. He's wearing his usual jeans and faded band T-shirt combo; today it's the turn of Nirvana. Rick smiles. 'Never for you, buddy.'

'Cool,' says Hawk, pushing his Red Sox ballcap up off his forehead. He orders a mineral water from the waitress, continuing to chew his gum as he does, and then looks back at Rick and gestures to his cell. 'You want to talk about it?'

Rick had trained with Hawk back in the day, and they'd been co-workers for a while before Hawk took a posting in Miami. They'd never lost touch, and since Rick moved to Florida they'd caught up over beers every couple of weeks. Well connected and discreet, Hawk was a useful guy to know when it came to off-the-books investigations. He knew the whole sad story about Estelle and her leaving, and he'd no doubt have some advice to give about handling her return, but Rick can't have that conversation right now. He needs to focus on the case. So, he shakes his head. 'Nope.'

'Well, alrighty then. I'll get to it. As expected, the local PD wrote the whole thing off as suicide from the get-go. I've seen the file, put together by the lead detective assigned – a Thomas B. Durcell – and it's light as a goddamn feather.'

'Nothing useful in there?' asks Rick, taking a sip of his Coke. 'Forensics? Crime scene analysis?'

'Not so much.' Hawk keeps working his gum. 'Just some process-following notes to show they didn't do anything wrong. The only thing of interest was a note from another detective, a Chester M. Golding. He said—'

'Golding?' says Rick, almost spitting his Coke out.

'Yeah, I know, weird, right?' says Hawk, grinning. 'His name being the same as that dude you came across in the other investigation.'

The other two investigations, thinks Rick, wondering if the two detectives are related. James R. Golding, one of the lead detectives at the police department that covered The Homestead retirement community jurisdiction, was a real pain in the ass. 'What did the note say?'

'So, here's the thing. Not a lot. But it contradicted the lead detective's conclusion.'

Rick leans forward, elbows on the table. Interested. 'Go on.'

Hawk pulls a small notebook from his shirt pocket and flips it open. 'In Detective Durcell's report, he said there were, and I quote, "no signs of an intruder" in the penthouse apartment, and, "in all aspects the scene was consistent with the victim taking their own life".'

'Okay,' says Rick, waiting for the punchline.

'But in the note from Chester Golding, which looked to be a copy from his official notepad, it noted, "black scuff marks on the balcony tiles" and, "three smashed champagne flutes, the contents spilled on the tiles, from the side of the table closest to the point where the victim fell from the balcony".'

'Signs of a struggle?' says Rick, nodding.

'Yep. I'd put money on it,' says Hawk, closing his notebook. 'But that detail didn't get into the main report.'

'Why the hell not?' asks Rick.

'Beats me,' says Hawk, shrugging. 'Could be the note got put into the file later, after the verdict was given by the coroner, because this Chester Golding guy didn't agree. Anyways I asked around about this Durcell guy and nothing I heard was complimentary. Nothing awful either, no total crossing the line, but one of those guys who does the minimum and cuts corners if he thinks he'll get away with it.'

Rick hates that kind of guy. 'He ignored the facts because it was easier to go with it being a suicide? Jesus.'

'Looks that way,' says Hawk, chewing faster on his gum. 'Makes me real mad.'

'Same.' Rick runs his hand across his jaw, thinking. 'You think it's worth reaching out to Chester Golding and seeing if he'll talk to us?'

'I don't know, man. Writing his thoughts down and sticking a copy in an archived file is one thing, talking to some private investigators out to prove one of his fellow detectives screwed up is kind of different.'

'I guess.'

Hawk stops chewing his gum for a moment. 'You *know* it. And have you even got your PI licence?'

'Not yet. Haven't gotten around to it.'

'None of you?'

Rick shakes his head.

Hawk lets out a long whistle. 'Then don't poke the bear, buddy. Do your thing, for sure, but stay clear of the police department.'

'You're probably right,' says Rick.

'You know I am.' Hawk grins, and drains the last of his mineral water. 'Now, I'd better get out of here, I've got a job to do myself. Call me if you need anything else.'

'Will do,' says Rick, raising his glass to Hawk. 'Appreciate it.'

As Hawk leaves, Rick puts the money for the drinks, and half again for the waitress, on to the silver plate, and gets up. The Coke has helped to settle his stomach, and the information from Hawk has convinced him even more that Jessie was murdered.

Rick can't let the Becktons go any longer without knowing the truth about what happened to their daughter. He knows what it's like to lose someone. When Alisha died it was as if a part of him had been amputated without an anaesthetic; the pain took months, years, to become bearable. And it must be a hundred times worse when your loved one is taken from you violently, and even tougher when you don't know why.

The Becktons deserve an answer.

He needs to work out who killed Jessie. And fast.

18

MOIRA

Phoenix Salford-Keynes' Girls Club Gym is a small unit sandwiched between a nail salon and a pet store. There's a huge four-foot-high Girls Club pink neon sign hanging in the window.

When Moira steps inside she's greeted by a young woman with a white-blonde pixie haircut and flawless skin, wearing white shorts and a pink vest emblazoned with 'Train like a Girl' in diamanté. 'Hi there, how can I help you?'

'Is Phoenix here?' asks Moira with a smile, opting for the casual approach.

'Do you have an appointment?' asks the woman, tapping on the iPad she's carrying. 'I can't see anything in her schedule.'

'Sorry, no,' says Moira. 'I'm an investigator and I'd like to speak with her urgently. It's about Jessie Beckton.'

'Oh, I . . . sure, she's out back,' says the woman, her smile faltering for a moment when she hears Jessie's name. 'We were all so sorry to hear about Jessie. She was one of the good ones, you know.'

'So can you get me in to see her?' asks Moira. 'It's really important.'

'Sure, Phoenix thought the world of Jessie. She'll want to speak with you. Please, come this way.'

Moira follows the woman through a door into the gym. It's a larger and airier space than Moira had imagined it would be. Very industrial-looking with exposed brick, ductwork and pipes, along with an array of equipment – hanging and free-standing punch bags, dumbbells, kettlebells, a TRX and a large mat space. On the mats, two women are practising their moves. An athletic, fifty-something woman giving instruction, her long hair in cornrows that have been twisted into a high bun, watches them.

The young woman beside Moira pauses on the edge of the mats and waits for the pair to finish their bout before speaking. 'Phoenix? There's someone to see you, it's about Jessie.'

The instructor looks round from debriefing the pair, and strides across to the edge of the mats. She puts her hands on her hips. 'What about Jessie?'

Moira takes in the woman's no-nonsense tone and powerful body language, and decides not to beat around the bush. 'I'm investigating Jessie Beckton's murder on behalf of her parents. There's evidence to suggest she was murdered.'

'I knew it,' says Phoenix, looking at the young woman who had escorted Moira into the gym. 'I told you, didn't I, Cameron?'

'You sure did,' says Cameron. 'We all loved Jessie here. Didn't believe for a second that she went over that balcony intentionally.'

'Exactly,' says Phoenix. 'Are you a cop?'

'No,' says Moira, shaking her head. 'As you've said, the official investigation concluded Jessie died by suicide, so the cops have closed the case. I'm one of a group of independent investigators, looking into what happened as a second opinion for Jim and Doreen Beckton.'

'Well, good,' says Phoenix, with a steely look in her eye. 'Anything you need from us to catch whichever asshole did this, you got it. Let's sit.'

Moira follows her across the gym to the weights area. Phoenix takes a seat on one of the weights benches and gestures for Moira to do the same.

Over in the corner, a woman in a yellow sports bra and navy leggings is dead-lifting what looks to Moira to be a huge amount of weight. She leans closer to Phoenix, lowering her voice to ensure they're not overheard. 'I've just been chatting to Brett Donaldson over at SSC Sports, he told me about a problem between Jessie and one of the parents. Did she tell you about that?'

Phoenix's expression clouds over. 'She mentioned it. Do you think the Fossways were behind her death?'

'I don't know,' says Moira. 'I'm just trying to find out what happened. Brett said Mrs Fossway accused Jessie of sending explicit messages to her husband. Was it true?'

'Yes. That son-of-a-bitch.' Phoenix clenches her fists. Anger clear in her tone. 'Carl Fossway had been chasing Jessie for a while and when she split up from that godawful Josh Stratton he stepped it up even more. He sent her roses, took her on fancy dinners out, the whole nine yards. And Jessie liked him, he was kind and considerate – and after Josh she needed that. Carl told her he was separated from his wife and, as his wife had never been to the sports club, and he seemed to be able to go out whenever she suggested, Jessie took his word on good faith and believed him. The first she knew any different was when Belinda Fossway turned up at the club and started getting all up in her face.'

'What did Jessie do?' asks Moira.

'Aside from kicking Carl to the kerb immediately? She told Belinda that she had no idea they were still together, but Belinda didn't believe her. That's when the messages on Instagram started – snide, mean things. Jessie knew Belinda and her friends had to be behind it – she'd overheard a couple of the moms at the sports club laughing about it – but there was nothing she could do to make

107

them stop. In the end she deleted her account, but that must have made Belinda really mad, because she came for Jessie again at the club – freaked out at her in the parking lot – yelling, pulling her hair, and trying to slap her.' Phoenix shakes her head. 'Jessie's got the patience of a saint, but she wasn't going to take that. She put that woman on the ground in a split second.'

Moira detects the note of pride in Phoenix's voice when she mentions Jessie's speed. 'So, she defended herself?'

'Exactly. It was instinct. Pure self-defence. Belinda didn't like it, but she sure didn't make the mistake of coming for Jessie again.'

'Is it right that Jessie died less than a week later?' asks Moira.

Phoenix frowns. 'That's right.'

'You said earlier you'd thought Jessie had been murdered. Did you speak to the police about it?' asks Moira. Over in the corner, the dead-lifter is clanking out a metallic rhythm: exhaling loudly as she lifts, and banging the huge round weights down on to the mat as she returns them to the ground.

'I tried to,' says Phoenix. 'But they didn't seem to care a damn about what I had to say.'

'What did you tell them?' says Moira, raising her voice slightly to be heard over the clanging of the weights hitting the floor.

'That Jessie wasn't suicidal and wouldn't have taken a dive off that building by choice.' Phoenix exhales hard. 'Jessie was an experienced fighter. She was good, great even. If someone attacked her there's no way she wouldn't have fought back.'

'But if she was so good, how could someone have overpowered her?' asks Moira.

Phoenix looks thoughtful. 'She was recovering from a shoulder injury, that could have limited her, but the thing with taekwondo is that it requires some distance to be effective. If someone got in too close too fast, she might not have been able to properly defend herself.'

What happened up on that balcony? Moira thinks. *Did the person who killed Jessie know about her skills and her injury? Did they act fast to limit her ability to fight back?*

Moira can't leave it any longer.

She needs to get into the penthouse and assess the crime scene for herself.

19

RICK

They ride the elevator up to the eighth floor. There's still tension between them, but with Moira having been following leads with Jessie Beckton's sports club and martial arts mentor, and him meeting up with Hawk for the insider intel on the police investigation, they'd both only just gotten back here a few minutes before they're due to view the penthouse. Rick knows he needs to tell Moira everything – how he threw himself into his work when Alisha had gotten sick; how Estelle begged him to stay home; and how they fell out immediately after Alisha's funeral – and he's going to, but it will have to wait until after the viewing.

'You ready?' Rick says, as they get out of the elevator and walk along the hallway to the penthouse.

'Of course,' says Moira, her expression serious. She sounds annoyed; frustrated by his question.

Rick feels a little more deflated. He hates the tension between them, but he knows he has to suck it up and get on with the job. 'Alright then.'

Moira reaches the solid oak door first and knocks firmly on it, twice.

The door opens almost immediately. The realtor smiles in greeting. 'Welcome. Please, come on in.'

Rick does a double take. It takes him a moment to respond. 'Er, thanks.'

The real-estate agent standing in front of them has platinum-blonde hair that falls straight and glossy to just above her waist. She's wearing a white pant suit, with red high heels and a full face of make-up. At first glance, she seems to be the spitting image of Jessie Beckton, although as Rick steps closer, he realises this woman must have at least ten years on Jessie.

As they enter the apartment, he looks at Moira. She raises her eyebrows and he can tell she's been thinking the same. He wonders who was copying who – Jessie or this woman.

'I'm Sindee McGillis,' says the woman. Her voice is as smooth as honey, her smile megawatt bright. 'I head up the team at Beachseekers and I'm thrilled to show you this premium property today.'

Rick knows the name. This is Jessie's boss. 'I'm Rick Denver, and this is Moira Flynn.'

'Hi,' says Moira. 'Good to meet you.'

Sindee takes their hands in turn. She holds Rick's for a fraction longer than is usual, and he's glad when she lets go. She's beautiful, and seems charming, but there's something about her that makes him suspect there's a cold, ruthless streak hidden behind the smile.

'So let me show you all the amazing features of this fantastic penthouse,' says Sindee, leading them through into the open-concept living area. It's immaculate and very modern for sure, but also rather clinical in Rick's view.

As Sindee talks about high-end finishes and chef-grade appliances, Rick nods in the right places but is more focused on the technical features of the apartment. He lets her rattle on for a while, then says, 'Can you tell us what security systems are installed?'

'Excellent question,' says Sindee. 'As you'd expect, this penthouse comes with state-of-the-art security. In addition to the cameras for the public areas which are monitored 24/7, you have your own intruder alarm, with sensors on every door and window, and panic buttons available in the main living space, master bedroom and all the bathrooms. If the alarm is triggered it alerts the security team here on-site, as well as the local police department. Access to the floor is via the elevator. There are stairs for use in an emergency situation, but the doors to the stairwell are alarmed and locked from the inside, so exit only.'

'Okay, thanks,' says Rick, making a mental note that the way the emergency stairs are configured seems to rule out the killer gaining access through the stairwell.

'Are there cameras in here?' asks Moira, looking around.

'Certainly, but they're very discreet. Let me show you.' Sindee walks across to the mantle over the fireplace, and taps a long, red fingernail against a spot in the centre. 'There's a micro camera in here, and others in the extractor over the range, the frame of the mirror in the master bedroom, and over the front and balcony doors.'

'Who sees the feed?' says Rick. The idea of being watched as you go about your business in your own home doesn't sound appealing to him, especially in the bedroom.

'You do,' says Sindee with a smile. 'The cameras aren't currently active, they'll be activated on purchase of the property and synced to the owners' smart device.'

'Okay,' says Rick. 'And you mentioned panic buttons. Are they active?'

A frown briefly crosses Sindee's face, but she regains her composure fast. 'No, again, they won't be activated until the purchase is complete. Now, shall we take a look outside?'

'Sure,' says Rick, following Sindee across the living space to the glass door. Moira falls in pace with him, but remains in the living space when he steps out on to the balcony to join Sindee.

'Isn't the view amazing?' says Sindee, stretching her arms out wide. 'This is what penthouse living is all about.'

It's impressive, for sure. Rick gazes out over the railing to the ocean. You can hear the sound of the waves crashing on to the sand even from up here on the eighth floor. Stepping closer to the edge, he looks down and sees the pathway Lizzie had described directly below. He agrees with her view: to hit the path, Jessie would have to have dropped down vertically from the railing. In his whole career, he never saw, or heard, of a jumper doing that head first.

He agrees with Lizzie. The coroner made a mistake; this was murder.

'Shall we go back inside?' says Sindee. There's tension in her smile now, and Rick notices she's stayed well back from the railing.

'Sure,' says Rick, stepping into the interior space. As he does, he catches Moira's eye. She's looking thoughtful. He wishes he could tell what she's thinking; she's not said anything to him since they entered the apartment. He reaches out to take her hand, but she moves away quickly, and goes out on to the balcony alone.

As Sindee starts listing all the amenities that come with the penthouse, Rick watches Moira out on the balcony as she paces the distance from the door to the railing, and then from one side of the balcony to the other. He wonders what she's thinking, if she's got a theory.

'So, what do you think?' asks Sindee, pulling him back into the conversation. She gestures towards the balcony. 'Your wife certainly seems to be enjoying the view.'

'She's not . . .' Rick swallows hard. Sindee referring to Moira as his wife throws him; it's wrong, and yet it feels strangely okay. 'I . . .'

Rick looks back at Moira. She's standing against the railing now, looking down. Suddenly her shoulders go rigid and she staggers backwards. Her hands fly to her chest as she turns towards the door. Her face flushes red. She's gasping.

Something's wrong.

She's having a panic attack.

Rick's heart rate accelerates. Fear flares inside him. Rushing to Moira, he puts his hands on her shoulders and looks into her eyes. 'It's okay, you're okay, I'm here with you.'

Her eyes are wide, panicked, her gaze darting side to side. She's struggling to breathe. 'I . . . everything I've tried so hard to repress . . . I remembered . . .'

'Slow breaths, deep and slow,' Rick says, trying to keep his tone calm and reassuring. 'Count in time with me.' He keeps his eyes on hers and starts to count, slow and steady.

It takes a while, but gradually her breathing settles and the fear subsides. She counts with him, able to speak again. They stop counting when they reach one hundred. Rick slides his hands down her arms and takes her hands in his. 'You okay?'

'I think so.' She squeezes his hands. Leans into him.

'You said you remembered something?' says Rick. He waits for her to tell him what it was, but she doesn't. Then he feels his cell phone vibrating in his pants pocket. He ignores it. Whatever it is can wait; Moira is more important. He puts his arms around her and they stand, hugging, for a long moment.

'I think I need to sit down,' says Moira, eventually, her words muffled against his shoulder.

'No problem.' Reluctantly, Rick lets go of Moira and turns back around. They go into the living space, and he closes the balcony door and then guides Moira over to the large sectional couch and helps her ease on to it. That's when he hears a strange noise coming from the armchair on the other side of the space and looks round.

It's only then that he realises Sindee McGillis is crying.

'Are you okay?' says Rick as he sits down.

'Yes . . . I . . . I just . . .' Sindee flaps her red-fingernailed hands at her face, as if hoping that will stop the tears. 'That balcony . . .'

'Someone died there,' says Rick. It's a statement, not a question.

Sindee dabs at her eyes with a tissue. 'One of my team – my top broker. It's still a little . . . raw. And then when your wife was . . . I just . . .'

'I understand,' says Rick, kindly. 'You were close?'

'She was my protégée. We weren't friends, but we respected each other.' Sindee shakes her head. 'It was a tragic accident. This is the first time I've shown the property since it happened.'

'Well, we appreciate you showing it to us,' says Rick. He glances at Moira but she's staring out at the balcony, her attention miles away. 'But I think it's a little too high up for our tastes.'

'I understand,' says Sindee, her tone becoming more business-like. 'I can find some other properties closer to ground level for you to look at, and set up a tour.'

'Thank you,' says Rick, looking at Moira again. She's still not following the conversation. Her skin looks flushed. 'Let us think on it.'

'Of course,' says Sindee. There's no trace of the tears now. 'Let me show you out.'

In the hallway, Rick scans the place for signs of a second eleva-tor, but sees nothing. If the stairwell is emergency only, and triggers an alarm if the door to it is opened, there must be another elevator that gives access to this level. Jessie's attacker didn't use the main elevator, and couldn't have used the stairs, so there has to be another way. As they walk along the hallway, he puts his arm around Moira. 'How are you feeling?'

'Dizzy,' she says, leaning against him for support as they reach the elevator. 'I need to lie down for a bit until it passes.'

Rick presses the call button. 'Let me help you back to your room.'

Moira nods. She seems exhausted.

He's worried about her and wishes he could do something more to help. As they get into the elevator and ride down to their floor, he holds her a little tighter and is encouraged that she doesn't pull away. He wants to ask her more about what triggered the attack; about this repressed memory from London. She's told him a little bit before about an operation that went wrong, and he knows she's reluctant to talk or even think about it, so perhaps it's something to do with that. He also needs to know if she discovered anything important while she was out on the balcony. But he doesn't ask. He knows how Moira is, she'll tell him when she's ready.

When they reach her room, he waits while she unlocks the door, and then loiters in the entryway until she's walked to the bed and sat down.

Moira gives him a small smile. 'Thanks, Rick. I'll be okay.'

'Look, if you want to talk about what happened, or the memory you mentioned, I'm here for you.' He hates leaving her like this, but it's clear from her expression that she wants to be alone. 'Anything you need, just call. I'll be right across the hall.'

'I will,' says Moira lying back on the bed and closing her eyes.

Quietly, Rick steps out of the room and pulls the door closed behind him, then moves across the hallway to his room. As he lets himself inside, Rick pulls out his cell phone and sees he's got three missed calls and voicemail. They're all from the same number. He dials his answer service and listens to the voicemail.

It's Estelle, and she's real angry. 'What the hell? You told me to call anytime. You said you'd always pick up. So where are you? Call me when you get this. Actually, scratch that. Don't bother. I've managed this long without you. I don't need you now. At least I know I can depend on myself.'

Wincing at the fury in Estelle's voice, Rick dials her number but it diverts after two rings to answerphone. He tries twice more;

each time the call diverts. He wonders where Estelle is, and what she needed him for. He hopes that she's safe, and that Bibi is too.

Tapping out a quick message telling her he'd been in an emergency health situation and apologising for not being able to call back immediately, Rick sets the cell phone down on the desk and waits for a response.

As the minutes tick past, he tries not to feel like a failure.

20

MOIRA

It's been months since Moira's last panic attack, so long in fact that she thought they'd gone for good, but now she knows she was wrong. This one was the worst she'd had in a long time, maybe the worst since that first attack in the aftermath of the undercover operation that left her team dead and her pensioned off on medical grounds. But it was different too. Instead of the flashback or nightmare preceding it seeming fuzzy, like a television that's become pixelated, this memory was in high definition and full sound.

She's tried so hard to block out the memory of what happened during the operation. It's bad enough that sometimes the memories force themselves into her nightmares, but even they have always been fuzzy and fragmented. That's why she refused hypnotherapy, and she wouldn't talk about it to the therapist the Met had paid for, fearful that if she did it would bring more memories of that fateful night flooding back, along with the overwhelming, suffocating feeling of panic.

She's even avoided tall buildings and balconies, despite the therapist telling her that if she truly wanted to heal she'd need to face her fear. But she hasn't. Couldn't. Today, on the balcony of the penthouse, all those fears came rushing back.

But it was different, somehow. It seemed as if it was trying to tell her something. Make her remember something. Something that's been lurking in her subconscious, just out of reach, all this time.

Lying on her bed in the darkened hotel room, Moira knows what she has to do. She can't have this hanging over her any longer. She needs to face her fears.

Closing her eyes, she forces herself to relive the memory. She recalls the way her vision had swum as she'd looked down from the eighth-floor penthouse balcony that afternoon. How her heart rate had accelerated and her breath had quickened. And how the memory had pushed its way into her mind's eye.

They're in a fancy riverside apartment in London at a meet with Bobbie Porter – kingpin of a vicious and prolific criminal gang. It's a first meeting, and they're here to bait a trap. There are two expensive white sofas facing each other. Moira and her colleague, Jennifer Riley, are seated on one, with Moira's colleague, and protégé, Al McCord, standing to the side of them. Opposite, Bobbie Porter – confident, and unmistakably female, sits calmly. It's the first time any team has got close to her; the first time the police have discovered she is a woman. This is the first real opportunity to take her down and collapse her empire of human suffering and exploitation.

Moira outlines the terms of the deal they'd like Porter to come in on while her heavies, one standing behind her, and two over by the door, look on. If Porter goes for the deal they'll have her trapped and when she hands over the cash for her half she'll be done. She'll go down for a long stretch and the team will be heroes.

Armed response is on standby, waiting in the stairwell a couple of flights down from the twenty-fourth floor.

McCord finishes his spiel. Now they need an answer. 'So what do you say?' he asks. 'Are you in?'

Porter shakes her head, but says nothing. She looks away from McCord, seemingly disinterested. It looks as if she's going to leave.

No, thinks Moira. *This can't happen; they can't walk away from this meeting empty-handed. Leaning forward, she catches Porter's gaze and says, 'What about your shipment due to leave on Thursday? Let us help you with that. Prove we know what we're doing.'*

Porter tilts her head to one side. Looks as if she's considering the idea.

Everything is riding on this.

Moira tries to breathe normally; not let the nerves show. But everyone except Porter seems tense. McCord is usually a cool operator, but today is different.

Then Porter's gaze flicks up to McCord and she nods. It's subtle, and for a moment Moira thinks she's giving the go-ahead for the deal. Then McCord pulls out a gun.

Everyone jumps to their feet.

Moira's confused; McCord isn't firearms certified. She thinks he's going to threaten Porter. But he doesn't. Instead, McCord aims the gun at Riley, his friend and colleague, and pulls the trigger. No hesitation.

Porter's heavies lift her over the back of the sofa and away.

Moira presses her hands against Riley's wounds but the bullet has hit an artery and she's bleeding out fast. Her blood staining the white sofa crimson.

Riley's dead in seconds.

Porter has gone.

Moira looks towards the balcony. She can see McCord out there in the pouring rain. Running across the apartment, Moira goes after him. It's dark outside. The wind buffets the building. The rain is torrential.

'What did you do?' screams Moira. 'What the hell did you do?'

McCord's crying. He points his gun at Moira's head. 'Get back. Leave me.'

Moira ignores him. Takes another step forward. 'Why did you kill Riley?'

McCord's hand is shaking. His expression is wretched. He moves back a couple of paces. Starts to lower his gun . . .

On the bed in her hotel room, Moira grips the duvet tight. This is the part of the memory she's fought so hard to repress; the most traumatic moment of her life. She's never been able to hear what McCord tells her. His words have always been muffled, incomplete; blocked by her subconscious as a self-protection mechanism. But this time it's different. She can't stop the horror playing out. The memory is vivid and clear.

. . . McCord's shaking his head. 'Don't trust Harry George. He blackmailed me. Forced me to do this. He wanted me . . . shoot you too, but I can't . . . I can't . . . I'm so sorry. You need to run. Don't trust Harry. He's . . . bad. You need to run.'

She can't believe what he's saying. Detective Superintendent Harry George is her mentor; he's like a father to her. 'You're lying. He can't—'

'Don't trust him,' says McCord. 'I've got proof. I've left it in your desk drawer. Expose him. End the corruption. Please.'

Then he turns and leaps over the railing, and is lost into the darkness.

On the bed in the hotel room, Moira cries out. Her heart rate accelerating.

Back in the memory, Moira runs to the balcony railing. It's twenty-four storeys down. She screams McCord's name. Behind her, a smoke grenade explodes in the apartment and the building alarm blares out as armed response storm inside.

But they're too late. Moira's team are dead. Riley's blood has stained Moira's hands red and McCord is gone. If what he said is true, this was a set-up, a way to get her and her team out of the picture and keep Porter's identity hidden.

If McCord is telling the truth, Detective Superintendent Harry George, her boss, a good man who's mentored her for almost her entire career, is a dirty copper. It can't be true, can it? The weight of it all slams into Moira like a wrecking ball to the chest. She gasps. Her eyes sting from the grenade smoke. Her throat constricts.

That's when she has her first panic attack.

Opening her eyes, Moira stares up at the textured ceiling of the hotel room and tries to calm her heart rate. She'd repressed so much; all those details of the conversation with McCord, hidden.

She exhales hard. Moira might have doubted what McCord had said at the time, but she knows now that he was telling the truth about Detective Superintendent Harry George. She learnt that the hard way: after she'd kept on pushing her colleagues to investigate, and try to catch, Porter, she'd been attacked on the street and then her home had been set on fire. When she'd started suspecting Harry George knew more than he'd said, she'd gone to his home unannounced to confront him – and she'd seen him with Porter, taking a cash bribe and agreeing to get Moira 'out of the way'.

She'd known the truth then, that Harry George was in league with Bobbie Porter. He'd manufactured Porter's escape when the trap Moira's team had set for her was closing in, and almost succeeded in having Moira killed. But she was alone in her beliefs, and there was no way she could prove them. That was why she really retired and escaped here to Florida. That's why she gave up the thing in her life that meant the most to her – her career.

But if what she now remembers McCord saying is right, she might have had the evidence she needs all along. She thinks back. She'd still have been traumatised when she'd retired. On that last day in the office she'd taken everything that wasn't police property from her desk drawer and stuffed it into a cardboard storage box. She didn't look at anything closely, and she didn't see anything obviously from McCord, but there might have been something in there.

She tries to visualise the contents of the box, but she can't; the memory is too murky, the stress she was feeling at the time dulling her senses. Could it be true, that she has evidence in her possession that could put Porter behind bars and expose Detective Superintendent Harry George as a corrupt, dirty copper? If it is, she could finish the job she started, but couldn't finish. She could get justice for Jennifer Riley and Al McCord.

Moira thinks of her walk-in closet back at her house in The Homestead. The box from her old desk – her old life – is buried somewhere in the bottom of the shoe cabinet. Sitting up on the bed, she glances at her small suitcase on the case stand on the other side of the room, open but still packed. It would take her five minutes to splash some water on her face and gather her things from the bathroom. Another five to call a cab, check out and get to the pick-up point at the front of the building. In less than two hours she could be back at her house, opening the box and searching for the evidence.

Making her decision, Moira stands up and hurries to the bathroom.

21

LIZZIE

They're due to meet at six o'clock in Lizzie and Philip's room to debrief on what they've each discovered. It's six now, and Lizzie's keen to get on with it, but it seems like she's the only one. Rick and Moira haven't arrived yet, and Philip is lying on the bed furthest from the murder board, snoring. He'd said he needed a nap as soon as they'd got back after lunch, and he's still out for the count. It really is most unlike him.

Lizzie starts arranging the armchairs and desk chair around the murder board. She misses not being at her own home, with her own belongings around her and her painting. It's nice being close to the beach, but the Shimmering Sands Resort community feels much less homely to her than The Homestead. It seems more like a holiday resort than a residential community. She wouldn't want to live here. She's just thinking about why that is when there's a loud knock on the door, and she flinches in surprise.

Over on the bed, Philip grunts loudly as he wakes up. 'What's that . . . are we . . . ?'

'It's probably Rick and Moira,' says Lizzie, walking over to the door and opening it.

'Hey,' says Rick, coming inside. He nods hello to Philip, then looks back at Lizzie. 'Moira not here?'

'Not yet,' says Lizzie. The pair seem to have been joined at the hip recently, she's surprised they haven't arrived together.

'Just going to freshen up,' says Philip, standing up from the bed and heading to the bathroom. 'It's jolly warm in here.'

Lizzie frowns. Usually, Philip would be pacing about complaining about people being late, but either he hasn't noticed or it isn't bothering him. Over the years him being a stickler for punctuality has grated on her at times, but now she's wondering what's changed. Also it's not at all warm in here; the air conditioning has been blasting away on the lowest setting for hours. Lizzie's had to put on a jumper to stop herself from freezing.

Rick takes a seat in one of the armchairs, ready to get started with the debrief, and Lizzie picks up one of the marker pens, poised to update the murder board as they talk.

When Philip returns from the bathroom it looks like he's washed his face, and at least he seems more alert than he was a few minutes earlier. 'No Moira?'

'Not—'

There's a knock at the door. Lizzie puts down the marker pen and goes to open it.

'Sorry I'm late,' says Moira as she comes inside. 'I lost track of time.'

'No problem,' says Lizzie, her irritation fading as she takes in Moira's blotchy complexion and bloodshot eyes. 'Are you okay?'

Moira doesn't quite meet Lizzie's gaze. 'Yeah, I . . . I had a panic attack earlier, on the balcony at the penthouse. I'm still feeling a bit peculiar.'

'That must have been horrible,' says Lizzie, ushering Moira over to the second armchair. 'Take a seat here. Would you like some sweet tea?'

'I'm fine, but thanks,' says Moira, sitting down on the chair. 'Let's get started.'

'Okay,' says Lizzie, picking up the marker pen again and looking across at Rick. 'Did you manage to speak with the Becktons?'

Rick nods. 'I did, but I'm afraid they don't have a key for Jessie's dressing table or know where it is. Neither of them has removed anything from her bedroom. They said they just haven't been able to face doing it.'

'That's understandable,' says Lizzie, her tone sombre. 'Okay, so who wants to go next?'

'I think we should hear from you, Lizzie,' says Rick.

'As I said before, Jessie was murdered. The evidence clearly points to that. The trajectory is as I suspected, consistent with her being dropped vertically from the railing. Nothing we've discovered since has persuaded me any different. There's no doubt in my mind, someone meant to kill Jessie Beckton.'

'Agreed,' says Rick. 'So our big questions to answer are who killed her, and how did they get in and out of the penthouse without leaving a trace?'

'They could have left a trace,' says Lizzie, thoughtfully. 'Fingerprints and DNA could have been left at the scene.'

'There wasn't anything useful in the police file,' says Rick. 'They either didn't take forensics, or they disregarded them fast.'

'Can they even do that?' asks Moira. 'That's destroying evidence.'

'They shouldn't, but like I said, there's nothing on file,' says Rick. 'And Hawk didn't hold any hope of tracking down extra intel. Said as far as the local PD are concerned the case is closed and buried, end of.'

'It's not good enough,' says Philip, sweat beading across his forehead as he slaps his palm down on to the arm of the chair he's sitting on. 'That young woman deserves better.'

'She does,' says Moira, her expression determined. 'And that's why we're here.'

Rick nods. 'There's another thing about the police file. Sometime, most likely after the case was closed, a file note was added. It gives details of some circumstantial evidence that wasn't put into the final report, and it rather gives a different spin on the crime scene.' He explains the details Hawk had told him – the broken champagne flutes and black scuff marks on the balcony floor tiles. 'And the kicker is the name of the officer who signed the note.'

'Who?' asks Lizzie, narrowing her gaze.

'Chester M. Golding,' says Rick.

'Golding?' Philip splutters, sitting up straighter. 'You think this Chester fellow is some relation to Detective James R. Golding from our local PD?'

'I reckon there's a strong possibility,' says Rick.

Philip curses under his breath. He and Detective Golding have never seen eye to eye. Lizzie knows that he loathes the man, and that the feeling is mutual. 'Well, that's just bloody typical, isn't it!'

'But what he's written in his note is useful,' says Moira. 'Scuff marks and broken glass found at the scene are more proof that the coroner's ruling is wrong. If there was a struggle then there were two or more people on that balcony. And if things got broken it's likely Jessie fought to try and free herself of the attacker.'

'That's what I thought,' says Rick.

'It would fit,' says Moira, taking out her phone and referring to the notes she'd made. 'When I spoke with Jessie's martial arts coach, Phoenix Salford-Keynes, she said Jessie was highly skilled, so it didn't make sense that she'd be easily overpowered.'

'Are there any photos of the marks and the damage? Something we can work with to see if it gives a clue as to how the struggle took place and the killer overpowered Jessie?' asks Lizzie.

Rick shakes his head. 'No, nothing.'

'How about talking to Chester Golding?' asks Lizzie.

Philip mutters under his breath. His face flushes beetroot red.

'Hawk warned me off doing that. He said it's a bad move to try and speak with an officer, especially given none of us have our PI licences.'

'And you agree?' says Moira, her tone indicating she doesn't.

'For now, yes,' says Rick. 'We don't know why these key details were left out of the police report. If there's something bad going on in the local PD then the longer we can stay under their radar the better.'

'I guess.' Moira exhales hard. 'Well, this might be relevant, the coach said taekwondo needs space to be fully effective. If the killer managed to get close to Jessie before they attacked it would have been much harder for her to defend herself. There wasn't much space up on that balcony, and if there was a table with champagne out there too, it would have been even more cramped. Jessie also had a shoulder injury. If the attacker got up close, and targeted her injury, it's possible they could have overpowered Jessie, even with her martial arts skills. But that assumes that they knew about her injury, and she trusted them enough to let them into the penthouse.'

Rick runs his hand across his jaw. 'So, she knew her killer.'

'Yeah, I think so,' says Moira. 'But that doesn't narrow it down much.'

Lizzie taps the marker pen against the whiteboard. 'Let's run through the people we've spoken to so far.'

'For sure,' says Rick. 'We spoke to her boss at Beachseekers, Sindee McGillis.'

'Sindee has a reputation for being a "hard ass", according to Elton Bruce, one of her agents who showed us the penthouse,' says Philip, still red-faced as he takes a bottle of water from the small fridge at the side of the desk and downs half of it.

'She does,' says Moira. 'But she seemed genuinely upset that Jessie died.'

'Well,' says Lizzie, 'Lucas B. Francis, the realtor with Ocean Nest who showed us around the apartment at the Golden Wave Seniors Community, said there's a rumour going around that Jessie was facilitating drugs and partying among some of her clients, and when the boss discovered – that would be this Sindee McGillis you met – she told Jessie if she didn't stop it, she'd end up dead. Apparently that was around a week before she died.'

'Interesting,' says Moira, raising an eyebrow. 'It's hearsay, but how reliable do you think your guy is?'

'He's not our guy,' says Philip, looking irritated. 'And I didn't take to him. I think he used the rumour to try and get us to work solely with him rather than because he believed it was the truth.'

'We should question Sindee McGillis on it though,' says Moira, glancing at Rick. 'I thought she'd seemed genuinely upset about what happened to Jessie.'

'For sure, but could be that she's a great actor,' says Rick. 'I agree she has to go on the suspects list.'

Lizzie writes Sindee's name on the whiteboard suspect list. 'Who else?'

'As I mentioned, I spoke to Phoenix Salford-Keynes, Jessie's martial arts coach at Girls Club Gym, and also Brett Donaldson, owner and head coach at SSC Sports, where Jessie volunteered as an assistant coach, along with his office manager, Norma,' says Moira. Using the notes she'd made on her phone, she talks them through what she'd been told. 'So, I'd say Belinda Fossway, and her husband, Carl, definitely need to be on the suspect list. Like I said, Belinda instigated a physical fight with Jessie in the car park at SSC Sports, and is the most likely source of the social media trolling too.'

'Agreed,' says Lizzie, adding the Fossways' names to the list. 'Anyone else?'

'The ex needs to stay on the list,' says Rick. 'Josh Stratton is a nasty son-of-a-bitch. He claims he's got an alibi for the time Jessie died because he was drinking at the Starfish beach bar, but we've yet to check it out.'

Lizzie notes that on to the board. 'And we still don't have any leads on Jessie's phone. That text she sent to her parents makes no sense if she was murdered. Why would she tell them she's sorry?'

'Unless the killer sent it to mislead the police,' says Moira.

'True,' says Lizzie, writing a note next to the word 'phone' on the murder board to that effect. 'I'd like to find a way to prove it though.'

'Shall we plan our lines of enquiry for tomorrow?' says Philip, flapping his hands towards his still-red face in an attempt to cool down.

'Good idea,' says Lizzie.

Rick takes his phone from his pocket and looks at the screen. He says nothing, but he looks anxious; his leg starts jigging up and down, and he fiddles with the pocket flap on the side of his cargo shorts.

Lizzie glances at Moira. She looks distracted as well. Lizzie hopes that whatever is going on between Rick and Moira resolves itself soon. Usually, they'd be bouncing ideas off each other, and finishing each other's sentences. Right now, neither of them seems fully on their game.

She taps her marker pen against the suspects list. 'Okay, so we've got actions here: one, find out more about Sindee McGillis at Beachseekers and whether she argued with or threatened Jessie; two, speak to the Fossways; three, check Josh Stratton's alibi; four—'

A loud knock on the door makes them all jump. Next moment they hear the sound of the electronic lock disengaging and the door to the room starts to open.

22

MOIRA

'Housekeeping.' A young woman appears in the doorway; her black hair is pinned up in a bun, and she wears a blue and white house-keeper's uniform.

'It's okay, we're fine,' says Lizzie, trying to stop the woman coming further into the room.

The housekeeper doesn't leave. Instead, she wheels a cart packed with cleaning products, fresh towels and replacement toiletries into the room and closes the door firmly behind her. When she turns to look at them, she looks worried, afraid almost. 'Are you the private detectives?'

'We are,' says Moira, intrigued.

The young woman hurries closer to them. Her name badge gives her name as Gabriella. She keeps her voice low. 'You are looking into why Jessie Beckton died?'

Moira nods. 'That's right.'

Gabriella's gaze moves to the murder board. Her eyes open wider. 'This is your work?'

'Yeah,' says Rick, his tone gentle. 'Did you want to see us for a reason?'

'I did,' says Gabriella. 'I liked Jessie, she was always smiling. She was nice to all of us who work here, not a bitch like her boss and some of the others. We were sad when she died.' Gabriella takes another step closer towards them. 'I didn't believe them when they said she jumped.'

'Why?' asks Moira.

Gabriella glances towards the door. Lowers her voice again. 'Because I saw her thirty minutes before she died, when she was on her way up to the penthouse. She was excited – it was her first time showing a penthouse on her own. She was thrilled about what it meant for her career, that her boss trusted her enough to do it alone.'

'Did you see anyone else go up to the penthouse?' says Moira.

'No,' says Gabriella. 'You see, they said she had to have died by suicide because she was in a locked apartment and the key was found in her pocket. But that doesn't mean no one else was in there.'

'How'd you mean?' asks Rick, frowning.

'I clean the apartments on the upper floors twice a week. Jessie Beckton did *not* have the only key to the penthouse. There are more.'

'How about access?' says Philip, dabbing at his brow with his hankie. 'Is there another way to the eighth floor that isn't watched by CCTV?'

Outside in the corridor there's a clatter that sounds like bottles falling from something. Gabriella glances towards the door again, and starts backing away. 'I'm sorry. I've said too much. If they knew I'd been talking to you I . . .'

'Wait,' says Lizzie. 'Is there another way to get to the penthouse without taking the main elevator?'

Gabriella bites her lip, looking conflicted. She glances towards the door. 'I . . . I must go.'

'Wait, please tell us,' says Lizzie.

'I'm sorry.' Gabriella pauses when she reaches the door. Turning, she looks back at Moira and the team. 'Find whoever did this to Jessie,' she says, her voice full of emotion. 'Make them pay.'

'We will,' says Moira.

Gabriella puts her hand to her heart and nods. Then she opens the door and takes her cart back out to the hallway, leaving them alone again.

'Well, that was different,' says Philip. 'Poor girl obviously took Jessie's death badly.'

'It confirms that there's something else going on here though,' says Moira. 'We need to know how many keys there are for the penthouse, and who has access to them.'

'And how they got up there,' says Philip.

'For sure,' says Rick. 'We know from what Jessie's boss, Sindee McGillis, told us that the penthouse and the hallways are fully wired for cameras, but they won't be activated until someone moves in. But the elevator to that level does have the camera switched on already – we know that from the police report – so if the killer used that route they would've been caught on the CCTV.'

'But they weren't, and the killer didn't bloody well levitate up to the eighth floor,' says Philip. 'So, either the camera feed got switched out or looped to enable them to ride the lift there and back unseen . . .'

'Or there's another way in that we aren't aware of,' says Rick.

'Agreed,' Moira says. 'And from the way Gabriella reacted when you asked her, I'm guessing there's an access route that the management aren't especially keen for the public to know.'

'For sure,' says Rick. He picks up the Surf-Sand Vista information directory from the desk, and flicks through it. 'It says here that there's a head of operations, I'll talk to them and get a sense of the way things are done, and I'll try to get a copy of the building schematics.' He looks across at Philip and then Lizzie. 'We also need to fact check what the housekeeper told us. There's a building manager for this place too. Can you do your prospective resident double act again and try to find out whether anyone other than the resident has a key that will open their apartment?'

'Good idea,' says Lizzie, writing it down on the board as an action. 'So, on our list to follow up on tomorrow we've got, one, find out more about Sindee McGillis at Beachseekers and the supposed argument between her and Jessie; two, speak to the Fossways; three, check Josh Stratton's alibi; four, get hold of the building schematics and speak with the management. Anything else?'

'Good, good,' says Philip, taking his hankie out again, and mopping his brow. 'Sounds about right.'

'I'll speak to the Fossways,' says Moira.

'Cool,' says Rick. 'I'll set something up with Sindee McGillis. I can take a walk down to Starfish too, and check on Josh Stratton's alibi.'

'Great,' says Lizzie, writing down who is going to do what on to the whiteboard. 'Then I think we're done for the evening.'

'Excellent work,' says Philip, checking his watch. He looks at Lizzie. 'We've got our dinner reservation at Spinners in twenty minutes. We'd better get going.'

◆ ◆ ◆

Leaving Philip and Lizzie to get ready for their dinner date at Spinners – a revolving top-floor restaurant at one of the nearby hotels – Moira and Rick head out to the hallway and back towards their rooms. They stop outside their doors.

'You want to grab a couple of beers, and watch a movie?' says Rick, the nerves that are clear in his voice seemingly at odds with his man mountain-like physical presence.

Moira looks up at him. She feels her heart flip as their eyes meet, but still she shakes her head. 'I'm feeling wiped out after earlier. I think I'm going to have a really early night.'

'Sure, good idea,' says Rick, clearly unable to hide the disappointment in his voice. 'Next time then.'

Moira nods. She hopes there'll be a next time, but until Rick can be fully honest with her about his family situation, she needs to keep a little distance. She's already let herself fall for him; she can't keep falling if his estranged daughter showing up is going to change everything. It's ironic, Moira knows that, what with all the secrets she's keeping from him. But the one thing she absolutely needs from Rick is the full truth.

Back inside her room, Moira orders a chopped salad with fries on the side from room service and then sits on her bed, staring at her suitcase on the case stand. Fighting the urge to head back to her house in The Homestead, pull the cardboard box with the contents of her old desk drawers in the Met out of the walk-in closet, and look for the evidence McCord might have planted before the operation, she picks up her half-read paperback, the latest Ian Rankin novel, and starts to read. She won't leave Shimmering Sands until she's finished this case, and got justice for Jessie Beckton.

Then she'll find the evidence and get justice for herself.

23

RICK

He's up by six for a workout in the gym before a quick breakfast of eggs over-easy, wheat toast and coffee, then figures he'll get out and at it. But getting any headway is harder than he thinks. His calls to Sindee McGillis are going straight to voicemail, and getting into the office belonging to the head of operations is like trying to talk your way into a super-max prison. Rick has to tell three different people who he is and why he wants to speak with the head of operations – first he persuades one of the reception team to let him through to the 'back-of-house' lower level, then shop-talks an ex-cop security guard with a few battle stories in order to be allowed to pass through another locked door into the office area. Then, finally, he turns on the charm to sweet-talk the operations assistant into escorting him through to speak to their boss.

The office is sparsely furnished, functional rather than stylish, and the only source of natural light is a long, thin window that runs high up across the back wall. A tall, broad man who looks to be in his early forties is seated behind a large oak desk.

'Sorry to interrupt you, sir,' says the operations assistant, a nervous wobble to her voice as she stops in the doorway of the office. 'But this gentleman was keen to speak with you.'

The man looks at the young woman and licks his lips. 'The man got a name?'

'No, I . . .' She glances towards Rick.

'I'm Rick Denver,' says Rick, stepping past her into the office.

'Okay then,' says the man. 'Thanks, Madison.'

The woman blushes, and turns away quickly, but not before Rick clocks the man's leering expression as he winks at her. If this is the head of operations, Rick's first impression of him is that he's a sleazebag.

'Good morning, Detective,' says the man, getting to his feet and stepping out from behind his laminate wood desk. He's got slicked-back brown hair, and is wearing a grey suit made of some kind of shiny, synthetic material that doesn't look like a smart choice for Florida weather. As he leans forward, his hand outstretched, Rick gets a strong whiff of flowery aftershave. The man smiles. 'I'm Adam Coulter, head of operations. How can I help?'

Rick shakes the guy's hand. He hadn't said he was a detective, but he knows after all the years as a DEA agent that he still gives off a law enforcement vibe, and he wasn't going to discourage that; he doubts he'd have gotten to see the head of operations so fast if he had. 'So you're the head guy in charge of operations here?'

'That's me, I oversee all our ops teams here at Surf-Sand Vista,' says the guy, with a touch of pride to his voice.

Rick keeps his tone all business. 'Good. I'm investigating the death of Jessie Beckton.'

Adam Coulter's smile droops. 'I thought the case was closed?'

'The police case, yes, sir,' says Rick, sitting down on one of the two moulded plastic chairs for visitors positioned in front of the desk. 'This is a private investigation on behalf of the family.'

Coulter cusses under his breath. Looks nervous. 'But it was a tragic incident, the coroner—'

'I'm well aware of the coroner's view,' interrupts Rick. 'My clients feel it was . . . too hasty.'

'Well, I told the cops all I know,' says Coulter, stepping back around his desk and sitting down. 'I've nothing more to add.'

Interesting, thinks Rick. The cops seem to have done a shoddy job of investigating the case, but they did speak to this guy. 'What did you tell them?'

'That Jessie Beckton was the only person picked up by the CCTV during the period they were interested in, and that all our risk assessments are up to date, and all the necessary building code approvals have been granted for this building.'

'Can you show me the tape?' asks Rick, keeping his tone light, friendly. 'I'd like to see the footage from the start to the end of the day.'

'Sorry, I'm not authorised to do that,' says Coulter, his eyes darting from Rick to the door. 'The bosses are very clear that we can't give out confidential data unless there's a warrant.'

Rick scans Coulter's desk; as well as a shiny computer, there are several piles of paper, a couple of notebooks and a few cold coffee cups. Beside the cup that still has steam rising from it is a half-eaten doughnut; a bunch of the sprinkles from it have fallen on to a stack of glossy hotel brochures. 'Did the cops get a warrant?'

'I . . . I can't answer that,' says Coulter. He picks up a pen from his desk and starts to fiddle with it. 'I'm not allowed.'

Rick clenches his jaw. He's pretty damn sure that means the police didn't get a warrant. Maybe they weren't so thorough after all, and just took Coulter's word about the CCTV footage. 'Okay, how about the schematics for the building, can I take a look at them?'

Coulter's eyes widen and he shakes his head quickly. 'I'm not allowed to share anything like that, I'm sorry. They're confidential, for security reasons.'

Rick holds Coulter's gaze for a long moment. It's possible he's telling the truth, but Rick wonders why the guy is so jumpy. There's nothing personal about this office, no family pictures or golf clubs to give Rick clues to the life Coulter leads away from the job; it's as if he doesn't want his co-workers, or his employers, to know any more about him than they have to. 'If you can't show me, maybe you can answer some questions? Is there more than one elevator that goes up to the penthouse level?'

Coulter swallows hard. 'Like I said, I can't tell you that sort of thing.' He leans closer to Rick, his voice lowered. 'Look, the big bosses made me sign a confidentiality agreement that prevents me sharing anything about the resort. Everyone had to. I'll get fired if I answer your questions.'

Rick narrows his gaze. This guy is looking increasingly skittish; his eyes are still darting side to side, his breathing's elevated, and there's sweat forming on his upper lip. 'Who owns the building?'

Coulter's nostrils flare. 'I—'

'Okay, okay, I get it – you can't answer the question,' says Rick, getting up. 'Thanks for your time, anyways.'

'No problem,' says Coulter, looking relieved. 'If it was up to me, I'd tell you all this stuff, but I just can't. I need this job, man.'

'Understood,' says Rick. As he walks from the chair back towards the door Rick hears Adam Coulter sigh.

'Oh, one last question,' says Rick, turning back towards Coulter. 'Did you ever meet Jessie Beckton?'

'I did not,' says Coulter, without hesitation. 'But she sounded like a . . . fine young woman. Please pass on my condolences to her family.'

'For sure.'

As he walks back along the corridor towards the exit into the public space, Rick clenches and unclenches his fists, trying to get rid of some frustration. Coulter's a sleazebag for sure, and it's obvious he's afraid of what his bosses might do to him if he shares the information Rick wants, but that only makes Rick all the more determined.

What are they hiding, and why?

24

MOIRA

The Fossways live in a new-build neighbourhood a few blocks from the beach. Unlike the pretty beach bungalows and cottage-style homes nearer the water, this neighbourhood of new builds seems rather beige. A neighbourhood for people who toe the line and don't like to stand out, perhaps? Which is an interesting choice given Carl Fossway's affair with Jessie, and Belinda Fossway's physical attack on Jessie in the car park; both unsavoury and distinctly un-beige acts.

Finding the Fossways' house number, she pulls Rick's jeep over to the kerb and parks. The house is cream stucco with white trim and looks well maintained; the front lawn is neatly mown and there are flowers in the borders lining the path to the front door and a swing chair on the front porch.

Moira takes a breath, then gets out of the jeep and heads up the path to the front door. This isn't going to be an easy conversation – neither of the Fossways are likely to be pleased that she's here to rake up uncomfortable memories – but it's important to get to the bottom of what happened. To get to the truth. And sometimes, getting to the truth *is* uncomfortable.

Stepping up on to the porch, she presses the button on the video doorbell and waits as the chime plays on the other side of the door. Seconds tick past, and she's just about to press the bell a second time when she hears a key being turned in the lock and the door starts to inch open.

'Hello?' A young girl of no more than ten years old in a pink flowery dress, blue leggings, and her blonde hair pulled into two plaits, peers nervously through the gap between the door and its frame.

'Hi,' says Moira. She's not had much to do with children and isn't sure how to speak to the young ones like this. She gives what she hopes is an encouraging smile. 'Is your mother at home?'

'Yes,' says the girl, fiddling with one of her long plaits.

'Can I speak to her?' asks Moira.

'Okay,' says the girl. She gives Moira a broad smile, then she shuts the door.

'Wait, I . . .' Moira stands on the porch, unsure what to do next. She's thinking about ringing the bell again when the door opens.

'Yes?' The woman frowning in the doorway has highlighted brunette hair looped up on her head with a scrunchie and is wearing a grey crop top and matching sweatpants. Her face is blotchy, and her eyes are bloodshot and a little unfocused. Moira wonders if she's only just woken up.

'Belinda Fossway?' asks Moira.

'Uh-huh,' says the woman, her frown deepening. 'Can I help you?'

Moira stifles a grimace. It's barely ten o'clock, but there's a distinct smell of alcohol on Belinda Fossway's breath – either hangover fumes or hair of the dog, it's impossible to know which. 'My name is Moira Flynn, I'm an investigator working on behalf of Jim and Doreen Beckton, looking into the circumstances of their daughter's death.'

'Oh hell no.' Stepping back, Belinda tries to slam the door closed. 'I am not doing this.'

Acting on instinct, Moira shoves her foot between the door and the frame and stops it closing. 'Mrs Fossway, please. It's just a few questions to get your side of the story about what happened with Jessie.'

'No comment,' says Belinda, shoving the door against Moira's trainer. 'Now get your damn foot out of my house and leave me the hell alone.'

'Please, Belinda,' says Moira, keeping her foot where it is and trying to ignore the pain as Belinda continues to batter it with the door. 'Jim and Doreen just want to know what happened to their little girl.' She lowers her voice so Belinda's daughter won't be able to hear what she says. 'If Wilma had died in tragic circumstances, wouldn't you want to know what really happened to her?'

Belinda curses. 'How can you . . . ?' She glances over her shoulder into the house, then hisses, 'That little girl is all I have. How could you say—'

'That's how the Becktons feel about Jessie. They lost their only child.' Moira holds Belinda's gaze. 'They just want to know the truth about how she died.'

Belinda glares at Moira for a long moment. Then she blows out hard, and opens the door. 'Fine. But you're not coming inside. We'll talk on the porch.'

'Okay with me,' says Moira, feeling relieved that Belinda has relented. She removes her foot and waits as Belinda puts the door on the latch and walks across to the swing bench. Belinda sits down, but Moira remains standing, leaning against the porch rail instead. 'So, what happened between you and Jessie?'

Belinda looks straight ahead as she answers, her voice monotone. 'She slept with my husband.'

After all she's heard about what happened, Moira's surprised that the anger she'd expected Belinda to be holding towards Jessie doesn't seem to be there. 'So, you went to SSC Sports to confront her?'

'I did,' says Belinda, nodding. 'I'd seen some dirty pictures on Carl's phone, they were from Jessie, and I saw red. Until that moment I thought I had a good marriage, a happy family. Those pictures, and Carl's messages back, showed me I'd been living a lie.'

Moira knows how it feels to have everything you thought you knew about someone close to you turned upside down. 'Is that why you launched an online attack?'

Belinda looks down. She doesn't deny it. 'I'm not proud. I believed she'd instigated things with Carl is all. Convinced myself Jessie had tempted him, you know? I told a few of the other moms, and we posted nasty comments on her Instagram but she wouldn't reply – didn't engage. She just deleted her account.'

'So, you decided to have it out with her in the car park at her workplace?'

'I was a damn fool,' says Belinda, shaking her head. 'But I just couldn't take it, her breaking up my family like that. I just . . . lost my shit. It wasn't until much later, after Jessie had died, that Carl told me what he'd done – how he'd been the one to chase her. How she'd only agreed to date him because she thought he was single.' She mutters *the asshole* under her breath.

Moira watches Belinda for a moment. She seems regretful, penitent for what she did to Jessie, but from what she's saying that's only happened since Carl confessed, and that took place after Jessie was dead. 'Where were you the evening Jessie died?'

Belinda's eyes widen. 'You can't think I—'

'I don't think anything, I'm just putting a timeline together,' says Moira, neutrally.

'I was with my daughter at her swimming class.' Belinda takes her phone from her pocket and taps the screen a few times, then turns it to face Moira. 'This is a video I took of Wilma – she was being assessed for her Elementary Lifesaver Badge.'

Moira watches the video playing. The date is the day Jessie died, and the time is 5.53 p.m. If Belinda was taking this video then, it would've been impossible for her to get to the penthouse in time to kill Jessie. She looks back at Belinda. 'This proves Wilma took a swimming assessment that evening, but it doesn't prove you were there.'

'Keep watching,' says Belinda.

Moira does as she says. As Wilma completes her lap of the pool carrying a rubber brick and stops, Moira hears Belinda's voice shouting 'good job' to her daughter. Moments later the camera view rotates and Belinda's face fills the screen as she does a big thumbs up to the camera.

Belinda switches the video off and puts her phone back into her pocket. 'You believe me?'

'Yes,' says Moira. The video is proof that Belinda was where she said she'd been. 'Was your husband also at the swimming assessment?'

'No,' says Belinda. 'I have no idea where he was, or who he was with.'

Moira looks towards the house. Movement in the large window to the left of the bench swing catches Moira's eye. The little girl, Wilma, is peeping out from behind the curtains, watching them. She moves out of sight when she realises Moira has seen her. Moira looks back at Belinda. 'Is your husband here? I need to talk to him as—'

'Carl's gone,' says Belinda, the anger and hurt raw in her voice. 'He left the day after Jessie died. He told me the truth about what he did with Jessie, then said he wanted a divorce and that he'd give me this house and the big car, but he wanted joint custody of Wilma.'

Moira's not sure what to say. 'I'm sorry.'

'I'm not. It was over the minute I found out about Jessie anyway.'

'Do you know where he's staying?'

'He's over in St Petersburg, staying with a golfing friend. I can give you his cell and the address if you want?'

'That'd be great.'

Belinda scrolls through her own cell phone, finding the information. Then reads it out.

Moira types the number and address into her own phone and saves Carl's details, then looks up at Belinda. 'Thanks.'

'No problem,' says Belinda. 'Do you think he killed her?'

Moira doesn't answer. 'Do you?'

Belinda exhales hard. 'I keep thinking about it, wondering. If you'd asked me last year if my husband could kill a person I'd have said no, but after everything I've learnt about him recently – all the lies – I don't know for sure.'

It's interesting timing that he left his family the day after Jessie's death, thinks Moira. 'We'll look into it.'

'Good. He played that poor girl just as bad as he played me,' says Belinda. Her eyes are a little tearful, but she forces a smile. 'I sure wish I'd known that before she died. I wish I'd known that before I did what I did on social media. Before I called her those things.'

Moira nods.

When a person's dead it's too late to admit you made a mistake and say sorry.

It's too late to take back what you did.

25

LIZZIE

It takes a bit of persuasion to get back-of-house, but Lizzie manages to get the security guy onside with her enthusiastic talk of the penthouse apartment and how excited she and Philip are to move to the Shimmering Sands Resort community. She tells him that they've just got a few questions about security before they finalise their offer, and that their real-estate agent told them to speak directly to the building manager. After a few minutes of over-the-top gusto, the security officer lets them through and directs them to Cal Staples' office.

Reaching the double doors into the maintenance department, Lizzie looks at Philip. 'Are you ready?'

'Yes, yes,' says Philip. 'Let's get on with it.'

Lizzie holds his gaze a beat longer than usual. Philip sounds eager enough, but he looks a bit tired, which is strange considering he was out like a light the moment they got back from dinner last night, and she'd had to wake him this morning or they'd have been late for getting on with the job. It's really not like him. Usually, he's the one up early and ready to go. She hopes he's not still feeling jet-lagged from the Australia trip as she gives him a smile and says, 'Okay, here we go.'

Pushing open the doors, they walk through into the maintenance department. It's a large open-plan space with several tables and benches along one side of the area, and the rest of the space taken up with various pieces of mechanical equipment. The walls are lined with floor-to-ceiling shelving filled with both plumbing and electrical spare parts and a number of metal toolboxes. The radio is playing some kind of dance music, and there's a group of overall-wearing maintenance crew standing around a large hot water urn, making coffee. Cal Staples' office is over in the corner.

The crew members barely look at them as they pass through the open-plan area to the office. There's a plastic nameplate on the door that reads 'Cal Staples – Building Manager'. Philip knocks firmly on the door, and a muffled voice tells them to enter.

The man sitting behind the light-oak laminate desk is wearing a Surf-Sand Vista branded baseball cap and polo shirt. He looks up at them and raises an eyebrow. 'Hey there, can I help you folks?'

'We're Lizzie and Philip Sweetman,' says Lizzie, rushing out her words as she fakes the role of overexcited home buyer. 'We're looking to buy an apartment here, on the eighth floor, one of those lovely penthouses, and, the thing is, we've just got a few questions about security, and our realtor, he's a lovely guy, you might know him? Elton Bruce? From Beachseekers? He said to speak with you because you know everything about the security here and so.' She takes a breath, smiling. 'We're here to talk to you.'

Cal looks a bit surprised by the verbal onslaught, but recovers quickly. He smiles. 'Well, sure, I know Elton. So, you're looking to move here?'

Lizzie's relieved Cal is nice; it makes it so much easier to not break character.

'Yes, yes,' says Philip. 'Jolly nice community you've got, and my wife does love the beach.'

'Well, great,' says Cal, a wide grin spreading across his lips. 'This here's a real nice spot – white sand beaches, quality amenities, good fishing – you've made an excellent choice. We don't have boat slips available on-site, but there are a bunch of great marinas nearby, and plenty of our residents have their own boats. There's even a fishing club that meets every Wednesday that seems really popular.'

'Thank you,' says Philip.

Cal leans back on his chair. 'So how is it I can help you good folks?'

'We're very security conscious,' says Lizzie. She notices that Cal has very little paperwork on his desk, and what little there is sits in a wire tray to the right of his computer. Aside from that, there's a large jotter pad, a couple of pencils, and a mug with a picture of a marlin fish on it. 'And we want to be sure that our apartment will be as secure as possible.'

'We have top-level security features on all our floors here at Surf-Sand Vista,' says Cal, his tone serious. 'You don't need to worry.'

'Good, good,' says Philip. 'But the thing is, my wife does worry, and she'd like to be reassured about who holds access keys to the apartment once we've purchased it.'

Cal's smile slips a little. 'Surely this is something your realtor can advise on?'

'Well, yes, and they've told us they'll hold a master key for the penthouse level until all the units are sold.' Lizzie glances at Philip then back to Cal Staples, and injects a bit more anxiety into her tone. 'But we wondered how many are held by the staff here – housekeepers, maintenance and everyone?'

'I can't tell you that,' says Cal, looking conflicted. 'I'd love to say more, but I just can't.'

'But you must know,' says Philip. 'A fellow like you, in charge of the whole building, you'd know about keys surely?'

'I do know,' says Cal, his expression earnest. 'But, like I said, I'm sorry but I'm not allowed to tell you guys.'

'Why ever not?' asks Lizzie, faking wide-eyed innocence.

Cal stands up, and walks around to the front of the desk.

'I'm sorry, but the boss won't allow it.' He gives a little shrug. 'They're worried the competition will get a hold of our operating secrets.'

Staying in character, Lizzie bites her lip, frowning. She puts her hand on Cal Staples' arm. 'Oh please, we really need your help.'

'Sorry, but like I said, I just can't,' says Cal, the anguish clear in his voice. 'If I tell you, I could get fired and, no disrespect, this is a good job, I just can't afford to risk it. You should raise any concerns with your realtor, maybe they can ask the owners for permission to disclose the information? I am so sorry I can't help more.'

It seems very odd that something so basic would have to be run past the owners of the Shimmering Sands Resort Community. Lizzie tilts her head to the side and gives him her most wide-eyed, sweet look. 'Not even for me?'

Cal shakes his head, sadly. 'Not even.'

'Well, thanks for your time, anyway,' says Philip, stepping towards the door. 'We'll talk to our realtor, like you suggest.'

Lizzie looks at Philip as they move out of Cal Staples' office and into the maintenance crew area. 'What now? Shall we take a walk on the beach?'

'The beach is always so hot, and there's no shade out there on the sand,' says Philip, grimacing. 'And I'm feeling a bit out-of-sorts, actually, so I think I'll take a nap. Shall we go back to our room?'

She'd rather take a walk along the beach, or a dip in the pool. It's hot outside, yes, but there's always a cooling breeze coming off the ocean. But Lizzie can tell Philip isn't feeling on top form, and the fact he's admitting it means a lot given his history of hiding health concerns from her, so rather than objecting she smiles and says, 'Of course.'

Putting her arm through Philip's, she leads him back through the maintenance area. As they reach the door, Lizzie glances over her shoulder towards Cal Staples' office. He's watching them, and when their eyes meet, he gives her a rueful smile and waves.

Waving back, Lizzie tries not to feel too disheartened that they didn't manage to get the information needed. It isn't so much what Cal Staples said, but the way he looked when they asked him for the information about the access keys that makes her think something about this place isn't right. The man was clearly afraid of the building's owners.

26

RICK

Outside in the hot Florida sun, Rick checks his watch. It's almost noon. The beach bar – Starfish – that Josh Stratton said he was drinking in at the time Jessie Beckton was killed opens at midday. Rick decides he may as well head straight there and catch the manager before the place gets too busy.

Slipping off his sneakers, Rick walks barefoot along the beach towards Starfish. It feels good to have his toes in the sand. Makes him think about the vacations he and Alisha had taken Estelle on back when she was a little kid; Myrtle Beach, Cape Cod, Virginia Beach, and Tybee Island had all been favourites. They'd pack up the car, book a little place close to the beach, and spend a week making sandcastles, swimming and surfing, and kayaking. Rick smiles at the good memories, then he sighs. Those times seem a world away from what's happened to their relationship since Alisha died.

Shaking his head, Rick forces himself to get his mind back on the investigation before emotion overcomes him. Pulling out his cell phone, he dials Hawk's number.

It's answered on the second ring. 'Hey, man.'

'Buddy, I need another favour.'

'I reckoned you might. Shoot.'

'I need the CCTV footage from level eight of the hotel for the day Jessie Beckton died. There should be tape of her in the elevator – it's referred to in the police report – but I'm thinking there could be other stuff on there that's useful.'

'Okay,' says Hawk, chewing on his gum. 'That all?'

'I need the schematics of the building.'

'You tried the property manager?'

'Yep, but it's a dead end.' Rick thinks for a moment. 'Actually, can you see if you can find anything on Adam Coulter, he's the head of operations at the building, and also any details on the owners of the Shimmering Sands retirement community?'

'Well, alrighty then, but that's four favours now.'

'Name your price,' says Rick, chuckling.

Hawk is silent for a long moment, aside from the chewing of his gum. Then he says, 'The next steak dinner is on you.'

'Deal,' says Rick, smiling. 'Beers an' all.'

'Oh yeah,' says Hawk. 'Okay, man, I'll let you know as soon as I have this stuff for you.'

'Appreciate it, buddy.' Rick ends the call.

Starfish is a few yards up ahead. It's a new-construction beach bar made to look like a massive tiki hut, but it's too shiny, and lacking the weathered, natural charm of the real thing. As Rick approaches, he can hear an old nineties rock song playing over the speakers rigged up under the canopy, coupled with animated chatter and clinking glassware. It's clear the place is popular, but not in the way Rick expected. The people here don't look much like vacationers. The furtive glances at him as he walks in, and the lack of anyone making eye contact, puts his retired DEA agent senses on high alert.

A long-haired guy in a grey T-shirt and camo shorts gets up from a table towards the back of the bar and hurriedly packs something into a carryall. He walks quickly towards the exit furthest away. As Rick watches, the guy glances back over his shoulder at him, speeding up further when he realises he's being watched. It seems real suspicious behaviour.

'What can I get you?'

Turning towards the bar, Rick sees the bartender is staring at him expectantly. He's a shaven-headed, muscular forty-something guy in a bright orange T-shirt with a large silver starfish across the chest. He gestures at the cocktail menu chalkboard that's sitting on the top of the bar. 'Lunchtime two-for-one special is running right now.'

Rick pauses for a moment before answering. The way the guy's looking at him as if he's a threat to be handled is in sharp contrast to the friendliness in his tone.

'A beer perhaps?' says the bartender. 'Or maybe you're lost and want to be on your way to a different bar?'

'I'll take a Coke,' says Rick, ignoring the man's comment about him being in the wrong place. He doesn't feel welcome, that's for sure, but he's got a job to do so he can't just turn and walk away.

He waits for the guy to serve his drink, conscious that he's still drawing furtive looks from the drinkers at the nearby tables. At the table closest to the bar, a couple of youths with buzz cuts and a large, white pit bull are staring at him with undisguised hostility. He tries not to let it get to him and asks, 'Were you working here the night that young woman died at the Shimmering Sands place along the beach?'

The bartender's expression remains the same. 'I'm always working.'

'You own this place?'

'I own the lease, have done as of the new year,' says the guy. 'And I'm the cheapest labour I've got.'

Rick nods. 'So you worked here that night?'

'Yep. It was busy – had a team of four on shift that night,' says the bartender, taking a cloth and starting to wipe down the bar. 'Business was going well until we saw the blue lights over at the Surf-Sand Vista. Then half our drinkers headed off fast.'

'Was this guy one of those drinkers?' asks Rick, holding up his cell phone with the picture from the KMP Auto Outlet website enlarged on the screen.

The bartender keeps wiping the bar. Doesn't look at the photo. 'I couldn't say.'

'You sure about that?' asks Rick.

'One hundred per cent,' says the guy. 'I'm not real good with faces, and it was a few months back. The nights kind of blend into one after a while.'

'So you've never seen this man?'

The bartender glances at the picture. Frowns. 'Maybe I've seen him, but I can't be sure.'

'What about CCTV, could I take a look at your footage from that night?'

'Don't have any,' says the bartender, shrugging. 'Sorry.'

Rick takes a sip of his Coke. It's clear this guy wouldn't help even if he was one hundred per cent sure he'd seen Josh. He shakes his head. 'Thanks for your help.'

'No problem,' says the bartender, evenly. He points to Rick's glass. 'Let me know if you'd like some rum in that.'

'Sure will,' says Rick, knowing that he'll be sticking with just Coke.

As the bartender moves down the bar to welcome a group of guys who look suspiciously underage, Rick thinks on what he's just learnt. He supposes Josh Stratton could have been telling the truth about where he was the night Jessie Beckton died, but it's unlikely he'll be able to prove it.

His alibi isn't solid, given the bartender can't vouch for him. So they need to keep him in the frame, for now at least, while they keep looking at the other suspects. What he really needs is for Hawk to get hold of the building schematics and CCTV fast. Because if Rick can figure out *how* the killer got to Jessie in the penthouse that evening, he might be closer to working out how to get proof of the identity of her murderer.

That's when he notices movement on the table across from the bar. The two young guys with the buzz cuts have been joined by a ballcap-wearing friend. They're speaking in hushed tones as they transfer packets wrapped in brown paper from his carryall to theirs.

Rick feels adrenaline firing through his body. There's a drug deal, or a re-up, taking place right here in the bar in full view of the bartender and the other drinkers. *That's bold*, thinks Rick. Real bold.

As Rick's watching, the ballcap guy turns to stare at him. Rick's trouble radar goes into overdrive. This feels bad; like these boys are going to threaten him, or worse.

Rick holds the ballcap guy's gaze. The guy keeps staring back, then raises his eyebrows and nods. 'What you looking at, old man. You want to come over here?'

It's a taunt, or an invitation to fight, depending on how you look at it. Neither is welcome.

He shakes his head. Keeps his tone neutral. 'I'm good here, thanks.'

'We don't think so,' says the ballcap guy. 'You're in the wrong bar.'

'Is that right?' says Rick, keeping his voice calm, not rising to the bait.

He doesn't want any trouble. These guys are at least forty years younger than him, probably more, and without any back-up nearby, he suddenly feels far more vulnerable than he ever has before.

Nodding, the ballcap guy takes the pit bull's leash from the others, and lets the muscular dog take a few paces towards Rick. The guy scowls. 'Yeah. It is.'

Rick glances round, looking for the bartender, but the man's disappeared. There's no one behind the bar right now. Looking at the other patrons, Rick sees they've all stopped looking his way. All of them seem very focused on their drinking companions or their drinks.

It's a bad sign. Real bad.

Gulping down the rest of his Coke, Ricks stands up. He fights to keep his voice steady. 'I guess I'm about done, anyways.'

He walks, not too fast but not too slow, across the bar area. The white pit bull strains at its leash as he passes, barking. One of the buzz-cut guys laughs; it's a joyless sound.

Rick keeps walking. Steady, alert, and ready to defend himself if needed.

It's not until he's a good hundred metres from the bar that he's able to breathe easy again. Starfish is a bad place. That was far too close for comfort.

27

MOIRA

They've regrouped in Lizzie and Philip's room after lunch, and are sitting around the murder board. The atmosphere is more downbeat than last night. Moira knows why. As the hours of their investigation tick by, the chances of discovering the truth of what happened to Jessie Beckton seem to be diminishing.

Rick stands and picks up a marker pen from the desk. 'Okay, let's get to it. I'll go first. I checked out Josh Stratton's alibi. Starfish is a real dive. I saw drugs exchanging hands in plain view and underage drinkers getting served without ID checks. The owner wouldn't confirm or deny anything. My thinking is that it's possible Stratton could have been at the bar, but there's no way we're going to get confirmation from any of the folks who were there.'

'So he doesn't have an alibi?' says Moira.

'Not unless there's any street CCTV of him,' says Rick. 'The bar itself doesn't have any.'

'He's still a suspect then,' says Philip. Unlike the previous murder board debriefs when he's taken more of a back seat, his bossy tone is back, along with a distinct air of 'officer in charge' attitude. 'What's our next move with him?'

'Not sure yet,' says Rick, scribbling the key points under Josh Stratton's name on the board. 'Let's move on and circle back to him later. I've also been trying to get hold of Sindee McGillis to fact check the intel from Lucas B. Francis on the drug rumour and Jessie, but I've had no luck so far, although she did message to say she'll be free later today if we want to talk then.'

'Okay, good, let's speak to her later,' says Moira. 'I visited the Fossways' place and spoke to Belinda Fossway. She was less angry than I thought she'd be. It seems she knows now that Jessie was a victim of the husband's lies and she regrets trolling her on social media and accosting her at SSC Sports.'

'So, she's in the clear?' asks Lizzie, slowly rotating her three rings around her wedding finger.

'Probably,' says Moira, thoughtfully. 'In terms of an alibi, she showed me a video she'd taken of her daughter's swimming assessment that was taking place at the time Jessie died. It has a date and time stamp from her phone, and Belinda's voice, and face, are clear in the video.'

'She can't be a suspect,' says Philip, his tone firm. 'Not if her alibi holds.'

Moira narrows her eyes. 'I haven't finished yet.'

'Well, go on then,' says Philip flapping his hand at her in a 'hurry up' motion.

Moira glares at him. How dare Philip act like he's her boss; they're all equal. He'd seemed to have mellowed a bit after his return from the Australia trip with Lizzie. Moira's disappointed that his old bossy traits seem to now be returning. 'She couldn't have got to the penthouse in time to kill Jessie, no, but although she now regrets what she did to Jessie, she didn't find out the real truth about her husband hounding Jessie into going on dates with him and telling her he was single until after Jessie's death.'

'Interesting,' says Rick. He finishes the point he's writing on the board, then looks at Moira. 'Belinda Fossway still had motive at the time Jessie was killed?'

'She did.'

'Yes, yes, but she has an alibi, this video, so we have to rule her out as a suspect,' says Philip, bossily.

'No, Philip, we can't rule her out,' says Moira, her tone sharp. 'Belinda might not have been there, but she could have hired someone. After all, she had no qualms about roping in her friends to help her troll Jessie.'

Philip gives a curt nod but says nothing.

'For sure,' says Rick.

Moira gestures to the name Carl Fossway next to Belinda's on the murder board. 'I didn't get to speak to Carl. Like I said, he told Belinda the full story about Jessie on the day after she died. He also told his wife he was leaving her and wanted a divorce.'

'You think the man has a guilty conscience?' asks Rick.

'Definitely,' says Moira. 'But the question is whether it's just because of what he did in pursuit of Jessie, and because he blew up his marriage, or whether it's because he threw her off the balcony. I've got his number but I haven't managed to speak to him yet. Belinda said she didn't know where, or with who, he'd been at the time Jessie died. So, I need to ask him.'

'For sure.' Rick adds the information beneath Carl Fossway's name on the board. 'As well as going to Starfish, I also visited with Adam Coulter, head of operations at the Surf-Sand Vista. He's a pretty sleazy kind of guy. He acted like a sexist creep with his assistant, and was kind of twitchy and nervous, refusing to give me a look-see at the CCTV footage or the building schematics.'

'He was obstructive?' says Philip, frowning.

'Yes, although it could have been coming from a place of fear. He said he'd be fired if he told me anything. It seems the owners of Shimmering Sands are real hard asses and like to control anything being said about the place. He told me that they'd only let him share stuff with the cops if they'd gotten a warrant.' Rick glances at Moira. 'Remind you of any place?'

Moira nods. The Homestead management committee had tried to stop any bad news stories being discussed or reported on. She hopes they wouldn't refuse to cooperate with a police investigation though. 'You think that means they're dodgy?'

Rick shrugs. 'Hard to tell. But we need to talk to them.'

'Definitely,' says Moira.

Rick writes 'Shimmering Sands Owners' on the list, then pauses. 'I've asked Hawk to find out who the owners are, and I've also asked him to find out background intel on Adam Coulter. There was definitely something about Coulter that seemed out of whack.'

'You think he knows more than he's saying?' asks Lizzie.

'Could be,' says Rick, making a note on the board. He looks back at Philip and Lizzie. 'How did it go with the keys?'

'We hit a dead end,' says Philip. 'The building manager, Cal Staples, was a nice enough fellow but he said he couldn't talk to us about keys.'

'That's right,' says Lizzie, nodding. 'He said we had to speak to the sales team at Beachseekers and see if they could get permission from the owners to release the information.'

'At least the two employees said the same,' says Moira.

'Just like your Adam Coulter chap, Rick, Cal Staples said he'd be fired if he spoke about anything to do with Shimmering Sands,' says Philip.

Moira doesn't like the sound of this. Why are the owners, and the staff, at Shimmering Sands so secretive? Surely, if they had nothing to hide, they'd be more open. 'Sounds like we should dig a bit more into the background of this Staples guy too.'

'For sure,' says Rick, adding Cal Staples' name to the board. 'I'll ask Hawk to get on it.'

'Yes, yes. Good idea,' says Philip; he looks at the murder board for a moment. 'After forty-eight hours on this job we've got a lot more people on our suspects list than we started with, and any of them could be our killer, or have orchestrated Jessie's death.'

'Maybe they could,' says Moira, thoughtfully. 'They're pissed off with her, yes, but whether any of them had a strong enough motive to kill her I'm not convinced.'

'Over my career I came to learn people don't always need much of a motive,' says Philip, shaking his head sadly. 'The punishment doesn't always fit the crime.'

If she's feeling generous, Moira could suppose that Philip doesn't intend to sound as condescending as he does. All four of them are experienced law enforcement officers with long careers to draw on; he's not the only one. 'And even if we thought one of them did kill her, how did they do it when the police seemed convinced no one else was in the penthouse?'

'True,' says Lizzie, giving a heavy sigh. 'We're still no further forward on that. Where do we go from here?'

'Like I said, we need that CCTV and the building schematics,' says Rick, determinedly. 'There could be stuff the cops missed; after all, it's clear they didn't put much effort into their investigation.'

'Yes,' says Moira. 'How's Hawk doing on that?'

'No luck so far,' says Rick, running his hand over his jaw. 'But he's working on it.'

'Well, we can't just sit here twiddling our thumbs,' says Philip. 'We must do something.'

'What do you suggest?' asks Lizzie.

'One of these people has to know more,' says Rick, circling the suspects group with the marker pen. 'We need to shake the tree. Put the pressure on harder and see if they cave.'

Moira raises an eyebrow. It's an interesting idea. 'What are you thinking?'

'We get all these folks in the penthouse together, and go through the reasons why each of them might be the murderer,' says Rick, his tone deadly serious.

'What, like Poirot in some Agatha Christie telly adaptation?' scoffs Philip. 'That's fictional drama, not how real police work is done.'

'For sure,' says Rick, evenly. 'But we're out of options until the intel we need from Hawk comes through. *If* it comes through. Getting all our suspects and witnesses together could help us out with this case. If one of them is the killer they'll be going back to the scene of the crime. We can put each one of them very publicly in the hot seat. If we also suggest that we've found new evidence and are close to unmasking the killer we can observe people's body language and see who gets spooked.'

'If you say so,' says Philip, his tone suggesting he isn't at all keen. 'But it sounds like half-arsed amateur-hour nonsense to me. I say we don't do this and we follow the tried and tested methods of traditional investigation like proper officers of the law.'

'Well, I disagree,' says Moira. She's fed up of Philip's increasingly pompous tone and him seeming to think he has the biggest say in the direction they take. 'We're not officers of the law any more, and we don't have to follow the rules. I think Rick's right. It's a good idea, given we've got nothing else.'

'Me too,' says Lizzie. 'It's worth a try.'

'Fine, fine,' says Philip, in a long-suffering tone. He puts his hands up in surrender. 'I'll play along if that's what you all want. But I doubt we'll get them to come along easily, I mean, you said it yourself, Moira, we're not officers of the law any more so we have no official capacity to ask them to do this.'

'We might not have police jurisdiction,' says Rick. 'But if these people want to help find the truth about what happened to Jessie they'll agree to meet us.'

'And if they don't care?' asks Philip, raising his eyebrows. 'I for one can't see the dodgy ex-boyfriend showing up.'

Moira meets Philip's gaze with a hard stare. 'Then that'll tell us something, won't it?'

'Will it?' Philip says, cocking his head to one side. 'Or will it just confirm what we already know?'

Moira blows out, frustrated. She doesn't understand why Philip is making such a big deal about this. 'If we tell them we've discovered new evidence, as Rick suggested, and that we need them to join us in the penthouse so we can exclude them from our enquiries, they'll come.'

Philip frowns. 'Sounds rather a stretch though, don't you think? I mean, what possible evidence could we have that means they need to come to that apartment, at that time, in person? It makes no sense.'

Moira looks at Rick. His irritated expression mirrors hers. There's nothing she'd like more right now than to have a go at Philip, but that isn't going to help the situation; she needs to get him onside. She tries to make her tone neutral as she says, 'Look, Philip, I do get what you're saying – we need the reason to be plausible. How would you entice them to join us?'

Philip thinks for a moment. 'I think your idea of needing to check something to eliminate them from our enquiries could work. And given you want to see their reactions at being in the penthouse at the same time of day Jessie was killed, we need a rationale for why, so the thing we need to check them against has to be in the penthouse.' He glances from Moira to Rick. 'Another tricky thing will be persuading them that they'll all need to be there together.'

'Perhaps we don't tell them we're gathering them all together?' says Moira, jumping in before Rick can respond. 'Maybe we tell them we're staging the balcony with a table of drinks, just as it was when Jessie died, and need to compare their stride length against the scuffs found on the balcony floor in order to eliminate them from our suspect list.'

Philip rubs his hand across his forehead. 'It could work. Obviously, it sounds rather far-fetched because it is, but, if they're anxious to be removed from our suspects list they might go for it.'

'Good, that's sorted then,' says Rick, looking relieved.

'Actually, there is another issue,' says Lizzie, cautiously. 'Philip has a good point about us not being here in an official capacity, how are we going to get into the penthouse?'

'I don't think that'll be a problem,' says Rick. 'Sindee McGillis, Jessie's boss, already said that she'll help our investigation. I'll give her a call and ask her to open the penthouse for us this evening at the same time the killer would have attacked Jessie.'

'And do you think she'll do it?' asks Lizzie, looking doubtful.

'She seemed to have really rated Jessie and was pretty cut up about her death, in her own way,' says Rick. 'I figure I'll be able to persuade her.'

As they work out who will call which suspects and witnesses, Moira hopes they're doing the right thing. It's unconventional, certainly, but sometimes the only way to find the truth is to do things that others won't.

Fortune favours the bold, or at least she hopes it does.

28

RICK

They were supposed to go into the penthouse at five o'clock, but it's twenty-one minutes past the hour, and they're still waiting out in the hallway and three people short. Rick dials Sindee McGillis's cell phone again, and again it rings twice and goes to voicemail. This is real bad. The group is getting restless. It took a lot of coaxing to get most of them here, and even more to keep them here once they realised they weren't the only suspect invited. If they can't get inside the apartment soon, Rick's worried they'll just leave. The rather morbid irony isn't lost on him either: this is the spot where all the real-estate agents who'd come to attend Jessie's broker's open event were waiting on the night she died; it's almost like history is repeating.

He looks at Moira and gives a little shake of his head, then turns to Elton Bruce, Jessie's co-worker and friend. 'Your boss still isn't picking up.'

Elton rolls his eyes, pouting. 'OMG, that's just so typical. It's a power move, all this making us wait around. She'll be here soon. I guess with Jessie gone it isn't like she can send her instead.'

Rick sure hopes Sindee will arrive soon. He's real glad they didn't invite Jim and Doreen Beckton to the meeting now. They'd considered it, but decided it might have been too difficult for them to be in the apartment their daughter was in when she was killed. With this delay, it was the right call for sure.

Aside from Sindee, they're missing Carl Fossway and Josh Stratton. Neither had been keen on coming here this afternoon. Rick checks his cell phone, but there's still no reply to the text he sent Josh Stratton just after five o'clock. On the call last night Josh had said he had nothing to do with Jessie's death and they couldn't force him to come to the penthouse. Rick thought he'd talked him into it by the end of the call, but given Josh isn't here maybe he hadn't been as persuasive as he'd thought.

Rick looks over at Moira. 'Any word from Carl Fossway?'

Moira shakes her head, grim-faced. 'He's not answering my calls or my texts.'

Dammit. Carl Fossway doesn't have an alibi for the time Jessie died. He'd told Moira on a call last night that he'd been at home working out in the garage at that time, but that doesn't fit with the story Belinda gave them. Right now, he's one of their top three suspects. Philip thinks Carl should be their top suspect but Rick isn't so certain; Carl seems too obvious a choice. Maybe he's overthinking it. Especially given the fact Carl hasn't shown up this afternoon. His absence indicates he's got something to hide, for sure.

'Do you know when we'll be able to go inside?' asks Brett Donaldson – owner of SSC Sports – who is standing opposite Moira.

'Sorry, no,' says Rick.

'Hopefully it won't be too much longer,' says Moira to Brett, giving him a reassuring smile.

Brett nods. He looks a little uneasy, but that could be because Belinda Fossway is nearby. It's got to be awkward, given the incident in the parking lot outside the sports centre, and Jessie's subsequent death. Brett isn't a prime suspect, but it's worth watching his reactions as he could know more about things than he's been letting on. In a case like this, it's never a good move to discount people too early.

Phoenix Salford-Keynes is next to Brett. Athletic and very attractive, she looks as if she'd have been more than able to lift Jessie over the balcony. But it's hard to think of her as a realistic suspect; she has no motive.

Lizzie is standing between Phoenix and Bethany Thompson. Bethany is another person without a motive, but she knew Jessie well having lived with her, and it's possible she knows something important without being aware of it. Bethany's head is bowed and Lizzie's got her hand on the young woman's shoulder and is giving her an encouraging rub. It must be tough for her, being here at the place her friend died.

In the middle of the group, near where Rick's standing, and halfway between the penthouse door and the elevator, are Elton Bruce and Lucas B. Francis. It's clear from their body language – turned away from each other, slight pouts, no eye contact – that they're not friends. Rick wonders if Elton is aware of the allegations Lucas has made about Jessie, and doubts he does. If he did, Rick figures there'd be a lot of shouting going on right about now.

At the end of the hallway, the elevator pings. Rick watches as the doors open, and Josh Stratton saunters out. He raises his eyebrows at the gathered crowd, then turns to Belinda Fossway who's standing nearby, and says something to her.

Also over by the elevator, a rather red-faced Philip catches Rick's eye and taps his watch. Rick nods. Right from the get-go Philip doubted they'd gather all the suspects here; now time's rolling on and it's almost a half hour since Sindee should have arrived to unlock the penthouse. They can't keep waiting forever. He looks at Elton. 'It's getting late. Is there anyone else who can open up the apartment for us?'

'I guess I could call the building manager,' says Elton. 'They might have a spare key.'

'I'd sure appreciate that,' says Rick.

As Elton makes a call on his cell phone, Rick turns his attention back towards the elevator and two of their top three suspects: Belinda Fossway and Josh Stratton. Josh is a big guy. Rick has no doubt he'd have zero trouble getting Jessie over the balcony railing against her will, and in his mind the alibi Josh gave them, saying he was drinking in Starfish, is patchy at best. Rick frowns as he watches Josh say something to Belinda, who giggles, her cheeks blushing pink. He's clearly flirting with the woman, and it makes Rick dislike the flash asshole even more. In his mind, Josh Stratton is the number one suspect. Jessie dumped him, hurting his pride and his reputation: two things it would be real hard for a man like that to stomach.

And if Josh Stratton is suspect number one, he'd put Belinda Fossway as number two. She might have an alibi, but a woman wronged is an age-old motive, and she's already admitted to starting a hate campaign against Jessie. At the time Jessie died, Belinda didn't know the lies Carl had told Jessie as he chased her. Belinda could have hired someone to do the job for her – from what they know, the Fossways have enough cash – and made the swimming assessment video with her kid because she knew soon she'd be asked about her whereabouts at that time. Rick exhales hard. Over the years he's seen people orchestrate murder for a hell of a lot less.

Elton ends his call, and waves to get Rick's attention. 'The building manager is coming up to let us into the apartment. He took a bit of persuading to let a large group in, but I told him it was agreed with Sindee and, given we have the right to show the place to as many people as we see fit, he has no grounds to refuse.'

'Great, thanks,' says Rick, relieved that Elton managed to get the building manager onside. Without any formal jurisdiction there's no way he or his retiree friends would have been able to get the building guy to open the place up.

'Anything for Jessie,' says Elton with a sad smile.

Next to him, Lucas B. Francis rolls his eyes and fakes a yawn.

Rick clears his throat. 'Sorry about the hold-up, folks. We've got someone on their way up now to let us into the penthouse, so please hold tight and we'll be inside very soon. It won't take us long to set up the table and mark out the scuffs on the balcony, and then we'll only need a few minutes of each of your time to do the comparison and elimination.'

Philip gives him a thumbs up and there are nods among the group, some rather nervous and others more irritated. Bethany grimaces and hugs her arms around herself. Lucas B. Francis gets out his cell phone and starts tapping the screen. Josh Stratton leans closer and brushes a strand of Belinda Fossway's brunette hair away from her eyes.

Rick glances back at Moira, but she looks deep in conversation with Brett Donaldson and doesn't return his gaze; Lizzie smiles at him as he catches her eye. Then he looks back along the hallway to the elevator. Waiting for the building manager to appear.

'I heard you folks had an access problem,' booms a male voice from behind Rick.

Rick turns, and sees a short, squat guy in a Shimmering Sands ballcap, a resort-branded polo shirt and navy work pants, heading his way from the opposite end of the hallway. 'Are you the building manager?'

'Indeed I am,' says the guy cheerfully with a broad grin. He taps the peak of his cap. 'Cal Staples at your service.'

'Appreciate you coming up to help us, Cal,' says Rick, wondering how the guy got up here to the eighth floor if he didn't use the elevator. Rick's assumption about a second elevator must be right.

He wonders where it is – there was no obvious sign of it when he and Moira looked around yesterday.

'No problem,' says Cal. He stops beside the door to the penthouse and gestures towards it. 'This the one you want open?'

'It is,' says Rick.

'Well, alrighty.' Cal blows out, looking conflicted. 'So I do want to help you out, man, truly I do, but I have to just double-check that Sindee McGillis okay'd this?'

'For sure,' says Rick.

Cal frowns. He glances at Elton. 'Where is she then?'

'Well, that's the thing,' says Elton, stepping closer to Cal. 'It's like I said on the phone, the boss was meant to be bringing our key. We arranged to all meet here at five but you know what she's like . . .' He shrugs. Getting out his cell phone he taps the screen a couple of times and then holds it towards Cal. 'This is the message exchange of her agreeing to let this group in together.'

Cal takes a moment to read through it. Then he laughs, and claps Elton on the back. Removing a small, plastic key fob from his pocket, he unlocks the door. 'I hear you, man. Your boss is a real force of nature. And, of course, I'm happy to help the Beachseekers team anytime.'

As Cal steps into the penthouse, Rick is surprised that he doesn't have a whole bunch of fobs on him. He'd not been one hundred per cent sure which door they wanted unlocked, yet he only seemed to have brought the one fob. He follows Cal into the penthouse. 'Is that a master key you've got there?'

Cal turns back to face Rick. 'Sure is. We have a couple of them for each level – so we can deliver our housekeeping and delivery services to all residents, and also for use in the event of an emergency.'

'Cool,' says Rick, although he thinks a master key that opens all the apartments on a level is anything but; he'd hate some stranger, or group of strangers, to have access to his property. Maybe that's why Cal didn't tell Lizzie and Philip about the keys when they'd asked him earlier; the owners don't like that information being told to prospective clients. Even so, it's strange the man has just told him about it, given he's with Elton and so surely it's to be assumed that he's a potential buyer. Rick shakes his head. If he lived here, knowing that, he'd never feel as if he had real privacy. It means that the Surf-Sand Vista crew members could enter the penthouse at any time.

He feels adrenaline spike his blood.

Maybe that's how the murderer got access and relocked the door.

Turning, Rick looks for Moira, wanting to tell her about the fobs and his theory. He catches her eye and is about to beckon her over when he hears Cal cry out.

Rick looks back towards Cal. He's in the open-living space, past the kitchen area; near the couches. There's no bravado, and no grin on Cal's face. Instead, he's gone pale beneath his tan and is thrusting his hand, palm up, towards Rick and the others. Rick wonders what the hell is going on now. They've had enough of a hold-up already. Telling Elton, and the others to wait a moment, Rick strides over to Cal. 'What's the—'

He stops mid-sentence. Not needing to ask the question any more.

Sprawled on her front, her face left-cheek down and her eyes staring sightlessly forward, is Sindee McGillis. Two circles of crimson have stained the back of her white, fitted dress and a pool of blood has spread from beneath her across the hardwood floor.

Beside him, Cal is mumbling to himself. Rick turns and meets Moira's gaze. He gives a little shake of his head, and knows that she gets it; something bad has happened. As he turns back to the crime scene, he hears Moira telling the group that they can't go into the penthouse and need to stay back in the hallway.

Rick takes out his cell phone and dials 911. He doesn't know who did this, and he doesn't know how long she's been here, but he is real sure about one thing.

Sindee McGillis is very definitely dead.

29

MOIRA

Keeping the group out of the penthouse is a tough job. It takes Rick and Philip physically blocking the doorway to stop them rubber-necking. Having radioed through to his boss, Adam Coulter, the head of operations, and updated him on the situation, Cal Staples is now sitting in the hallway, head in his hands. While they wait for the cops, Moira and Lizzie work the crime scene. There's not much time, but they need to get any intel they can before the police arrive and force them to clear the room.

They're careful not to touch anything; not wanting to disturb any forensic evidence. As Lizzie studies the blood splatter and pool-ing, Moira takes a few pictures of the scene on her phone so they can refer to them later, then stands for a moment, analysing what she sees. There are no signs of a struggle; nothing is broken or dis-turbed. Sindee McGillis's handbag is on the sofa, with her phone and wallet clearly visible. Whatever this was about, it doesn't look like a robbery.

Moving across the room to join Lizzie, Moira crouches down opposite her on the other side of Sindee's body. Other than the bloodstains, and a chipped nail on the index finger of her left hand, there's no obvious secondary damage. Moira looks at Lizzie. 'What do you think?'

Lizzie's expression is grim. 'She's been stabbed. The blade has gone in through the back, between the ribs. I'd say she bled out pretty fast. From the positioning of the wounds, I'd say whoever did this knew what they were doing.'

Moira hasn't found the murder weapon in the apartment. 'Any idea what sort of blade they used?'

Lizzie shakes her head. 'I can't tell without disturbing her clothing, so we'll have to see if Hawk can get us a copy of the autopsy report. I can't give a specific time of death either, but from the coagulation of the blood I'd guess she was killed sometime within the last two hours.'

Moira looks at Sindee's body. She was a healthy woman – fit and toned – and from what they've heard about her she had a lot of energy and a kick-ass attitude. 'Any sign that she fought back?'

Lizzie crouches lower to the floor, looking at Sindee's hands. 'There might be some skin scrapings beneath her nails, but I can't tell properly without touching and lifting her hands.'

Moira hopes Sindee fought back. She hates to think of the killer getting away too easily. Although either way, they have got away; Sindee's dead, and they're in the wind. Moira clenches her fists. Two women are dead. There has to be a connection. 'Do you think it was the same killer?'

Lizzie shrugs. 'It's a different MO. Unless there's forensic evidence to connect the two deaths there's no way to be—'

Rick coughs loudly, and Moira knows that's the signal for them to get out of the room. She and Lizzie hurry back to the doorway and stand just behind Rick and Philip. Seconds later two uniformed officers and a pair of suit-wearing detectives push their way through the group in the hallway.

'Clear the way,' says the guy in front. He has close-cropped salt and pepper hair and his navy suit fits just a little too snugly. His mouth is downturned and he has a surly frown that, from the deep lines seemingly grooved into his skin, looks as if it's his permanent expression. He turns to the uniforms behind him and snaps, 'Get control of the scene. Move these people back to the elevator.'

They allow themselves to be ushered back along the corridor as the two suited detectives – the fifty-something guy, and his willowy, twenty-something partner with unruly curly brown hair down to just below his collar, and wearing a brown suit that looks a size too large for him – enter the penthouse. Moira wonders if these are the detectives who handled Jessie Beckton's death and, if so, which of them is Chester Golding, the detective who added a note to Jessie Beckton's file with evidence not included in the main report. From the way the older guy is acting, he's the lead detective in the duo, so that would make Chester the younger man.

'Can we go?' asks Josh Stratton, his question directed to the uniformed officers. 'I've got a busy schedule and I need to get back to work.'

Beside him, Elton Bruce, his red-rimmed eyes still wide from shock, curls his top lip, his disgust at Josh's lack of empathy clear from his expression. Bethany Thompson is standing with Elton now, and she looks just as appalled. A few feet away from them, Cal Staples stands, head down, his whole body still shaking. On the other side of the hallway, Brett Donaldson, Phoenix Salford-Keynes and Lucas B. Francis are watching the situation unfold silently.

'Not right now, sir,' says a broad-chested cop with his cherub-like face partially obscured by a pair of mirrored sunglasses. 'The detectives might want to ask y'all some questions.'

'But I didn't see anything,' says Josh, waving his arms to emphasise his words as he moves closer to the officer. 'We were just standing in this hallway. I haven't even been inside that god-damn apartment.'

'Take a step back, sir,' says the cop's partner, a muscular guy with a close-cropped Afro and at least a couple of inches on Josh.

His tone is firm but amicable, his body language assured. 'We need you to stay right here.'

Josh looks from one cop to the other, and curses under his breath. The cops stare back at him, impassive. Neither looks ready to yield. Josh clenches his fists. A muscle is pulsing in his neck. A few beats pass. Then Josh sighs loudly and stomps back to the elevator, cursing.

Interesting, thinks Moira. He might have backed down this time, but Josh Stratton certainly does have a temper.

Beside her, Rick leans in closer. 'Find anything useful in the penthouse?'

Moira keeps her voice low. 'She was stabbed twice. Lizzie thinks whoever did it knew how to handle a knife to inflict maximum damage. Sindee's handbag was still in there – wallet and phone still inside. This wasn't a burglary gone bad. The MO might be different, but—'

'Which of you found the body?' yells the older detective from the doorway of the penthouse.

Rick and Moira glance at each other and then raise their hands. Cal stays motionless, as if he's not heard the question.

The grumpy detective beckons them towards him. 'Get over here.'

'Cal was there too,' says Rick, gesturing to the building manager, who is still slumped against the wall with his head bowed. 'It's hit him bad.'

'Then get him over here too,' says the sullen detective, raising his voice at Cal, and clearly ignoring Rick's comment about how Cal is feeling. 'We've got questions.'

Rick puts his hand on Cal's shoulder. 'Come on, buddy, let's go.'

As Rick helps a stunned-looking Cal along the corridor, Moira walks on ahead. The younger detective ushers the three of them further along the corridor, as the sullen detective shouts to the uniformed officers to guard the door to the penthouse. Then he strides after his partner, Moira, Rick and Cal.

'You got a key for these other rooms?' asks the older detective, scowling.

'Yes,' says Cal, his voice shaky.

'Open one up.' The detective looks pointedly at his watch. 'And fast.'

With trembling hands, Cal removes the fob from his pocket. He's just about to unlock the door to the apartment that's next along the corridor from the penthouse when there's a ping at the end of the hallway and the elevator doors slide open. A broad man with slicked-back hair and a rather shiny-looking grey suit marches along the corridor towards them. The group of witnesses and suspects part quickly to let him through.

'I came as soon as I could, Detective Durcell,' says the man as he joins them, reaching out to shake the grumpy detective's hand. 'Adam Coulter, head of operations. We met last time you were here, you might remember? Anyways, whatever you need from us here at Surf-Sand Vista, just ask.'

'Yep.' Durcell ignores Coulter's outstretched hand and looks unimpressed. 'Your man here was attempting to open this apartment for us.'

'We need somewhere private to speak to the people who found the body,' adds the younger detective. 'We can't use the crime scene.'

'For sure,' says Adam Coulter, smoothly. He takes a fob from his jacket pocket, unlocks the door and pushes it open. 'As I said, anything to assist.'

As they follow Adam Coulter into the apartment, Moira catches Rick's eye and nods. The older detective is the guy who led the half-arsed investigation into Jessie Beckton's death. It's a good opportunity to see how he works, although he's probably going to be annoyed when he finds out what they're doing here.

Detective Durcell gestures to the couch. 'Sit.'

They do as he says. Moira takes a seat on the far side of the large corner sofa, and Rick sits beside her. Cal sinks down on to the sofa next to him, clearly still shaking. Adam Coulter takes a seat on the other end of the sofa. He sits bolt upright, feet planted firmly on the ground. He's almost in the exact same spot as Sindee McGillis would have been sitting in the other apartment before she was attacked.

Moira shudders. This apartment has the same layout and furnishing as the penthouse next door. It's weirdly disorientating, and feels as if they're in the penthouse but Sindee McGillis's body has somehow disappeared.

The detectives remain standing. The lead detective, Durcell, positions himself next to the fireplace, one hand on the mantle. The younger of the two detectives leans against the island unit. The brown woollen suit he's wearing looks far too heavy for the Florida temperatures.

'Which one of you was first to see the body?' says Durcell, his voice deep and rasping, like a dog's bark.

No one speaks for a moment. Rick and Moira look at Cal. Cal keeps his gaze on the floor, his sunny demeanour long gone.

'Come on, it's not a hard question to answer,' snaps Durcell, slapping his palm against the mantle. 'Who found it?'

Moira grimaces. Sindee McGillis was a woman, not an it.

'Cal was first to set eyes on her,' says Rick when it's obvious Cal isn't going to speak up. 'I was right behind him, and Moira was behind me.'

'Is that right?' says Durcell, his tone gruff as he addresses the question to Cal.

Cal nods, but says nothing. He doesn't meet the detective's gaze.

Durcell looks back at Rick and Moira. 'What were y'all doing up here anyways?'

'We were bringing all the potential witnesses and suspects connected to the murder of Jessie Beckton up to the penthouse to recreate the set-up on the balcony from that afternoon, and measure their strides against the scuff marks found on the balcony,' says Rick.

Over at the island unit, the eyes of the detective in the brown woollen suit widen. His cheeks redden and he runs a finger under the collar of his shirt.

'We were also going to observe their behaviour while being in the apartment where the murder took place, and hoped to prompt new memories, and extra information,' adds Moira.

'The murder of who now?' says Durcell, scowling.

'Jessica Beckton.' Moira holds the detective's gaze, refusing to let him off the hook. It's only a few months since Jessie died and he was the lead investigator on her case; surely he remembers?

There's a slight hint of recognition on Durcell's face. 'Died by suicide, yeah?'

'No.' Moira's tone is granite tough. She's had enough of this guy already. 'She was murdered.'

'That's not what the coroner's report said,' says Durcell, a smug expression on his face.

'That's right,' says Adam Coulter, nodding. 'You're wrong about a murder, little lady.'

Moira frowns. Little lady? Really? It takes all her willpower not to snap back at this Coulter guy. Instead she ignores him and looks at Detective Durcell. 'The coroner was wrong.'

'Is that right?' Durcell raises an eyebrow. He glances across at the younger detective. 'My partner and I worked that scene. There were no signs of foul play.'

Moira clenches her fists. 'Really? What about the smashed champagne flutes and the scuff marks on the balcony? Didn't they indicate a struggle?'

The younger detective shoves his hands into the pockets of his over-sized suit and shifts his weight from one foot to the other, looking uncomfortable.

A brief expression of surprise flits across Durcell's face, before he covers it with a glare. 'The girl would have knocked the glasses as she jumped. The scuff marks would have been easily made as she tried to climb over the balcony railing.'

'Was she wearing black-soled shoes then?' asks Moira, knowing that, on the list of personal clothing and items on her body, Jessie Beckton's shoes had been described as Christian Louboutin heeled pumps: shoes that would have had the designer's trademark red soles.

'I don't . . . I'm the one asking the questions here.' Durcell waves the question away. 'Was Sindee McGillis supposed to be at your gathering in the penthouse this evening?'

'Yes,' says Rick. 'She was bringing the key to let us into the apartment, but she never showed, or rather she must have arrived earlier, and been killed.'

'What time had you agreed to meet her?' asks Durcell.

'Five o'clock, same as all the others,' says Rick.

Durcell nods. 'And what time did you yourselves get to the penthouse?'

'Five to five,' says Moira. 'We knocked and rang the doorbell, but no one answered so we assumed Sindee hadn't arrived yet.'

Durcell shifts his gaze from Rick to Moira. 'Did you hear any noises from inside the penthouse while you were outside?'

'No,' says Moira.

'Did anyone leave the apartment while you were waiting in the hallway?' asks Durcell.

Rick shakes his head. 'No.'

'Okay, that's it for now. You can go.'

'Go?' says Moira, confused. 'You don't want to ask us anything else?'

'I said we're done,' says Durcell, a growl in his voice, gesturing towards the door. 'Get out of here.'

Moira glances at Rick and he raises his eyebrows. She can tell he's thinking the same as her: if this is the detective's idea of how to conduct an investigation no wonder Jessie Beckton's killer is still on the loose. She turns back to Durcell. 'Don't you want our contact details or for us to give a written statement?'

Ignoring her, Durcell looks at Adam Coulter. 'I'm going to need your camera footage.'

'You got it,' says Adam. 'But all we'll have is the elevator, the public areas, and levels one to seven. The cameras up on this level aren't active yet.'

'Why the hell not?' says Durcell, his frown deepening. 'I recommended you activated them after the last unfortunate incident here.'

'No one lives on the eighth and ninth floors yet,' says Coulter. 'I told the management your recommendation, but they didn't want to switch the cameras on until the levels are occupied due to cost.'

'Well, that's going to make my job a whole lot harder,' says Durcell, exhaling hard. He looks at the younger detective, who is still leaning awkwardly against the island unit. 'Golding, go see those people in the hallway and take their statements.' He gestures at Moira, Rick and Cal. 'You can start with these as they're so keen to keep talking.'

Detective Chester Golding nods, and gestures for them to follow him out of the apartment.

As they move towards the door, Rick stops and turns back towards Durcell. He's standing with Adam Coulter, speaking too quietly to be overheard. Rick raises his voice. 'What's your take on this, Detective? Two women killed in the same apartment; you've got to have a theory?'

'I'm not sharing it with you,' says Durcell, curtly. 'There might have been two deaths here, but only one was a murder.'

'You real sure about that?' says Rick.

Beside Detective Durcell, Adam Coulter raises his eyebrows. Ahead of them, Detective Golding gives a tiny shake of his head.

'Totally,' says Durcell, his tone defiant as he looks Rick up and down as if he's a cockroach that's just crawled on to his shoe. 'For all I know, *you're* the guy who killed Sindee McGillis.'

Moira bites her lower lip to stop herself from telling this idiot detective just what she thinks of him. Detective Durcell seems to be as much use as a paper bag in a rainstorm. It's clear he just wants to do the minimum and get out of here. Moira has no faith that he's going to do a good job and get justice for the two women who've died.

She clenches her fists tighter.

Someone needs to stop the murderer before they kill again.

30

PHILIP

They reconvene in Philip and Lizzie's room after they've finished giving their statements. It's just gone eight o'clock but the evening already feels like a complete washout. Philip feels most unlike himself; light-headed and sometimes short of breath. His heart has been rather jittery for the past few hours too, and no matter what he's wearing, or how high he turns up the air conditioning, he still feels jolly warm. Maybe he's coming down with something. He hopes not. As much as he doesn't like to admit it, he's been feeling more than a little peculiar ever since they got back from the trip to Australia.

'. . . don't you think, Philip?' says Lizzie, her words jolting him from his thoughts.

'I'm not sure,' Philip splutters, not wanting to admit to the others that he'd tuned out of the conversation for a moment. 'What's your take on it?'

'It's hard for me to say really, isn't it, as I wasn't in the room with them,' says Lizzie.

Philip guesses she's talking about the detectives and takes a punt. 'Me as well.' He turns to Rick and Moira. 'What do you think?'

Moira grimaces. 'I think Detective Durcell is the kind of guy who'll do the absolute minimum to get by until he can retire on his pension. I can't believe he didn't ask us more questions, and the scowl never left his face, it was like he thought he shouldn't have had to be dealing with the murder.'

'Yes, yes, that chap, Durcell, looked like a bulldog that'd swallowed a wasp,' says Philip, nodding vigorously and then regretting it as a wave of nausea hits him.

'For sure,' says Rick. 'He's a lazy son-of-a-bitch according to Hawk's intel.'

'There was an odd dynamic between the detectives,' says Moira. 'Durcell was very definitely in the lead role and after asking those few preliminary questions only seemed interested in getting us out of the way fast. But the impression I got of Chester Golding was different. He was quiet, and didn't say more than a few words even when taking our statements, but he was watching, listening and taking everything in.'

'You think he's under this Durcell chap's thumb?' says Philip, reaching for his mineral water on the nightstand and gulping down half the bottle.

'Yes,' says Moira. 'But I think if we could speak with him away from his partner he'd have more insight to offer on the cases.'

'For sure,' says Rick, nodding. 'Question is whether he'd be willing to do that. Talking behind your partner's back, that's an asshole move that'd have him blackballed by the other cops if it got found out. Even if he disagrees with the line his partner is taking, I reckon it'd take a whole lot more than us asking nicely to get him to speak out of turn.'

'So, we're buggered then?' says Philip, feeling the sweat starting to bead across his forehead.

'No, we'll find a way to solve this,' says Moira, her voice full of determination. 'We have to.'

'Agreed,' says Rick. 'Hawk will let us know the results of the autopsy once they're in, but for now his intel says the only person on the elevator CCTV in the three hours leading up to her death is Sindee McGillis.'

'How did he find that out so fast?' asks Moira. 'The cops could barely have had time to review the footage.'

Rick shrugs. 'Hawk has connections. His sources are good, loyal. And I told him this was urgent.'

'So where does that leave us?' says Lizzie, gesturing to the murder board.

'Back at square one, I'd say,' says Philip. 'We may as well wipe this off and start again.'

'You think this puts all our previous suspects in the clear?' asks Lizzie.

'Potentially,' says Philip. 'They can't very well have murdered Sindee McGillis *and* have been standing in the hallway with us now, could they?'

'But then who did kill her?' says Lizzie. 'We're out of suspects.'

'Not necessarily,' says Moira. 'We don't know the exact time of death yet, but even if it happened when most of our suspects were in the elevator or up on the eighth floor with us, Josh Stratton turned up nearly half an hour late, and Carl Fossway didn't show at all. Add to that the fact we now know for certain that Adam Coulter and Cal Staples both have access to master key fobs that open the doors on that level so they could have let themselves into the penthouse even if it was locked from the inside, and I'd say we've still got a minimum of two previous suspects and two new suspects in play.'

'I suppose,' says Lizzie.

Philip nods. Moira makes a good point. 'I think you're right. And this Carl Fossway chap seems a really bad egg. My money is on him, at least for Jessie's murder.'

Rick frowns. 'Josh Stratton is a grade-A asshole. He's more likely to be the killer in my book.'

'What we need is evidence rather than opinion,' says Moira, sternly.

'Yes, yes, you're right,' says Philip, nodding.

'Okay, so we need to find out why Josh Stratton was late,' says Moira. 'And interview Carl Fossway properly, I only spoke to him on the phone – we haven't even had a face-to-face with him yet.'

'For sure,' says Rick, getting to his feet and starting to add some notes to the board. 'And Cal Staples got to the eighth floor using a different route to the main elevator so, as I'd previously suspected, there *is* a different way up to that level – we just need the building plans to see where it is and how it's accessed.'

'What about the stairwells?' says Moira.

Rick takes a sip from his beer, thinking. 'Yeah, could be. When Sindee showed us the apartment, she told us the stairs were alarmed and exit only, but maybe those master key fobs can open the emergency doors too. My money is on there being another elevator; otherwise surely Cal Staples would've used the residents' elevator if the only other choice was to walk up the stairs?'

'We need to find out,' says Philip, taking out his handkerchief and mopping his brow. His green polo shirt is clean on after returning from the penthouse fiasco, but it's already damp and clammy against his skin. 'Either of these two employee chaps could be our man.'

'But what motive could Cal or Adam have to kill Jessie and Sindee? It makes no sense,' asks Lizzie, shaking her head. 'Neither of them knew Jessie. We don't even know if they knew Sindee.'

'We can't be certain at this point that the person who killed Sindee is the same as Jessie's murderer,' says Moira.

'It's a weird coincidence if it isn't though,' says Lizzie, frowning.

'Be that as it may,' says Philip, trying to keep his mind on the case even though it feels like he's burning up. 'We can't just leap to conclusions. We need to proceed on the basis that the murderers *might* be linked but could be entirely separate.'

'Agreed,' says Rick, nodding.

'Good, good. And then there's the fact that the housekeeper told us there were other keys,' says Philip, thinking back to the woman who'd burst into this very room twenty-four hours earlier. 'More people than just Staples and Coulter could have access to those penthouses.'

'There must be thirty or more people who work at the Surf-Sand Vista; if they all potentially had access . . .' Lizzie throws up her hands. 'Where do we go from here?'

It's a good question, thinks Philip. One that needs proper thought, but right now he feels like he's becoming increasingly sluggish in the brain department. There's an uncomfortable feeling in his arm, like pins and needles. He rubs it, trying to rid himself of the sensation.

'There is something else we haven't talked about,' says Moira. 'We've got two women dead in the same apartment, less than four months apart, and I'm pretty sure that's not a coincidence. Both women had long platinum-blonde hair and a very similar style.'

'You think they were targeted because of how they look?' asks Rick as he finishes the notes on the board summarising their conversation.

'I think that it's possible,' says Moira.

Rick runs his hand across his jaw. Putting his beer down on the desk, he moves to the left side of the whiteboard, where a photo of Jessie Beckton is stuck alongside a new photo – a printout of Sindee McGillis's picture from the Beachseekers website. 'Facially they're real different, but, from behind, they could have been mistaken for one another.'

'So, Jessie might not have been the original target?' asks Lizzie, frowning.

'Maybe,' says Moira.

It's an interesting theory, thinks Philip, but it still leaves the question why someone would want to kill Sindee, and who had the opportunity? He starts saying this out loud, but his mouth feels weird, his lips difficult to move; as if he can't get his words out properly.

'Are you okay, buddy?' says Rick, looking concerned.

'Philip,' says Lizzie, putting her hand on his arm. There's panic in her eyes. Her voice is getting louder, but yet she seems to be getting further away. 'Philip, please, look at me. Stay with me. Don't . . .'

Philip can't catch his breath. He feels a crushing pain in the centre of his chest. His vision blurs, and then he's falling.

After that there's only nothingness.

31

LIZZIE

Blue lights. Siren. Speed.

Lizzie twists round in the front passenger seat of the ambulance so she can watch the paramedic work on Philip through the small window between the cab and the body of the vehicle. She'd wanted to be with him in the back, but the emergency medical technician told her it was against protocol. She hates it that she can't be right alongside him, holding his hand.

The EMT driving is focused on the road ahead. They've already radioed through to despatch telling them their ETA at the emergency room, and now they're hurtling along the highway, overtaking cars and lorries, pushing the ambulance to its maximum speed.

'Is he going to be okay?' asks Lizzie.

'We'll do all we can, Mrs Sweetman,' says the EMT; her tone is kind but there's a firm set to her jaw and Lizzie wonders if she knows more than she's letting on.

Lizzie turns in her seat, looking again through the glass into the back of the ambulance. Philip is strapped to the gurney while the paramedic works on him. She can't see what they're doing but there's a mass of wires attached to him; stuck to his chest, something on his finger, and a canular in his arm. Philip's eyes are closed. He looks so pale beneath his tan. So lifeless.

It takes all Lizzie's strength not to cry.

She thinks about the minutes between Philip collapsing and the ambulance arriving. How Rick had called 911 as Moira had started CPR. How Rick had then called Cal Staples in the building office and Cal had rushed to wait at the hotel entrance to meet the paramedics and escort them to Philip and her room taking the fastest route, and how he'd done the same to get them quickly out to the ambulance. Lizzie had felt frozen to the spot the whole time, unable to move; useless. It had been Cal who'd helped her into the ambulance and told her things would be okay. Despite the horror of finding Sindee murdered just hours earlier, he had been professional and efficient. His kind reassurance that the paramedics would save Philip had meant a lot.

She really hopes he's right.

Now, they approach a four-way crossing and the ambulance swings into the middle of the road to overtake a line of vehicles waiting at the lights. They accelerate on across the junction. Lizzie grips her seat. She has no idea where they are but she hopes that they're nearly at the hospital. Hopes that all the machines attached to Philip, and whatever the paramedic is doing to him, help him hang on to life.

Lizzie swallows hard, stifling a sob.

Please let him hang on.

She can't lose him.

32

MOIRA

She's in shock, and from the expression on Rick's face Moira knows that he is too. Moira had thought Philip had been looking a little tired, but she'd hoped it was because of the case or that he was still recovering from the trauma of being taken hostage during their last investigation. Now she remembers how shocked she'd been when she'd seen him at The Homestead residents' meeting earlier in that week, and how she'd thought he'd lost weight and looked pale, and realises they were warning signs. The four of them have been so focused on the Jessie Beckton case that it'd slipped to the back of her mind. Now she wishes she'd taken Philip to one side and checked how he was really feeling.

'You did a good job,' says Rick, his expression serious.

Moira nods. She'd kept the breaths and chest compressions going until the ambulance crew had arrived to take over. 'I just hope it was enough.'

'For sure,' says Rick.

It seems strange to be in Philip and Lizzie's room without them here, but the ambulance had only allowed one family member to go with them, and Lizzie had insisted she'd call as soon as there was news. Rick is sitting in one of the armchairs next to the murder board; Moira is on the bed. They are just a few feet apart, but it feels like miles. It's as if they've forgotten how to speak to each other.

The silence grows between them. Moira feels increasingly awkward.

'I should—'

'Do you want—'

They speak at once, and are both cut off by Rick's mobile ringing. Moira's stomach flips as Rick pulls it from his pocket and reads the screen. He glances at her and gives a brief shake of his head before he answers the call.

Not Philip or Lizzie.

'Honey, are you okay?' says Rick, with a gentle concern in his voice.

Moira can't hear the words of the person calling, but she can tell they're a woman and they sound really pissed off.

Rick's nodding as the woman speaks. He looks stressed. 'Of course, I get that, honey, I really do. I didn't mean for you to—'

The woman cuts him off. Her voice sounds louder, angrier.

Rick swallows hard. 'No, I guess I didn't.'

He listens as the woman talks. It takes a while, but then Moira thinks the woman's voice starts to sound a little calmer.

Rick's nodding again. 'Another day or two, I guess. Could be longer. I'll let you know when I'm on my way back, for sure. But in the meantime, anything you need, just call. I'm here for you.' He pauses as the woman says something else. 'I know, honey. But I can't let these people down.' Another pause. Rick exhales hard. 'I get that and I am real sorry.'

As his call ends, Rick looks back at Moira. 'It was Estelle.'

'I guessed that,' says Moira.

'She thinks I should go back home,' says Rick, with a sigh. 'She just doesn't understand why the case is so important.'

192

'Do what you need to do,' says Moira. She doesn't want him to go, but she'd understand if he wants to. Estelle is his daughter and, from what he's said, Rick hasn't seen her in years. It's understandable he'd want to spend time with her and find out what's been going on in her life. 'I'm not going to stop you.'

Rick takes a breath. 'Look, I owe you an explanation, Estelle and I—'

'Not now,' says Moira, putting her hands up, palms out, to stop him talking.

'But I need to tell you. I should have—'

'Don't. Please,' says Moira, looking up at him. She can't do this now; doesn't have the emotional capacity for this conversation right after Philip's been carted off to the emergency room. 'Just hold me, will you?'

As Rick wraps his arms around her and pulls her close, Moira allows herself to sink into his warmth and pretend, just for a minute, that everything is okay; that the killer, or killers, of Jessie and Sindee aren't still out there, possibly planning their next victim; that Philip isn't critically ill on the way to the emergency room; that the evidence to expose her ex-boss and mentor as a dirty copper isn't in a box in her walk-in closet back home; and that the fledgling romance she and Rick had isn't complicated and messy now.

Sometimes, when you're in the eye of the storm, you have to take a moment to breathe, in order to get the strength to survive what comes next.

33

PHILIP

The beeping is very annoying.

He's flying a fighter plane over the English Channel on a special mission. He's the top pilot in his squadron, and the winning of WW1 depends on him. The view is amazing from up here, but he's a tad worried about how chilly it is. He feels ice cold, even through the thick leather and sheepskin of his flying jacket. He needs to put it from his mind and focus on the job he's been tasked with, and he'd be able to if it wasn't for the relentless beeping that's still driving him crazy.

Philip peers through the thick glass of his heavy flying goggles at the dials and switches in the cockpit, trying to work out which one is causing the incessant noise. Aha! He sees it – a pesky switch with a red light flashing on and off over to the right of the console. Reaching out, he flicks the switch.

Pain, dull and heavy on his chest, takes his breath away. He gasps. Groans loudly. And wonders why the bloody beeping hasn't stopped.

'Philip?'

He hears Lizzie's voice, somewhere to his left, and wonders what she's doing in the plane. Moving his head towards the sound, he realises his eyes are closed, so he opens them. He winces. It's bright, and he blinks, trying to adjust to the light. That's when he realises he's not in the fighter plane any more.

'Oh my God,' says Lizzie. She's standing over him. She looks worried.

That's when he realises he's lying down.

'Lizzie, I . . .' His words won't come out. His throat feels like sandpaper.

He feels pressure on his arm. Sees more people scurrying around him; all wearing light-blue scrubs.

'What's . . . what's . . .' It hurts when he speaks; his mouth is so dry.

'You had a funny turn,' says Lizzie. Her eyes are red-rimmed and bloodshot. There's a tremble in her voice. 'We're at the hospital now. Remember?'

Philip can't remember. Instead, he looks around the white-walled room with the monitors and IV pumps and all manner of other technological equipment and he feels one overwhelming emotion.

Fear.

34

RICK

The knock on his door comes at just before 7 a.m.

Last night, he'd gone to bed sometime after midnight when Lizzie had messaged him and Moira. By that point Philip had been stabilised and transferred to a room, and Lizzie had decided to stay with him until the morning. Rick hadn't slept well and after hours of feeling restless he'd gotten up at 5.30 a.m. He's already had an hour-long workout in the gym, a shower, and had been getting ready to go and get breakfast.

He assumes, as he goes to answer the door, that Moira's checking in to see if he wants to head down to the restaurant together. But he's wrong. It isn't Moira waiting on the other side of the door.

The man's wearing a black suit and aviator shades, and looks like he's FBI, although Rick knows he isn't. It's Detective James R. Golding.

'What the—'

'You want to invite me in, Denver?' says Golding.

'You want to tell me why I should?' replies Rick, crossing his arms and not moving from the doorway an inch. He's not seen the detective since the last case they'd worked a few months back. He'd have preferred it if things had stayed that way.

'There are two reasons,' Golding says, his expression real serious. 'Jessica Beckton. Sindee McGillis.'

Rick narrows his eyes. Doesn't move. 'What about them?'

'Come on, let's not do this dance,' says Golding, running his hand through his unruly brown hair. 'I know you're here looking into the death of Jessica Beckton, and you and your senior pals were right outside the penthouse when Sindee McGillis got killed yesterday.'

Rick says nothing. Keeps a poker face.

'And you know that a young local detective, Chester M. Golding, is working that homicide with his partner, Detective Thomas Durcell.' Golding pauses for a moment, watching for Rick's reaction. When he doesn't see one, he continues. 'That young detective is my nephew. He's a good boy. A solid detective, even if a little green. And he's got a bunch of concerns. When he told me about four seniors who were poking their noses into a closed case of his I asked him for the names, and when he messaged them across and I saw it was y'all I figured I should get myself on out here.'

'So you're here to get heavy with us again and tell us to back off your nephew's case?' says Rick. 'Hell of a long drive to do that. You could've just called.'

Golding shakes his head as he lets out a long breath. 'Nope. That isn't why.'

Rick narrows his gaze. 'What then?'

'I'm here to offer a truce.'

Fifteen minutes later, Rick is seated at a breakfast table in the poolside terrace restaurant with Moira and Golding. They must make for an odd grouping: Rick in cargo shorts, a blue Hawaiian shirt, and flip-flops; Moira wearing her usual leggings, Nike top and sneakers; and Golding in his black suit and shades. They wait for the server to pour their coffee and take their food order, then they get down to business.

'You said you wanted to call a truce,' says Rick, looking at Golding. 'What's that about?'

Golding takes a long drink of coffee, and carefully places the cup back on the table before speaking. 'I meant what I said – we call a truce. No more arguing or trying to solve the case first. We work together.'

'On what?' asks Moira, pouring herself a glass of orange juice from the pitcher on the table. 'You're way out of your jurisdiction here.'

'True,' says Golding, smiling. 'But I'm not here on official business, I'm just spending a few well-earned vacation days at the beach.'

Rick glances at Moira and she raises an eyebrow.

'The question remains,' says Rick. 'What are we supposed to collaborate on?'

'Well, shit, the murders of Jessica Beckton and Sindee McGillis, obviously,' says Golding.

'But Jessie Beckton's death wasn't ruled a homicide,' says Rick, cautiously. Golding's always taken a hard line about Rick and his friends investigating cases, and has been antagonistic at best, what with Golding being real keen on finding ways to throw their asses in jail. This change of tack is unnerving and Rick sure as hell doesn't trust the detective.

Golding rolls his eyes. 'Yeah, sure. But all of us here know that's bullshit, right?'

'Right,' says Moira, taking a sip of her orange juice. 'But your nephew's case file ruled out murder.'

Golding's expression darkens. 'Let's just say my nephew doesn't have himself the best kind of partner.'

Rick leans forward in his chair. 'If we get into this, we're going to need to know everything that your nephew does, what he's gotten from the two crime scenes, and who he thinks could be in the frame.'

'He'll do that,' says Golding. 'He's with us on this.'

'Then where is he?' asks Moira, clearly suspicious. 'How are we to know this isn't just some scheme of yours to get *us* behind bars?'

'You've got my word,' says Golding, giving her and Rick a slightly forced smile.

Moira shakes her head. 'Forgive me if I don't think it's worth much.'

Rick takes a sip of coffee. Golding wants to help his nephew out, Rick can understand that, but Chester let Jessie's coroner's report, and the closing of the police investigation, go unchallenged. Why does he suddenly care? 'What I'm thinking on is why?'

'What do you mean?' asks Golding, pushing his aviators on to the top of his head.

'Why are you getting involved? Like Moira says, you're way out of your jurisdiction, and your nephew's known that there was evidence missed out from Jessie Beckton's file for over three months,' Rick says, squinting at Golding as the sun continues to rise behind him. 'So, why are you getting involved now?'

'Chester's older sister, Krista, went to high school with Sindee. Sindee used to hang out around their place almost every night and weekend. I reckon it's likely the kid had his first crush on that girl. Now she's dead and his sister's in bits.' Golding exhales hard. 'Chester doesn't trust that his partner is going to do things right; he cuts corners every chance he gets and doesn't give a damn about his case clearance rate, never mind bringing killers to justice.'

'So, it's personal,' says Moira, nodding.

Golding's expression is real serious. 'Yeah. It is. You guys, you get results. While I sure as hell don't agree with your off-the-books, taking-the-law-into-your-own-hands way of operating, I can't deny that y'all are effective.' He looks at Rick. 'You know how it is with family, you want to do whatever you can to help them? Well, Chester and me, we need your help on this one.'

An image of Estelle and her little daughter, Bibi, floats into Rick's mind's eye. Yeah, he gets what Golding is saying; you do want to protect your family, and help them through the tough times.

Rick's silent for a long moment. He looks at Moira, trying to work out how she feels about this. She meets his gaze and gives him a small nod. Rick half smiles back. Then he turns to Golding and wonders if he can put all the stunts the man has pulled behind them. It takes a short moment. But, he figures, if it helps bring a killer, or killers, to justice, working with Golding will be worth the hassle.

He holds out his hand. 'Okay. You got yourself a deal.'

35

MOIRA

Having left Rick to walk Golding through their investigation so far, Moira takes the jeep and heads out on the I-275 to St Petersburg. She's sceptical that the truce with Golding will last; the man is too lazy and antagonistic to work well with them for long, but Chester, his nephew, seems to have a good heart even if he isn't bold enough to challenge the way his partner, Detective Durcell, is handling the investigation. And right now, if teaming up will help get justice for Jessie, and Sindee, then it's worth the extra effort needed to get along with James R. Golding.

While Lizzie stays with Philip at the hospital, and Hawk tries to get hold of the intel they need to move forward with the investigation, Moira has a suspect to chase down. It takes just under half an hour to get to the address where Belinda Fossway said her estranged husband, Carl, is now living. Moira hasn't called ahead, figuring that as Carl didn't show up last night, and has been dodging her calls ever since, he's unlikely to be up for arranging a meeting. Her best chance of speaking to him is by catching him unawares, and she intends to do just that.

The house is in the Jungle Terrace neighbourhood, and as Moira pulls up outside she can see it must have cost a bit; it's a big, square-fronted new-build property with four pillars along the front porch, light-grey stucco, white-framed windows and a dark-grey roof. It must easily have four bedrooms and the double garage, broad driveway and lush landscaping all look well tended.

Stepping up on to the front porch, Moira walks to the door and presses the buzzer. She hears the bell chime inside, followed by a woman's voice calling to an Annie and a Cleo to get their school bags ready. A few moments later the door opens and a harassed-looking woman appears. She's make-up free, her brown hair in a ponytail but already pulling loose, and a dark-pink stain that still looks wet blooming across the pale shirt she's wearing over jeans. 'Can I help you?'

Moira gives her a non-threatening smile. 'Hi, I'm Moira. I'm looking for Carl Fossway? Belinda said he's staying here.'

'Sure, he's in the pool house,' says the woman, waving her inside. 'Come this way.'

Moira follows her through a classy, but toy-strewn, open-plan living and dining space, to the bi-fold doors that lead into the garden. The woman opens them, and gestures across the garden. 'Go past the pool and you'll see the pool house on your right.'

'Thanks,' says Moira, giving the woman another smile. She's surprised she's just let her through her home so easily without even asking Carl if he wants to see her, but she's thankful for it. It'll made it harder for Carl to avoid speaking to her if she's already on the property.

She takes the paved walkway across the lawn, then steps up on the decking and walks around the side of the pool. It looks new; the water sparkles in the sunlight and the turquoise and blue mosaic tiles glisten. There are four sun loungers set up poolside; they look very enticing. But Moira can't rest right now; there's a job to get done – a killer to catch.

The pool house is a small, one-storey building to the side of the pool deck. It looks like a miniature version of the main house with its light-grey stucco and dark-grey roof tiles. Reaching out, Moira knocks twice on the white door, then takes a step back and waits.

She hears a key turn in the lock and the door opens. 'Hello?'

The man standing in the doorway looks confused. Moira appraises him. He's medium height, athletic build, with short ginger hair, black-framed glasses, a surfer brand T-shirt and board shorts. He's not a huge guy, but looks strong enough to be capable of pushing Jessie off the balcony. 'Carl Fossway?'

The man frowns. 'Yeah.'

'I'm Moira Flynn. We spoke on the phone the other day.'

Carl's eyes widen. For a moment Moira thinks he's going to either slam the door in her face or run. Then he shakes his head. 'What the hell are you doing here?'

'Why didn't you show up yesterday?'

'I never said I was coming,' says Carl.

Moira holds his gaze. 'I think you did, or you certainly implied it. So why didn't you?'

Carl's expression hardens. 'What gives you the right to show up here and start questioning me? You're not the cops and you're trespassing anyways. You shouldn't—'

'I was invited in and shown where to find you by the lady in the house,' says Moira, calmly. She needs to get Carl to simmer down and cooperate; to not see her as the enemy. She softens her tone. 'I'm not trying to give you a hard time, Carl. Like I said before on the phone, I just want to be able to eliminate you from our list of suspects so I can focus on finding Jessie's killer. You understand that, right?'

'I . . . yes, I get that, but I . . .' Carl looks away, his eyes downcast. 'I just . . . couldn't meet you at the penthouse. Going into that apartment, the one where Jessie died.' He shakes his head again. 'It would've been a lot, too much.'

'So why not answer my calls and do me the courtesy of telling me that?' asks Moira, her tone still gentle, coaxing.

'I . . .' Carl swallows hard. 'Look, I really liked Jessie, okay. I know you probably think I'm a real asshole, and I've behaved badly, I know that, okay, but I did like her.'

'Yet you lied to her about your personal circumstances.'

'Yep. Like I said, I acted like an asshole and I'm not proud. You must think I'm a total . . .' He curses under his breath. 'And I bet Belinda told you a whole bunch of shit about me. I mean, nothing was ever good enough for her, and everything was always my fault and I just—'

'Look, Carl, I'm not here to judge you on how you conduct your life and your marriage. My job is to find out what really happened to Jessie so her parents can at least get some sort of closure. That's what I'm interested in. Your issues with your wife are between the two of you.'

Carl holds her gaze for a long moment, then nods. 'Okay.'

'I need to know where you were when Jessie died, and where you were yesterday afternoon and early evening,' says Moira, maintaining eye contact with him. 'And, Carl, I need the truth.'

'Yeah, okay.' Carl gestures towards the wicker sofa. 'Look, you'd better sit down.'

Moira does as he suggests and waits while he fetches a couple of glasses of water from the kitchenette. He looks rattled by her being here, but not afraid. That could mean he's got nothing to hide, or it could mean he's good at hiding his emotions. Hopefully, with a little more discussion and information, she'll be able to get a handle on which.

When Carl has set the glasses down on the coffee table, and has taken a seat in the wicker armchair, she fixes him with a firm stare and says, 'So tell me what happened.'

Carl swallows hard. 'Okay, so Belinda and I, look, our marriage was a big mess. I lied to Jessie to get her to go on that first date with me, yeah, I hold my hands up to that, but I did like her; a lot. Belinda had been having affairs for a while – she thought I didn't know but I always did – and I was fed up of being the faithful husband while she was getting it on with her personal trainer and tennis club buddies.'

'So you decided to pursue Jessie?'

'Yeah.' He shakes his head. 'It was clear she'd never get involved with a married man, so I told her I was separated. It was so great being with Jessie, so easy and fun. I felt alive again after years of feeling, just kind of numb.'

'And you never told Jessie the truth?' says Moira, taking a sip of her water.

'I couldn't. I mean, I wanted to, but I knew that unless I left Belinda she'd want nothing to do with me and I was . . . I was too weak.' He runs his hand through his hair.

Moira nods. 'But Jessie found out you'd lied to her anyway.'

'Yes.' Anger flares in his eyes. 'Belinda attacked her. Called her these awful names and tried to hurt her.'

'And what did Jessie do? Did she confront you? Push you? Get angry?'

'No, never,' says Carl, quickly. 'She'd never do anything like that. She was such a gentle soul, I loved that about her. But she told me we couldn't be together.'

'So did you push her?' says Moira, not prepared to back off yet. 'From the balcony?'

'Dear God, no. I wouldn't.' Carl looks as if he might vomit. 'I just . . . couldn't ever hurt Jessie. She meant the world to me, but after Belinda attacked her she ended things and blocked my calls. She even refused to see me when I turned up to try and speak with her. I knew what I'd done was bad, so I said I'd respect her privacy, but I hoped she'd find it in her heart to forgive me if I just gave her a bit of time.'

'And did she?' asks Moira.

'No, she didn't get the chance. When I found out she was dead I . . .' His voice cracks as he says the word 'dead'. He blows out, his breath shaky. 'I couldn't believe it. It felt like my life was ending too. And when they said that she'd died by suicide I . . . I felt . . .' A sob catches in his throat.

Moira studies him. He's playing the part of the bereaved boyfriend pretty convincingly. 'You felt responsible?'

Carl nods. 'That's why I left Belinda and came here. Things hadn't been right for such a long time, but I just hadn't faced up to it. It was Jessie's death that was my big wake-up call. I needed to start over. I'm hoping to get joint custody of our little girl, and I'll always be the absolute best dad that I can be, but as far as Belinda and me are concerned, we're done.'

'So where were you when Jessie died?' asks Moira, keeping her gaze firmly on Carl.

He fidgets in the armchair. 'I told you before, on the call. I was at home in the garage, working out in my home gym.'

'You said that,' says Moira. 'But the problem is, Belinda says you weren't at home and that she doesn't know where you were.'

Carl curses under his breath. 'That's a lie. She knew I was at home.'

Moira holds his gaze, but says nothing. Philip thinks Carl should be their top suspect, but now, having met him, Moira isn't so sure. He seems too gentle to have thrown Jessie over the railings to her death. Although appearances can be deceiving – she should know that better than anyone after what happened back in London with her ex-boss and mentor, Detective Superintendent Harry George – her gut is telling her Carl isn't the killer.

'Look, I can prove it.' Getting up, Carl walks across to the kitchenette and grabs his phone from the counter. He flicks through it, then walks back to Moira and holds the screen out. A video is playing. It's from a home security system, the camera focused on Carl lifting weights in his home gym. The time period covers the time of Jessie's death. 'This is from the house CCTV. There's more from cameras in the hallway and kitchen showing me walking to the garage and making a protein shake afterwards.'

It seems pretty conclusive to Moira. 'Can you forward a copy of the footage to the number I called you from the other day?'

'Sure.' Carl taps the phone a few times. Moments later Moira's own phone pings to alert her to a new text. 'It's with you now.'

'Great.' Moira takes a breath. 'So what about late afternoon yesterday – where were you then?'

'Ah,' says Carl, shaking his head. 'That's a little trickier. You see, I was out fishing.'

'Alone?' asks Moira.

'Yeah. After talking to you on the call it brought everything back about Jessie and how I screwed up so badly.' He shakes his head. 'I needed to get away from things, so Paul said I could borrow his boat for the day.'

'Paul?' says Moira.

'My buddy, the guy who owns this place.' Carl gestures around the pool house. 'His wife, Christina, was the person who let you in.'

'Okay.' Moira thinks for a moment. 'Does Paul's boat have any cameras or tracking? Anything that can place you out on the ocean at the time Sindee died?'

Carl thinks for a moment. 'I'm not sure about the boat itself, but I had to sign in at the reception of Sunset Cove Marina when I arrived, and my car was parked there for the day. They've got security cameras on the parking lot and the boat slips, so I reckon there'll be footage of me.'

'Okay, I'll look into getting hold of that,' says Moira. If he's telling the truth, and the footage corroborates his story, then they'll have to rule him out as a suspect for both murders. 'Is there anything else you think I should know? Anything you remember that might help us find Jessie's killer?'

Carl frowns, thinking. 'Look, there is this one thing, Jessie mentioned it a couple of times but I just put it down to the guy being a bit overly familiar, you know?'

'What guy?' asks Moira.

'That's the thing, I don't know his name. All Jessie said was that there was this guy at the Surf-Sand Vista place who was kind of creepy.'

Moira leans forward. 'Did he do something to her?'

Carl shakes his head. 'No, not that Jessie mentioned. She said he just had this way of looking at her, like he was undressing her with his eyes. It made her feel uncomfortable.'

This is new information, thinks Moira. There hasn't been any talk of a man at the building where Jessie, and now Sindee, died who acted like a creep. 'Was he a resident?'

'No, not a resident,' says Carl. 'Jessie told me he was someone who worked there.'

36

RICK

In the KMP Auto Outlet parking lot Rick shuts off the engine of Philip's Toyota. He finished bringing Golding up to speed earlier than he'd reckoned on and, having lent Moira his jeep, Rick figured Philip and Lizzie wouldn't mind him borrowing their ride. Before jumping out, he reads Moira's text and then sends her request for video footage from the Sunset Cove Marina on to Hawk. If Carl Fossway has video evidence of his whereabouts during the times Jessie and Sindee were killed it'll put him out of the frame for both murders, so that's even more reason to confront Josh Stratton about his tardiness yesterday and his sketchy alibi at Starfish.

As Rick approaches the chrome and glass sales building, he can just make out Josh Stratton sitting at his desk towards the back of the offices. Just seeing him makes anger flare inside Rick. The egotistical smugness of the man, and the appalling way he treats women, really grates on him. He takes a breath, knowing he's going to have to fight hard to keep his emotions in check.

The automatic doors slide open, but before Rick can enter the foyer Josh Stratton leaps up from his desk and hurries towards him.

Rick nods hello. 'Josh, just the—'

'Not inside,' hisses Josh, his features set in a forced smile. Clasping a hand to Rick's shoulder, Josh forces him to turn and move further outside, away from the building and down between two lines of silver and grey cars. 'I told you not to come to my place of work. What the hell is wrong with you?'

Shaking himself free of Josh's grip, Rick halts beside a silver BMW. 'Don't touch me again.'

'Or what?' says Josh, his tone full of macho bravado. Tilting his chin up, he eyes Rick with undisguised contempt. 'You shouldn't be here. I should call security.'

Damn. Rick knows he needs to pull the situation back. Getting Josh riled up isn't going to help get the truth out of him. Rick makes a show of brushing down his shirt. 'Look, Josh, I'm just here to clear up a few things. It won't take more than a couple of minutes of your time.'

Josh eyes Rick with suspicion. 'Like I said, I told you not to come back here.'

'I figured you'd prefer me coming here to the cops,' says Rick, amicably.

Josh frowns, grim-faced. 'Why would the cops come here?'

'The cops were asking a lot of questions last night, Josh, but I didn't want to drop you in it,' says Rick, careful to keep his tone real conversational.

'Drop me in what?' asks Josh, looking confused.

'You were thirty minutes late arriving yesterday. For all I know you'd killed Sindee and were cleaning yourself up during that time.'

Josh cusses loudly. 'Killing Sindee? Why the hell would I do that? I didn't even know the woman.'

'You sure about that?' says Rick, raising an eyebrow. He knows he's treading a fine line, but needs Josh to believe he's better off confessing to him than the cops; at least that way he can get something done rather than leaving it to chance with this ineffective Detective Durcell.

'Yes, I'm damn sure.' Josh clenches his fists, scowling. There's sweat beading across his forehead; Rick's not sure if it's due to the heat of the sun or a reaction to his question. 'I've never even spoken to this Sindee woman.'

Rick takes a little of the hardness from his tone. 'Then why were you late, Josh?'

Josh shakes his head, still scowling. 'That's my business.'

'Fine,' says Rick, shrugging. 'I'll tell the cops you arrived half an hour later than everyone else, and that your alibi for Jessie's murder isn't watertight.'

'Woah, hold up there,' says Josh, throwing up his hands. 'My alibi is rock solid, I was partying at Starfish when Jessie died, just like I told you.'

Rick shakes his head. 'That's not the way the manager tells it.'

Josh cusses again. Kicks the toe of his shoe against the asphalt. 'I was there.'

'So prove it,' says Rick, holding his gaze.

Josh says nothing. Kicks his toe against the asphalt again.

'You've got to know this looks bad, Josh,' says Rick, his tone kinder, more conciliatory. 'The cops here are real sloppy, and I doubt they'll dig around much for more suspects if I tell them what I know about you. Hell, I reckon they'll bite my hand off for the intel.'

Josh blows out hard. Clenches and unclenches his fists a few times.

Rick can tell he's on the verge of telling him something – the truth – but he needs a bit more incentive. So he shrugs again, and turns back towards where the Toyota is parked and starts walking. 'Okay, Josh. I'll give the cops what I know, but don't say I didn't try to help you out. I've given you every chance to—'

'Mary-Beth Eastfield,' says Josh. He sounds deflated, the macho bravado of earlier gone.

Rick stops and turns back around. The name seems vaguely familiar but he can't place it. 'Who is she?'

'She's the woman who can alibi me,' says Josh, his voice subdued.

'For yesterday afternoon, or for when Jessie was killed?' asks Rick.

Josh exhales loudly. Shakes his head again. 'For both times. I was drinking with Mary-Beth at Starfish, and I was with her at her home yesterday afternoon, if you catch my drift?'

'Yeah, I get it,' says Rick, taking out his cell phone. 'I'm going to need her contact details so I can verify this as the truth.'

Nodding, Josh recites Mary-Beth's address and cell phone number. 'Just be discreet, okay?'

Rick frowns. From what he's seen of Josh so far it's not like him to give a damn about a woman, and that's gotten him real curious. 'Why?'

Josh holds Rick's gaze for a long moment. 'Because her husband won't like it.'

37

MOIRA

There's something bugging Moira that she can't shake. It came from a throwaway comment Elton Bruce made when they were waiting for Sindee McGillis to show up to let them into the penthouse. Moira wants to find out what he meant by it, so she's decided to swing past the Beachseekers office on the way back to the Surf-Sand Vista.

After finding a parking spot just along the street from Beachseekers, Moira locks the jeep and walks down the pavement to the glass-fronted unit. She hadn't been sure they'd be open today, given Sindee's death, but Moira had called on the drive here from Carl Fossway's place and been assured they were very much open for business.

The automatic doors slide open as she approaches, and as she steps inside she's immediately blasted with cold air from the air conditioning vents in the ceiling above. She pauses, just over the threshold, scanning the room. The offices are designed to look like a high-end New York loft, with exposed brick walls, industrial ducting and high vaulted ceilings. An iron spiral staircase to one side of the open-plan space leads up to a mezzanine level. There are four white leather sofas around a glass coffee table to her left, and ahead is a work area with eight light-oak desks with grey Herman Miller chairs, and the latest edition MacBooks.

Only three of the desks are occupied: two by slim, leggy blonde twenty-somethings wearing tight skirt suits and the best blow-dries Moira's ever seen, and the other by Elton Bruce. Elton's already getting up, concern on his face as he hurries over to her.

'Is-everything-okay?' says Elton, his words coming out fast. 'Has something else bad happened?'

'No, nothing else has happened,' says Moira, trying not to think of Philip – stable but still in hospital undergoing tests, and Lizzie, worried sick, with him. 'I just wanted to see how you're doing and ask you about a couple of things you might be able to help me with.'

The relief is clear on Elton's face. 'Oh, sure, anything you want.'

'Is there somewhere here we can talk privately?' asks Moira.

'Upstairs is good,' says Elton. 'This way.'

Moira does as he asks, and follows him up the spiral staircase and on to the mezzanine. The space is half the size of the downstairs area, but still bigger than any room you'd usually find back in London. There's more exposed brick up here, three purple velvet and chrome sofas, and the back wall is covered in modern art – mainly big canvasses of bold colours and abstract shapes.

She sits down on the sofa facing the street.

'Can I get you a drink?' says Elton, gesturing to a fancy-looking coffee machine sitting on the light-oak side unit that runs along the left-hand side wall for the whole length of the space.

'Black coffee, please.'

'Coming right up,' says Elton, rather too cheerfully. There's a puffiness around his eyes, and they look a little bloodshot. Moira would put money on him having been crying.

'How are you doing?' she asks, once Elton has made the drinks and sat down on the sofa to the left of her.

214

'I'm fine,' says Elton, rather too brightly.

Moira doesn't speak for a moment, letting silence prompt him to say more. After just a few seconds it works.

'It's so awful about Sindee. I mean, she was a bitch sometimes, for sure, but to die . . . and like that, stabbed, it's just so . . .'

Moira nods, sympathetically. 'It must have been a real shock.'

'Do you think the killer is targeting realtors? Could all of us here at Beachseekers be in danger? Do we need protection?' asks Elton, his eyes wide. 'Or do you think the killer has some kind of attachment to that specific penthouse at the Surf-Sand Vista and they don't want us to sell it?'

'Do you?' asks Moira.

Elton unbuttons his waistcoat, revealing the perfectly ironed shirt beneath. He shakes his head. 'I just don't know, but my anxiety is through the roof over it. I'm popping Xanax like candies.'

'I understand,' says Moira, her tone kind and reassuring. 'And we're doing everything we can to find who's doing this.'

'Thank you,' says Elton, reaching over and taking Moira's hands in his. 'I really appreciate it.'

Moira looks down at his hands around hers. Gives a little smile, and then slowly disengages from him. 'How's the mood here in the office?'

'Kind of low, and pretty tense. Most of the team didn't like the boss so much, but they didn't want her dead.' He bites his lower lip. 'And who knows what's going to happen to the agency now. It could be we're all going to be out of a job really soon. It's just . . . a lot.'

'I'm sorry to hear that.'

'At least I'm not dead, hey?'

'There is that,' says Moira, nodding. 'So, look, there's something I wanted to ask you about. Yesterday evening, when you were talking to Rick in the hallway while we were waiting for Sindee to show up, you said, "I guess with Jessie gone it isn't like she can send her instead." What did you mean by that?'

Elton blows out hard. 'I don't like to speak ill of the dead, you know? But I guess I'm only telling you the facts. The truth of it is, Sindee didn't always do her own showings. If she'd gotten a better offer – you know, like a hot date or a tip-off about a designer sale, she'd push her showings schedule on to one of us. Oftentimes it was Jessie who took the majority of the extra work – she was kind natured and super keen to do well. Sindee exploited that.'

Moira feels a hit of adrenaline hit her bloodstream as some of the pieces of the puzzle click into place. 'Did Sindee do that with the penthouse broker's open scheduled on the night Jessie died?'

'I'm not sure, but give me a moment and let me check the schedule.' Lifting his MacBook on to his lap, Elton taps the keys a few times and then turns it so Moira can see the screen. 'She did. If you look here, you can see that the broker's open in the penthouse was originally booked in by Sindee – she was going to be the host – but, if you look here.' He points to lower on the pop-up window on-screen. 'It shows that the booking was changed to be hosted by Jessie. The change was made at 15.23 that afternoon.'

'Just a couple of hours before the broker's open was due to start,' says Moira, thinking.

Elton nods. 'Yes.'

Moira thinks about the pictures of Jessie and Sindee back on the murder board in Lizzie and Philip's hotel room. They're both around five feet six inches, both slim with toned, athletic figures, and they both have waist-length platinum-blonde hair which they usually wear long and straight. When she and Rick had been speaking with Bethany, she'd told them that Sindee once referred to Jessie as her 'mini me'. Moira looks at Elton. 'Did Jessie and Sindee have a similar sense of style?'

'Sure. I mean, at first not so much, but after her first couple of weeks working here we all noticed how Jessie started wearing similar outfits to Sindee.' He shrugs. 'They could have been sisters, even if Jessie was no way the bad-ass bitch that Sindee was.'

Sisters.

Two women who looked similar from the front and, as she'd said at the debrief last night, from behind would've looked nearly identical. Both were victims of a killer, or killers, who found their opportunity for murder in the exact same location: Jessie, dropped head first over the railings of the eighth-floor balcony, and Sindee stabbed twice in the back. Two different kill methods, yes, but the attack was the same – from behind.

She doesn't believe in coincidences.

Her heart rate accelerates, and adrenaline spikes her blood again.

Moira knows why Jessie was murdered.

38

LIZZIE

She was only in the bathroom for five minutes, ten at the most, so that she could freshen up after spending the night sleeping in the armchair in Philip's hospital room. Not that she slept hardly at all, of course, and that's mainly the reason she'd felt the need to splash some water on her face, to try to get herself more alert, before they spoke with the doctor.

But the doctor must have come early, or Lizzie had taken longer than she'd thought in the bathroom, because as she pushes the door open to Philip's room she sees the petite black-haired woman in a white coat, with a stethoscope around her neck, talking to Philip, and she sees Philip's expression – serious and watery-eyed – and knows it must be bad news that the doctor is telling him. Suddenly Lizzie's legs feel wobbly, like they're made of not-quite-set jelly, and she feels as if she might keel over. It's all she can do to stagger across the room to Philip.

Turning towards her, the doctor gives her a reassuring smile. 'Mrs Sweetman, hello, I was just updating your husband on how I see his situation.'

Lizzie feels her breath catch in her throat. 'Thank you for everything you've done.'

'It's my pleasure,' says the doctor. There's real warmth in her voice. 'Philip says he feels well enough to be discharged so he can rest at home. It's kind of fast for a patient to leave hospital within twenty-four hours after a health episode like his, but your husband has made a persuasive case. Are you happy for him to be discharged?'

Lizzie looks at Philip. He looks tired and pale, but he smiles at her encouragingly, so she nods. 'If that's what he wants.'

'Alright then,' says the doctor. 'I'll put together the necessary paperwork and get the nurses to start the discharge procedure.' She looks back to Philip. 'You can collect your meds from the dispensary before you leave, Mr Sweetman. Make sure you get into a routine like I've said, and take your blood pressure reading twice a day. You should have a follow-up appointment with your physician before the end of the week.'

Philip nods earnestly, like a good patient. 'Absolutely, Doc.'

Lizzie waits for the doctor to leave the room before asking, 'What did they say?'

'You know, just the usual,' says Philip, easing himself off the bed. 'Pass me my clothes, will you, I can't very well go back into society dressed like this.'

Lizzie smiles, eying the blue, open-backed hospital gown. 'Might be a bit draughty.'

'I should say so,' says Philip, chuckling.

She feels nauseous and jittery as she takes his underwear, trousers and polo shirt out of the small cabinet beside the armchair and hands them to him. As he goes to take them, she holds on to the clothes for a moment longer, forcing him to look at her. 'What did the doctor say?'

'I told you.'

'No, you didn't.'

Philip frowns for a moment, then shakes his head. 'It was like I just said, the usual – eat healthily, not too much salt, take some exercise, blah, blah, blah.'

'That blah blah could save your life,' says Lizzie, sternly, letting go of Philip's clothes. 'You need to listen to the doctor, this isn't the first heart attack you've had.'

'It wasn't a proper heart attack,' says Philip petulantly.

'Philip,' says Lizzie, her tone stern.

'Yes, yes, alright.' Philip turns away and starts dressing. 'They're going to adjust my meds, up the dose a bit, the doc thinks the dosage wasn't doing enough for me. I'll be fine, don't worry.'

As Philip gets dressed, Lizzie takes the other few items from the cabinet – his watch, wallet and phone. She can't help but feel uneasy. Philip seems too chipper. Usually, he's a real worrier if he gets sick, and this might not have been a full-blown heart attack, but he's had one of those before – it's one of the things that forced him into retirement – so he knows this is serious. But he's not treating it that way; he seems strangely unbothered, blasé even. And Lizzie doesn't understand why.

◆ ◆ ◆

Forty-eight minutes later the discharge process is completed and Lizzie pushes Philip in a wheelchair through the foyer and out towards the patient collection and drop-off point. It's warm outside, and Lizzie wishes she wasn't wearing the heavy sweatpants and jumper that she'd had on last night.

'Right, let's get back to the case,' says Philip, as soon as they're through the doors. 'We can't let Rick and Moira do all the work.'

'But you're meant to be resting,' says Lizzie, unable to hide the worry in her voice. 'I promised the doctor I'd take you home.'

'Nonsense,' says Philip, his tone businesslike and full of bluster. 'Like I said, it was just a mini heart attack, not even a proper one. And, anyway, I feel fine.'

'You don't look fine,' says Lizzie.

Philip raises his eyebrows. 'That's not a very nice thing to say.'

'You know what I mean,' says Lizzie, shaking her head. 'You're not well, and you need to rest. A mini heart attack is a big deal. You have to take it seriously.'

'Yes, yes, well, I can rest from our room at the Surf-Sand Vista then,' says Philip. 'All that sea air, it's bound to do me the world of good, yes?'

Lizzie takes a breath. She recognises the signs: the stubborn tone and the defiantly tilted-up chin. Philip's not going to concede defeat on this without a fight and, given he's supposed to be keeping stress to a minimum, fighting with him isn't a very good idea. 'Fine.'

'Well, good that's settled,' says Philip, giving her a smile. 'When's Moira getting here?'

Lizzie checks her watch. 'I said noon, so any minute now.'

'Good, good,' says Philip, leaning back in the wheelchair. 'Lizzie, there's something I wanted to say. I've been thinking about our vow renewal, and us doing it on the beach like you wanted, and if that's what you'd like then let's go for it.'

'You don't mind the sand?' says Lizzie, surprised. He hates getting sand on himself, and he'd been so against a beach ceremony when she'd raised it a few days ago she'd thought he'd never come round to the idea.

Philip shakes his head. 'No, no. I think it sounds romantic, and you deserve to have everything exactly as you want it. If you want us to renew our vows on the beach, I'm in. And let's do it soon, shall we? No time like the present and all that, eh? I want to celebrate our marriage together.'

Reaching out, he takes her hand and presses his lips to her palm. Lizzie forces a smile as she fights back the urge to cry. She'd love a beach ceremony, really she would, but she can't help wondering what's brought about Philip's sudden change of heart. A few days ago it had taken a lot to coax him on to the beach for just a walk. Now he's agreeing to a ceremony on the sand, and is keen for it to happen soon. What's the urgency?

A cold fear grips her, despite the warmth of the Florida sunshine. Did the doctor tell him something that he hasn't shared with her? Does he want the renewal of their vows brought forward because his health is deteriorating and he doesn't have long?

She looks at Philip in the wheelchair. He's pale and tired-looking, but other than that he looks remarkably okay. Still, looks can be deceiving; this past twenty-four hours have highlighted that. She hadn't realised anything was seriously wrong until he'd been about to hit the floor.

Emotion builds like a pressure in her chest and Lizzie blinks hard, trying to stop the tears from falling. He might be pig-headed and obstinate, even pompous at times, and driven almost to obsession by the cases they take on, but he's a good father and a loyal husband, and even after everything they've been through, she still loves this man.

Now she's terrified that she might lose him.

39

MOIRA

They're back in Philip and Lizzie's room. It's almost like déjà vu, except Philip's in bed this time, at Lizzie's insistence, and Moira's the one standing by the whiteboard with the marker pen in her hand.

She looks from the board to her friends. 'So, what have we got?'

'Not a whole lot more than yesterday, I'm guessing,' says Lizzie. She's sitting on the edge of the bed beside Philip, holding his hand. There are dark circles under her eyes, and she sounds tired.

'Actually we've been pretty busy,' says Moira. 'At our last debrief, we agreed Carl Fossway and Josh Stratton were still very much in the frame for Jessie's murder, and could potentially have been responsible for Sindee's death too. Well, this morning I tracked down Carl Fossway in St Petersburg, and Rick paid our friend Josh Stratton another visit.'

'And what did you find?' asks Philip, his voice sounding weaker than usual.

Moira takes a breath. 'Well, Carl Fossway has video evidence that he was at home, working out in his garage, at the time of Jessie's death. It seems his estranged wife, Belinda, didn't tell us this because of the bad feelings between them.'

'Why didn't he show up yesterday then?' asks Lizzie, frowning.

'He said he couldn't face being in the same place that Jessie died, and that he went out on his buddy's boat for the day.'

'And you believe him?' says Philip. 'You know I had him as our number one suspect.'

'I've seen the video from the time Jessie was killed, and I do think he's out of the frame for that, but we haven't managed to get any CCTV that confirms him as being at sea when Sindee died. Hawk is working on that at the moment. So he's still a possible for Sindee's murder, although my gut is telling me he's not our guy.'

Rick nods, ruefully. 'Yeah, and as you know Josh Stratton was my top suspect for Jessie's murder, but he's alibied out for the time of her death, and the four hours preceding him arriving at the penthouse with us yesterday.'

Lizzie frowns. 'But I thought the manager at Starfish wouldn't give him an alibi?'

'They wouldn't, but he gave me another name – a woman – who has, and she checks out. Seems the alibi is genuine.'

'But why didn't he just give us her name before?' says Lizzie. 'Seems a bit odd.'

'I thought that too, but the woman, Mary-Beth Eastfield, is the wife of Remmy Anderson.'

'The famous football guy who's doing his first season as coach in Tampa?' asks Philip. 'He's a really big guy. Isn't his name "The Juggernaut"?'

'That's the one,' says Rick. 'Anyways, it turns out that Josh and Mary-Beth have been sleeping together for a while, even going back to the time when Josh and Jessie were together. I'm guessing that's why Josh was so cautious – I certainly wouldn't want to get on to the wrong side of The Juggernaut.'

'Okay, so that takes Josh Stratton off the board as a suspect,' says Lizzie. 'So what else are we left with?'

'You've got a theory, right?' says Rick, looking at Moira. 'Do you want to update on that?'

'Sure,' says Moira. She'd debriefed Rick on her conversation with Elton Bruce as she'd driven from the Beachseekers office to the hospital to pick up Philip and Lizzie. She turns towards them. 'I think Sindee McGillis was always the killer's target.' She taps the photos of Sindee and Jessie with the end of the pen. 'Both women were approximately the same height, body type and dressed with the same style. They both had platinum-blonde hair, usually worn long and straight. We've been told that Sindee McGillis even referred to Jessie as her "mini me".'

'You're basing a theory on the fact that they looked similar?' says Philip, sitting up a little straighter in bed.

'Yes,' says Moira, feeling irritated that he's questioning her before she's finished explaining, but trying to hide her frustration, given he's not well. 'And, also, on the evidence. Sindee McGillis was the organiser of the broker's open in the penthouse. She asked Jessie to stand in for her as host just a few hours before it was due to start – I confirmed this on the Beachseekers scheduler this morning. We know from Jessie's parents that Jessie was really excited about hosting a penthouse open for the first time, but the invitations and the arrangements with the Surf-Sand Vista had all been made in Sindee's name.'

'What, so Jessie's death was a case of mistaken identity. The killer went to the penthouse that evening expecting to find Sindee preparing for the event?' says Philip, frowning. 'Yes, yes, I suppose I can see that's possible, but wouldn't the killer have realised he'd got the wrong person before tipping her over the balcony?'

'Perhaps,' says Moira. 'But if the broken glass and the scuff marks show us where a struggle took place, he'd got very close to her before he pushed her. Maybe she was standing with her back to him, or perhaps he'd already said or done something incriminating by that point, and he couldn't let her live. Either way, I don't think she was the intended target. I think that was always Sindee.'

Rick lets out a long whistle. 'She was collateral damage? Jeez.'

'I think so,' says Moira. 'But that's where my theory ends, I don't have a motive for why someone wanted to kill Sindee.'

'She was nicknamed the Boss Bitch by her team,' says Rick. 'And described by more than one person as a hard ass and ball breaker. It's possible she pushed someone too far, or got the wrong person pissed at her.'

'It's possible, but is someone pissing you off really enough of a reason to kill them?' says Lizzie, doubtfully.

'Possibly,' says Philip. 'But if Sindee was the real target, why wait almost four months between the first and second attempt to kill her?'

It's a flaw in her theory, and Moira knows it. 'That's a good question, and I have no idea, although perhaps the person who killed Sindee is different to Jessie's killer.'

Rick nods. 'It's certainly possible.'

'Well, what do we know for certain?' asks Philip. His voice has his normal bossy edge to it, but it sounds fainter, wheezier than usual; as if he can't quite catch his breath.

'I've gotten a few updates from Hawk,' says Rick, pulling a napkin out of his pocket with some notes scrawled on it. 'He hasn't managed to get us the CCTV recordings or the building schematics yet, but the results of Sindee's autopsy match what you thought, Lizzie. She was stabbed from behind with a seven-inch, smooth-edged narrow blade, most likely a filleting knife like the sort used to gut fish. It was inserted between the ribs, twice, in an upwards trajectory. One of the wounds was fatal. The time of death was estimated at between four thirty and five thirty that afternoon.'

'So, any one of the people with us in the hallway could have killed her before joining us at five o'clock?' says Moira.

'Yep,' says Rick. 'And anyone who wasn't with us could have done it too.'

'Carl Fossway was out on a boat fishing at the time of Sindee's murder,' says Lizzie. 'Isn't it rather a coincidence that the murder weapon is a fish-gutting knife?'

'Perhaps,' says Rick. 'We need the marina footage to check if he really was out on that boat the whole time.'

'But it's possible he sailed the boat to Tampa, moored it and came here undetected to kill Sindee, isn't it?' says Lizzie.

'I guess it is possible,' says Moira, unconvinced. 'But there's something else. Carl Fossway told me that Jessie had mentioned feeling creeped out by someone, a man, who worked here at the Surf-Sand Vista. He didn't have a name, but apparently she'd mentioned a guy behaving in a creepy way towards her – staring and looking her up and down, that sort of thing.'

'Would have been more useful if he'd had a name,' says Philip. 'Otherwise it's just as likely he made that up to try and cover his tracks.'

'But why would Carl have killed Sindee?' says Lizzie. 'Did he even know her?'

Moira thinks for a moment. 'He really liked Jessie. If he'd suspected Sindee of being behind Jessie's death it might have been enough for him to take revenge.'

'How about that Elton Bruce chap?' asks Philip. 'He didn't seem to like his boss much.'

Moira shakes her head. 'He's alibied out for Jessie's death; he was showing an apartment and the people he was with have confirmed that. I suppose he could have killed Sindee and then joined us outside the penthouse at five o'clock, but it seems rather a stretch. He's gone out of his way to be helpful and—'

'Just because someone seems nice, it doesn't mean they're not a killer,' says Philip, condescendingly. 'There've been plenty of charming and "nice" serial killers.'

Moira clenches her fists. She's about to reply when Lizzie beats her to it.

'I'm not sure this is helping,' says Lizzie, shaking her head. 'It seems like we're slipping back into the guesswork again. Was the knife recovered from the crime scene?'

'That's a negative,' says Rick. 'There were a whole bunch of fingerprints in the apartment and the cops are working through them, trying to eliminate the people who've entered the unit in the course of their work or as prospective buyers, but given Beachseekers have been showing that penthouse for a number of months it's going to take a while.'

Moira thinks about what Rick's just told them as she adds the information to the whiteboard. 'Did they give any thoughts on the person who carried out the attack?'

Rick consults his notes. 'Right-handed. Could have been male or female. Height was hard to ascertain as the trajectory was an upwards motion, but they estimate between five foot six inches and six foot one inches. One thing they did say, is that whoever did this, they knew how to use the knife to create maximum damage.'

'Ex-military?' says Philip.

'Could be. That or an experienced hunter of some kind. Anyways, that's not all. Hawk found out who owns the Shimmering Sands Resort Community. It's a group of investors rather than one person – Mr and Mrs Dale Velmon, Ms Roberta Wright, Mr Cameron Webster, and a Mr Anthony Oxford. The chief executive role is taken by Anthony Oxford, so I'm guessing he's the guy Staples and Coulter were referring to when they talked about "the boss".'

'Do we know where these people live?' asks Moira.

'All out of state,' says Rick, consulting the notes of his napkin. 'The Velmons are in Cape Cod, Ms Wright lives in Texas, and Mr Webster is based in London, England. Anthony Oxford has a number of homes, but for the past five months has been based in New Zealand. All their business is apparently conducted via video calls.'

'Did Hawk check whether they'd travelled recently?' asks Lizzie.

'For sure,' says Rick. 'None of them has caught a flight.'

'So, Oxford and Webster can't be in the frame for the murders,' says Moira, summarising what Rick's just told them on a fresh section of the whiteboard.

'It seems real unlikely any of them would be,' says Rick. 'But it's interesting Oxford has such power over his team even working remotely. Cal Staples and Adam Coulter became very anxious when we asked them to give us information about this place.'

It's an interesting observation, but Moira doesn't see how that helps them with the case. 'Okay, so where does this leave our investigation?'

'Still a hell of a long way from a prime suspect,' says Rick. 'There are a lot of work colleagues and associates in real estate who might have had a grudge against Sindee, and we still have the list of people who were angry with Jessie. Josh Stratton is alibied out, but Carl Fossway is still a possible for Sindee's murder, and the theory that Belinda Fossway could have hired someone to kill Jessie is still a possibility. But, if your theory is right, Moira, and Sindee was the real target, we need to appraise their attitudes and interactions with Sindee and cross-reference their movements for the time of both murders, especially that half-hour window from four thirty until they joined us in the hallway outside the penthouse.'

'Things are getting far more complex now we could be looking for two killers,' says Lizzie, sounding rather defeated. 'We really need something that conclusively ties the two crime scenes together – DNA or fingerprints, ideally.'

'Agreed,' says Rick. 'But whether we get that or not, we'll find the truth.'

'Thinking more about it, my money is on Adam Coulter now,' says Philip, firmly. 'He fits the creepy guy profile, and there's just something rather off about him in my book.'

Moira frowns. Philip was gunning for Carl Fossway at the start of the debrief. 'The head of operations, really?'

'Yes, yes. He had opportunity,' says Philip.

'But not motive?' says Rick.

'Not one we've uncovered yet, no,' says Philip, wheezing between his words. 'But Jessie and Sindee both would have interacted with him when showing clients the apartments here. I've got a nose for this sort of thing. He was far too unruffled yesterday – the man hardly reacted to the fact that a second young woman had been killed in his building, and in the exact same apartment no less. He smells guilty to me.'

Moira thinks back to how calm Coulter had been at the scene of Sindee's murder yesterday evening. He's flashy, certainly, and a little oily, perhaps – that 'little lady' comment was fairly revolting – and he hadn't seemed fazed about being close to death, but there really wasn't any evidence of him having a motive. 'I'm not convinced.'

'Maybe he had a thing for Ms McGillis? Perhaps he came on too strong and she told him she'd report him to the boss that he's so afraid of,' says Philip, his voice getting fainter at the end of the sentence, making him start coughing.

Moira knows Philip's keen to stay working the case, but she wonders if he's really up to doing it. After the twenty-four hours he's had, he really should be resting.

Lizzie passes him a tissue. She looks really worried.

Philip takes the tissue, but continues talking. 'Maybe Coulter tried it on with Jessie first and he pushed her from the balcony as she tried to fight him off?'

'Some predators are good at flying under the radar, and Coulter certainly seemed keen to stay on the right side of the boss when I spoke to him,' says Rick, thoughtfully. 'There could be something to your theory, Philip.'

'But then why stab her twice in the back?' says Moira, doubtfully. 'Surely if it was a crime of passion or retaliation, he'd have been facing her?'

Rick runs his hand across his jaw. 'That's a good point. And there weren't any signs of a struggle.'

Philip starts coughing again, and takes a long drink of water.

'So, we're still nowhere near solving this then,' says Lizzie, clearly exasperated.

Moira gets it. Lizzie's worried about Philip. They all are. And he really should be back at home, recovering. 'No, I think we're getting closer. We know that—'

She's interrupted by a loud rap on the door.

'Are you expecting anyone?' says Rick.

'No,' says Lizzie. She walks across the room and opens the door. 'What the . . . ?'

'Good to see you, Mrs Sweetman,' says James Golding, stepping into the room. He nods towards Philip. 'Mr Sweetman.'

Philip's cheeks redden and he tries to sit up taller. 'What the bloody hell are you doing in my room?'

Golding puts his hands up, as if in surrender. 'I'm working with you guys now, didn't Denver here tell you?' He pushes his aviators up on to his head and grins. 'We're all on the same team.'

40

RICK

The situation's gotten real tense real fast, and Rick feels like it's on him to cool things down. He explains to Philip and Lizzie how James Golding, Philip's nemesis, is related to Chester Golding, the young detective who worked Jessie Beckton's death, and is now working Sindee McGillis's murder; and that's why James Golding is here. But it isn't going well; every word seems to make Philip angrier and more red-faced.

Rick keeps his tone soothing, trying not to aggravate Philip any more than he already has, as he summarises the situation. 'So, James, here, came to help. He wants to support Chester, and us, to find the killer and get justice for Jessie and Sindee.'

Philip's expression grows even more thunderous. His voice gets louder. 'And you agreed? After everything this bloody man has—'

'Look, buddy,' says Golding, holding up his hands. 'I'm asking you for a truce, so we can work together on this. I'm not real happy about working with you seniors either, but I'm prepared to put our differences aside for a little while for the sake of my nephew. Surely you can do that too, or are you just too damn petty? I mean, you can go right back to hating on me once we've caught the son-of-a-bitch.'

'I'm not your damn buddy,' Philip mutters. 'And I'll keep on hating you the whole time, don't you worry.'

'It would be helpful to have more people on this case,' says Lizzie, rubbing Philip's arm. 'And if we know what the cops know, we'll be able to move forward faster.'

'I suppose so,' says Philip, grudgingly. 'But I'm not being bossed about by this . . . fellow.'

'Like your wife says, you need me, right? So tough shit,' says Golding, his smile so fixed that it's more of a grimace. He turns back to Moira and Rick. 'Let's get down to it. I've got intel from Chester and a plan.'

'Sure,' says Rick, trying not to bristle at the detective's increasingly overbearing tone. He gestures for Golding to talk. 'Walk us through what you've got.'

Golding takes a folded sheet of paper from inside his suit jacket. Opening it up, he spreads it out on the bed beside Philip.

Frowning, Philip purses his lips together, but says nothing.

Golding gestures to the paper. 'These are the building plans. If you look right here.' He taps his index finger on the diagram. 'You'll see there's a service elevator.'

'As I suspected,' says Rick, squinting at the plans.

'Yeah, but I was the one who got the intel, right?' says Golding.

Rick clenches his jaw, hating that Golding is gloating like this; they're meant to be on the same team now, that's the point of the truce, but the detective seems hell-bent on point scoring. He shakes his head. It would've been a hell of a lot easier if Coulter or Staples had just given them this information when they'd asked for it instead of getting all evasive; would've saved a lot of time, and maybe helped them work out the identity of Jessie's killer before they'd had the chance to get to Sindee. 'What else?'

Golding's smile broadens. 'This elevator requires a key fob to operate above the seventh floor. There is CCTV inside the elevator car, but when the cops checked the recording from yesterday, it'd been deleted.'

'And when Jessie Beckton was killed?' asks Moira.

'Same,' says Golding.

'Jeez,' says Rick, glancing at Philip. 'Looks like it could be an inside job.'

Philip nods. But still doesn't speak.

'Yep, it's obvious really,' says Golding. 'There are three master key fobs that give access to the elevator, and open the units, on the eighth and ninth levels. Adam Coulter and Cal Staples have one each, as they do for the other levels of the building, which you'd expect given their roles. The last fob is kept in a lockbox and available for use by the housekeeping and maintenance crews – they sign it out as and when they need it.'

'Did anyone sign it out around the times Jessie and Sindee died?' asks Philip, begrudgingly.

'Nope, but then they're hardly going to do that if they're the killer now, are they?' says Golding, his tone implying Philip's question was stupid.

Philip reddens. 'We need to cover all—'

'Yeah, sure,' says Golding, dismissively. 'But let's get real here. The way I see it, the only people we know for sure had opportunity are Coulter and Staples. Yeah, other folks working at the Surf-Sand Vista might have been able to get access to the eighth floor via the service elevator, and could've taken one of the master key fobs, but it would've been harder and riskier for them, what with having to sign out the key and all.' Golding runs his hand through his hair. 'In my experience, usually the easier route is the route that's taken.'

'Sounds like the way you operate alright . . . the easiest route and all that,' mutters Philip under his breath, clenching and unclenching his fingers around the edge of the bedsheets.

'You want to share that with the room?' says Golding, narrowing his gaze.

'I want to share it with you,' says Philip, his voice increasing in volume. 'You're the laziest detective I've ever met, and yet here you are, waltzing in on *our* investigation, asking *us* for help, and then throwing your weight around with all your facts and pontificating, as if—'

'Well, Jeez, that's a real nice thank you,' says Golding, sarcastically. 'And there I was playing nice.'

'You aren't nice,' shouts Philip. 'You're an arsehole, and I don't want you in my room or around my friends, or dirtying my investigation.'

'Really?' says Golding, smirking. 'You're throwing me out?'

'Yes, really,' Philip shouts, gesturing towards the door. 'Go.'

Lizzie puts her hand over Philip's, and gives it a squeeze. Golding doesn't move.

'I said go,' screams Philip, spittle flying, breath coming in gasps. He shoves Golding away from the bed. 'Get out of my room.'

Golding steps back, getting his balance. He glances at Rick and shakes his head, then looks back towards Philip, sneering. 'You need to chill out, old man. Otherwise your next heart attack will kill you.'

Philip's face flushes red. He grabs the full glass of water on the bedside table and hurls the contents at Golding. 'Get the hell out!'

With Golding gone, slamming the door behind him, Philip leans back against the headboard, eyes closed, and takes some deep breaths. Lizzie's gripping his hand as if her life depends on it. Moira's looking shell-shocked. And Rick has no idea what to do next.

This is a real shitshow. Rick regrets agreeing to work with Golding, for sure. He should have guessed it wouldn't work out. But he'd thought the detective would've made more of an effort with Philip, not carried on like a kid in the schoolyard. Problem is, he can't deny that the intel Golding's bringing them is useful. Rick hates to admit it, but they need Golding right now.

Rick clears his throat. 'Philip, we need the police information, and without Golding telling us we're—'

'I know, I know,' says Philip, wheezing. 'But the man's an arsehole.'

'True, he is that,' says Rick. 'But it'd be good if you could find a way to work with him.'

Philip exhales hard. Shakes his head.

Lizzie looks up at Rick, her expression furious. 'He can't take this stress. He's not meant to be getting upset or excited. It could kill him.'

'It's okay, I'm okay,' says Philip, patting her hand. He meets Rick's gaze. 'If Golding agrees to be less of a condescending dictator, I'll try to put my issues with him to one side until we solve this case.'

Twenty minutes later, and after a lot of persuasion from Rick, Golding rejoins them in Lizzie and Philip's room. The atmosphere is still tense, but after Philip's begrudging apology for throwing the water, at least he and Golding are making more of an effort to get along and the tone they're using with each other is less antagonistic. Rick doubts it'll last, but if they can just work together for long enough to share intel it'll be something.

'Okay, so shall we summarise our position?' says Golding, raising his eyebrows. 'Phil, do you want to do the honours?'

Philip tuts. Rick knows why: it's because he hates people using the abbreviated version of his name. Rick braces himself for Philip to launch another verbal attack, but it doesn't come. Instead Philip holds Golding's gaze for a long moment, then shakes his head and says, 'You carry on.'

'Well, alright then. So—' Golding is interrupted by the loud ring of a cell phone.

Rick feels the buzzing in his pocket and pulls out his cell. He reads the name on the screen and looks at the others. 'I need to take this.'

Answering the call, he listens to the information he's being given, making a mental note of everything. He thanks the caller, ends the conversation, and looks back at Golding. 'That was Hawk, my law enforcement contact. He's been doing some digging on Cal Staples, the building manager, and Adam Coulter, the head of operations. Nothing has flagged on Staples, but Coulter's a different story. Apparently, the guy's ex-military. He spent eighteen years in the army before getting busted on a drugs charge when he was posted out in Germany. The record says he resisted arrest and was also charged for punching a police officer. He served a ten-month sentence and got himself a dishonourable discharge from the military in 2014. He's been a civilian since then, taking jobs mainly in the service industry running operations back-of-house in hotels and leisure facilities, and had no further arrests.'

'Like I said earlier,' says Philip, a smug tone to his voice, 'Adam Coulter's our man.'

'Good call, Sweetman,' says Golding, nodding. 'Sounds like he could be.'

'But what's Coulter's motive?' says Moira. 'Aside from the military training meaning he'd know how to use a knife, there's nothing more to suggest it was him rather than Staples or anyone else with the opportunity to get their hands on the access fob. We need more than a hunch; we need a motive and some proof.'

She's right, thinks Rick, running his hand over his jaw. They've got a bunch of circumstantial evidence, but nothing concrete. 'But if there's no useful forensics, and the CCTV's been wiped, how do we get more watertight evidence?'

'We need to lure the killer into the open,' says Golding. 'Set a trap.'

'Okay,' says Rick. 'But how?'

Golding smiles. 'I've got an idea. It's risky, and . . .' He turns towards Moira. 'I'm going to need your help to make it happen. You feeling brave?'

Rick frowns. Risky and involving Moira? He knows Moira's a great detective, and fearless in her pursuit of justice, but he sure doesn't like the sound of this.

Moira holds Golding's gaze. 'What's your plan?'

41

PHILIP

'I'm fine, stop worrying,' says Philip, although in truth he feels anything but fine. Having taken the short walk from the lift to the entrance, and on to the Surf-Sand Vista office area, he's already out of breath and feeling light-headed. He can't let Lizzie know that though; she'll only worry more.

Lizzie looks at him, her concern obvious on her face. 'You should be in bed.'

Philip rolls his eyes. He hates being treated like an invalid. 'I'll go back to bed later, yes?'

'Fine,' says Lizzie, with a small shake of her head.

He walks alongside his wife in silence. He knows she's annoyed with him and anything he says now will just exacerbate the situation. She's going to put her foot down soon, he can tell, but he can't miss the sting operation. This is the best bit: catching the killer and bringing them to justice, and they're part of it. Even if he's a bit disappointed they're not the ones laying the bait by delivering the message to Adam Coulter – the prime suspect. Philip would've loved to have seen the look on that man's face when they told him. After all, a man like that – who doesn't show a flicker of emotion when he sees the body of a woman lying dead on the floor – has to be up to no good.

'You ready then?' asks Lizzie as they approach the door to the maintenance crew area.

Philip nods, wishing that his heart would stop racing. 'Of course.'

Lizzie pushes open the double doors in the maintenance department, and they walk through the open plan to Cal Staples' office in the corner.

A few of the maintenance crew are sitting around one of the benches, drinking coffee and listening to some kind of sports commentary on the radio. They nod as Philip and Lizzie pass, but don't question why they're there. News of their investigation has travelled, supposes Philip. Maybe that's a good thing – given what they're about to do.

Lizzie knocks twice on Cal Staples' door before opening it. Cal is sitting hunched over behind his desk. His baseball cap is pulled down low over his eyes as he stares at a video playing on the screen of his computer. He flinches when he sees them in the doorway, and quickly shuts whatever he was watching, knocking over the marlin coffee mug as he does so.

'Ah, Cal, good to find you here,' says Philip, ignoring the coffee spreading over the desk, and injecting a friendly, jovial tone to his voice.

'Lizzie, Philip, good to see you. Sorry to be such a butterfingers,' says Cal as he finishes mopping up the spilt coffee with a tissue from the box in his top drawer. It looks as if he's aged ten years in the last twenty-four hours. There are dark circles under his bloodshot eyes, and although he smiles up at them it can't disguise his haunted expression. He looks broken. 'It's good to see you up and about, Philip. You gave us a real scare. I truly hope you're feeling better.'

Philip nods. He doesn't want to get into his health. 'I'm doing well. Thanks for helping Lizzie and the emergency crew out, much appreciated.'

Cal waves away the thank you. 'Anytime, I'm always happy to help out a guest in need.'

'Good, good,' says Philip.

'Cal, we wanted to see how *you* are,' says Lizzie, kindly, as she steps further into the office ahead of Philip. 'It must have been awful finding Sindee McGillis the way you did.'

'I . . .' Cal rubs his eyes. 'It was awful. I can't sleep, and when I do sleep I'm having nightmares about it.'

'I'm so sorry,' says Lizzie. 'I hope you've got some support? Someone to talk to?'

'Yep, the boss is paying for some therapy. I've got my first session tomorrow.'

'Good,' says Lizzie. 'I hope it helps.'

'Me too,' says Cal, his eyes becoming watery. He looks down at his desk, and fiddles with the placeholder ribbon of a large paper diary that's beside the computer keyboard.

Sensing a lull in the conversation, Philip takes a breath, readying himself to lay the bait. Positioning himself in the centre of the doorway, and raising his voice, so his words will reach the crew members out in the open-plan area too, he says, 'If it's any consolation, I think we're very close to unmasking the person who killed Jessie Beckton and Sindee McGillis.'

Cal looks up at Philip. There's hope in his eyes. 'Really? How?'

'We've discovered some new evidence. Our colleague, Moira, is on her way up to the penthouse now, just to double-check it, but we're pretty certain it gives us proof of the killer's identity. Once Moira's confirmed it, she'll call the cops and, if we're lucky, there'll be an arrest before the end of the day.'

'That's good news,' says Cal, looking thoughtful as he pushes the brim of his Surf-Sand Vista baseball cap up a little higher. 'Can I help you in some way? Let your friend into the penthouse or something?'

'No need, no need. Our realtor friend, Elton, has already opened the apartment for her,' says Philip, making sure that the crew are listening as well – after all, although Adam Coulter's their main suspect, it could be that a crew member used the spare master key fob to access the penthouse and carry out the murders; it's even possible it was Cal Staples, although looking at the state he's in Philip very much doubts that. He looks back at Cal. 'Luckily for us he was coming this way anyway to do some showings on the units for resale on the lower levels this afternoon. Says he can close up the penthouse later this evening once he's finished.'

'That is lucky,' says Cal, nodding. 'I hope you find what you're looking for.'

'We will, we will,' says Philip, working hard to keep the confident edge to his voice, even though, with all this standing and talking, he's feeling increasingly breathless.

'Anyway, we should leave you to your work,' says Lizzie, putting a hand on Philip's arm. 'We just wanted you to know that we're thinking of you, and that we'll do whatever it takes to catch the killer.'

'I really appreciate that,' says Cal, giving a slightly strained smile. 'Good luck, and do keep me posted. It would be such a great relief to us all here if you could bring these awful murders to an end.'

As they leave the maintenance area, and walk back towards the guest area, Philip smiles at Lizzie, and squeezes her hand. 'Good work. Everyone in the maintenance area will have heard the bait.'

'Yes, it went well,' she says, looking relieved. 'Cal looked in a bad way, though.'

'Indeed. The poor fellow looks crushed.'

'Finding Sindee must have hit him really bad,' says Lizzie. 'I do hope the counselling helps.'

Philip nods. Leaving the service area, and returning to the guest space, they head across to the lifts and press the call button.

Lizzie turns to face him. There's worry in her eyes. 'We need to get you back to bed now.'

'Not yet,' says Philip. 'Let me see this through. I'll rest afterwards. I promise.'

Lizzie looks uncertain. 'Do you really feel up to it?'

Forcing a smile, Philip squeezes her hand again, and tries not to let the nausea show. 'Absolutely.'

Turning away, he tries to catch his breath without Lizzie noticing. He can't bail on his friends at this stage, health issues or no. Philip's always been an all-or-nothing sort of person and he's going to finish this case, even if it kills him.

He just really hopes that it doesn't.

42

RICK

Rick checks the time on his watch; it's almost three o'clock. Philip and Lizzie should be with Cal Staples now, so it's time for him to get moving. Heading over to the reception desk, he finds it's a whole lot easier to persuade them to let him through to the 'back-of-house' lower level than it had been before, and when the ex-cop security guard waves him through the locked door into the office area, and the head of operations' assistant immediately buzzes him through to Adam Coulter's office, Rick knows word of their investigation must have filtered through to the whole team working here. Which is exactly what he'd hoped, because it means what he's just told each of them should spread through the staff like wildfire.

When Rick walks in, Adam Coulter is standing over on the far side of his office, putting a book back on one of the bookshelves. It's gloomy in the office, so Rick can't see the title of the book but if he had to guess he'd say it was one of those 'get rich quick' or 'build your multi-million-pound business in a month' type books. Coulter gives an oily smile when he sees Rick. 'Detective Denver, good to see you again.'

'Rick will do just fine, sir,' says Rick. He knows Coulter is aware he's not a police detective, but whatever his reason to keep up the pretence, it never hurts to be courteous, and he sure doesn't want

Coulter to get suspicious of what's about to go down. The plan depends on him believing everything Rick is about to say is true.

'Rick, then,' says Coulter, still smiling. 'I assume you're here about the investigation. How can I help? Like I told the other detectives, anything you need, you got it.'

'And we appreciate that, sir,' says Rick. He studies Coulter. His hair is slicked back as usual but he's wearing a different suit; this one is navy, but seems to be made of the same shiny, synthetic material as the grey one. *It's interesting,* thinks Rick, *that even though there's been a second murder in the building the guy seems visibly less nervy than the last time we spoke in this office, and much more the calm, helpful person he'd presented to the cops last night.* Rick wonders which one is the real Adam Coulter; or whether they're both fake personas. 'But there's no need for you to take any action.'

Coulter walks across the office to his desk. The desk looks messier than when Rick was last in here; along with the take-out cups of half-drunk, stagnant coffee, there are some Chinese food cartons and a couple of scrunched-up, and obviously used, napkins. There's a musty, mouldering smell coming from an old fried chicken box, and he tries not to grimace.

'Then how can I assist you?' asks Coulter, pulling out his desk chair, but not sitting down.

'I just wanted to stop by and give you an update,' says Rick, as he sits down on one of the hard, moulded plastic chairs in front of Coulter's desk. 'We're real close to catching the killer.'

'That's quick,' says Coulter; a brief flash of surprise passes across his face before he rearranges his expression into something more neutral. Taking a seat, he leans across the cluttered desk towards Rick. 'Tell me more.'

Rick fights the urge to sneeze as he gets a strong hit of the guy's flowery aftershave. 'We've gotten some new evidence. My associate, Moira, is heading up to the penthouse, and once she's confirmed it's genuine, she'll call the cops. I'm thinking there'll be an arrest before the end of the day.'

'Is that right?' There's a hint of suspicion in Coulter's tone.

'For sure,' says Rick, pleased that he's got the guy's attention now. 'Good news, right?'

Coulter smiles, but it doesn't quite reach his eyes. 'Yeah. Very. And you say, Moira, your colleague, is in the penthouse now?'

'Yeah, she's . . .' There's a beep from Rick's cell phone. He pulls it from his pocket and reads the message on-screen. Smiles as he looks back at Coulter. 'She's found what she was looking for and she's called the cops. The detectives are a half hour away. I'm going to head out front to meet them.'

'That's great, really great,' says Coulter, his smile looking increasingly strained. 'Looks like you're going to catch your killer.'

I sure hope so, thinks Rick, as he bids Coulter goodbye and heads out towards the front of the building. *I sure hope so.*

43

MOIRA

This is it.

Moira tries not to think about what happened the last time she was involved in a sting operation, back when she was still an undercover detective in London; how two of her team were dead within minutes, and her career was over a few months later. This isn't about her; it's about getting justice for the two women who've lost their lives in this penthouse. It's about catching a killer who thinks they're too clever to be caught.

Sindee McGillis's body is long gone, but the apartment still bears the scars of violent crime. There's a space on the sofa where the seat cushion should be, and although it's clearly been scrubbed, the hardwood floor has a large patch of discolouration in the spot Sindee's body had been found. Moira isn't squeamish, but she'd prefer not to look at the bloodstain, so she walks through the living space to the open door on to the balcony and looks out at the view of the ocean. 'Can you hear me?'

'Loud and clear,' says Chester Golding, his calm, steady voice coming from the tiny earbud in her left ear. 'Visuals are good too. Are you still okay to do this, Moira? You know you can pull out if you want.'

'I'm fine,' says Moira, giving a thumbs up. There's no way she can pull out now, but it's sweet of him to say so. She has to admit Chester Golding is a breath of fresh air compared to his uncle; kind, compassionate and diligent at his work, he did a quick job wiring the penthouse with cameras, even if he's acting alone and his partner has no idea what's going on. Turns out, for Chester, today was the perfect time to stage the sting operation; Detective Durcell is taking a couple of planned vacation days. 'We need to do this.'

'Yep. We do,' says James Golding, his tone abrupt and bossy. 'Don't get too comfortable, Moira, you're not on vacation here. Be ready for action.'

Clenching her jaw to stop herself saying something about teaching his grandma to suck eggs, Moira looks at her phone. There are four new messages. Once Elton had let her into the penthouse and the Goldings had everything set up, she'd messaged each of the people they'd previously spoken to about Jessie – witnesses and suspects alike – telling them she's got some further intel that shows the identity of both Jessie and Sindee's killer, and once she's double-checked one last thing in the penthouse, she'll be ready to tell the cops who the killer is. The replies each say a variation of the same thing – good luck. Bethany Thompson, Phoenix Salford-Keynes, Brett Donaldson, and Carl Fossway have sent them. The others – Belinda Fossway, Josh Stratton and Lucas B. Francis – have read her message, but not replied. Moira thinks it's more that they don't give a damn than that they're guilty. But when they'd been planning this operation, they'd decided to give the bait to everyone they'd ever suspected or interviewed. After all, they could be wrong.

But Moira doesn't think so. Given the intel they've received about the master key fobs and the CCTV in the service elevator being deleted from the times around each of the murders it's most likely the murderer is someone who works here at the Surf-Sand Vista. Still, it doesn't hurt to be thorough.

'You still hanging in there okay, Moira?' asks Chester, his voice a little tinny in her earpiece.

'Sure,' says Moira, nodding.

'I really appreciate you doing this,' says Chester. 'It's so great to work with professionals who give a damn.'

'Likewise, Chester,' says Moira, and she means it. Chester's uncle, James Golding, might feel more like a liability, but working with Chester has been nothing but a good experience.

'Quit with the lovefest, yeah?' says James Golding, the bossy tone of his voice grating on her. 'Keep your mind on the job.'

For the sake of the operation, and Chester, Moira bites her lip instead of giving James Golding what for. Turning her attention to the case, she thinks about Philip's absolute confidence in his theory that the killer is Adam Coulter; something even James Golding is agreeing with him on, despite their hatred of each other. Moira knows it's possible. Most likely, even, that Coulter is the killer. But something in Moira's gut tells her it isn't him. Yes, he's slick border-ing on smarmy, and he was unnervingly calm last night when faced with a dead body, but then he's ex-military so he's trained for that. Still, her money is on another member of the team.

There's only one way to find out who's right.

And so, she waits.

Seven minutes later, there's a noise at the door. Moira holds her breath, listening. She hears the lock disengage, and sees the door handle being slowly pushed down.

Her heart rate accelerates.

It's time. They're here.

Stepping away from the balcony, she moves into the living space and across to the sofa. She doesn't want to be too easy a target, but it has to look as if she isn't expecting anyone until the police arrive in a while. Leaning down, she pretends that she's inspecting something to the left of the bloodstain.

The door opens. 'Hey there.'

There's nothing intimidating about this guy. Nothing that screams danger. Yet Moira knows she has to be on her guard.

She pretends to look surprised. 'Hi. I wasn't . . .'

'I heard you were up here checking out some new information, and wondered if you needed any help?' he says, smiling as he closes the door behind him. 'I always like to help the pretty ladies.'

'I'm fine, thanks,' says Moira. She smiles, trying to act as natural as possible and forcing herself not to rise to his casual, slimy sexism. 'No help needed.'

'Your friends not here?' he says, looking around.

'No, not right now.'

'Good,' he says, coming closer.

That's when she sees the hunting knife poking out of the end of his sleeve.

He sees her notice it, and gives a little shake of his head. 'I'm afraid I can't let you win this fight, you know that, right?'

She'd expected it to be him, but the change in demeanour from last night is so striking it takes her aback for a moment. This man can *really* act. And she needs to act too. So, she plays her part, shaking her head as she backs away towards the master bedroom with the door that locks from the inside only. 'Cal, I don't . . .'

He moves fast, blocking her path. He's far quicker than she'd thought he'd be, and she's further from the bedroom than originally planned. It's not a good combination. She opens her eyes wide. Acting the innocent. 'What are you . . . ?'

In her earbud she hears James Golding say, 'We've lost visuals.'

'I'm trying to get them back,' says a panicked Chester Golding, in her earbud. 'The system isn't responding.'

Smiling a loan shark grin, Cal holds up a small plastic box with a red light illuminated on the side. 'Signal blocker, just in case you and your friends thought you'd be staying in touch.'

Moira swallows hard. She's glad James Golding persuaded them to go old school – radio mics rather than Bluetooth or wi-fi. 'I don't understand.'

Cal's grin widens as he shakes his head. 'I'm sorry, Moira. But I think you do.'

It happens so fast.

Cal lunges at her with the knife and she jumps back, trying to avoid the long, dagger-sharp blade. He thrusts the knife at her again, aiming for her chest, and as she dodges sideways, he follows her, blocking her path to the door. 'Not so quick.'

She raises her hands. 'Why don't we talk about—'

Ignoring her words, he rushes towards her. She's in a bad position, trapped between him and the sofa, so she makes the only move she can, pushing herself forward and hitting him straight in the chest with her shoulder, her hand reaching for his wrist to block him from using the knife.

Her momentum throws Cal backwards, off his feet, and he hits the wooden floor hard, pulling Moira down on top of him. The knife's still in his hand and Moira closes her fist around his wrist, pushing it away. But he's strong; far stronger than he looks. Twisting beneath her, he throws his weight sideways, unbalancing her. As she falls, she clings on to his wrist, knowing that if she lets him get his knife hand free it'll all be over. He straddles her, flapping his knife hand back and forth against the floor, trying to get her to release him. She lifts her knee, aiming for his genitals. Can't get as much power into the move as she'd like but she hits her target.

'You little . . .' Spittle hits her face. Cal drops the knife and it slides across the floor out of reach. His face is a mask of anger and pain.

'Didn't Jessie and Sindee fight back?' hisses Moira, trying to goad him.

'They didn't get the chance,' says Cal, smugly.

He lets go of her arm. Then his hands are around her throat and he's squeezing.

She thrashes beneath him, but she's got no breath; no voice. Her energy is fading.

Cal presses harder. Choking her.

In her earbud, she can hear Rick's voice. 'Moira? You okay? Confirm.'

'Moira, can you hear us?' asks Chester, the fear obvious in his tone. 'What's happening? Please respond.'

'Moira?' says Rick, in her earbud. 'Confirm you're okay?'

But she doesn't answer. Can't breathe. Spots dance across her vision.

She won't last much longer.

44

RICK

'Don't rush in there trying to be the goddamn hero,' growls James Golding. 'She'll be fine. We need to get more from Staples on tape, more that'll incriminate him.'

'We've got enough,' says Chester Golding, looking at Rick, wide-eyed.

The fear is clear from his expression, just as Rick knows it will be in his own. Only James Golding seems unbothered, but he's not the boss, and Rick sure as hell isn't going to wait for his approval. He sprints for the door of the apartment they've been holed up in, throws it open and races to the penthouse next door. His heart is beating like it's going to burst clean out of his chest. He has to get to Moira.

There's no time for the key. It takes him two hard kicks to get the doorframe to break, rendering the lock useless, and another one to break the door free and clear.

Shoving the door aside, he hurtles into the apartment, ignoring the pain in his leg from the impact with the door as he searches for Moira and Staples. They're across by the sofas, on the floor. It takes him a moment to take in the situation.

'It took you long enough,' says Moira, looking up from binding Staples' hands behind his back with a lace from one of her sneakers.

'I thought you were in trouble?' says Rick, peering at Staples, and trying to figure out if he's conscious. It doesn't look as if he is.

'For a hot minute, I was. He was trying to throttle me.'

'So how did you . . . ?' Rick gestures to the prone form of Staples.

'Headbutt.' Moira smiles. 'I hate them, but it was the only thing I had left that might work. He thought I was half-dead already, so he wasn't expecting it. That helped.'

Rick looks at the red mark on Moira's forehead that he knows is going to turn into an impressive bruise soon. 'I'm real sorry I didn't get in here earlier.'

'It's okay. I'm fine.' She smiles as she pulls the lace tighter around Staples' wrists. 'Did you get what he said on tape?'

'Loud and clear,' says Rick. 'The video was taken out by the signal blocker Staples activated, so the only bit that was difficult to interpret was when he attacked you. Golding, well, both Goldings, wanted to make sure he'd said and done enough to ensure a water-tight case, but when the talking stopped, I feared . . . well, I wanted to get in here.'

'Thanks for coming to check on me,' says Moira, as she finishes tying the lace cuffs around Cal Staples' wrists and stands up. 'But I can handle myself.'

'I know,' says Rick. And he does.

They stare at each other for a long moment. Rick wants to take her in his arms and tell her how he feels about her; how he's sorry about not telling her about the situation with Estelle and all the stuff that happened for their relationship to be where it's at now. He wants to apologise for not being completely honest, and promise that he will tell her everything from now on, always.

Then Staples groans, and as Moira gets to work binding his ankles, Chester Golding sprints into the apartment.

'Oh Jeez, Moira, are you okay?' says Chester, breathing hard. 'Did Staples hurt you?'

Moira meets Rick's gaze one last time, and gives him a small smile.

Then the moment is gone.

45

MOIRA

They meet over breakfast. The Becktons have already been told the official police story by Detective Chester Golding, but they deserve to know everything, and there are things that can't be disclosed officially. As far as they know a suspect is in custody and will likely be charged with Jessie's murder. They haven't been given any details.

They gather for breakfast at the same table where they first met five days ago, the one at the furthest end of the terrace restaurant, closest to the pool. It's only eight thirty but the air is warm, the sun stronger than usual for this time of day. The light glints on the water, and Moira wishes she'd had the time to use the pool for a swim at least once during their stay. It's too late now, though. They'll be leaving straight after this meeting is finished.

There are five of them today; Chester Golding has joined them as an honorary member of the group. He's here in his own time, off duty, but his uncle James Golding has been told to stay away. Moira doesn't know exactly what happened in the aftermath of the operation, but she knows that it started with cross words and ended with Rick punching the off-duty detective in the face. Given Rick is always keen to resolve things non-violently, she's guessing James Golding must have really overstepped to provoke such a reaction.

Without James Golding here, the body language between them all is relaxed and calm. Chester is a good influence: smart, kind and collaborative rather than dictatorial. Even Philip said that he enjoyed working with him, and that's high praise coming from him.

'Thanks for coming,' says Rick, rising to his feet as Jim and Doreen Beckton approach. He gestures to the two empty white wicker seats. 'Please, join us.'

'Thank you,' says Jim Beckton, as he takes the seat closest to Rick. He looks even more gaunt than he did the first time they met. The stress of the situation is clearly continuing to impact.

Doreen Beckton's unruly greying curly hair is pulled back into a scrunchie, but is already escaping from it. As she sits down between her husband and Moira, and pulls her navy cardigan tighter around herself, she gives them a strained smile.

'Hello again,' says Philip. 'You know Rick, Lizzie, Moira and myself, of course, and Detective Chester Golding is joining us in his own time, not in his capacity as a detective.'

'But you are the detective on Jessica's case?' says Doreen, turning towards her husband. 'He visited with us at our home last night, didn't he?'

'He did,' says Jim. 'So why are you here in an unofficial capacity, son?'

'It's a little delicate,' says Chester.

'As you know, Chester led the operation yesterday,' says Rick. 'But officially he's only able to give you a certain limited amount of information, whereas we, as retirees, aren't bound by those rules. Still, we thought it was important that Chester was here, as he and his uncle were the brains behind yesterday's operation to catch the killer.'

'Thank you,' says Doreen. She looks around the table. Her eyes becoming teary. 'Thank you, all of you, for what you did. And please pass our thanks on to your uncle, Chester.'

'I will, ma'am,' says Chester, solemnly.

'Chester didn't tell us how you did it, but he did say that Cal Staples killed Jessie and her boss, Sindee, and that he wouldn't have solved the case if it wasn't for your assistance,' says Jim, looking at each of the retired detectives in turn. 'How did you know Cal Staples was behind the murders?'

'A bunch of things pointed to it being someone with access to the back-of-house areas in this building,' says Rick. 'It could have been a few people, and it was only by setting up the sting operation to draw them out that we found out which one was the actual killer.'

'Moira used herself as bait,' says Lizzie.

Chester nods. 'She was incredibly brave.'

'Yes, yes, we spread the word that we'd got more evidence and Moira was double-checking it in the penthouse alone before calling the cops,' says Philip, proudly. 'The Staples fellow fell for the ruse, and stormed up to the eighth floor to silence our Moira. But, of course, he got far more fight back than he was planning on.'

'Is that how you got that awful bruise?' says Doreen, looking at Moira's forehead. 'It looks very painful.'

Moira gives her a smile. 'It's a small price to pay for bringing Staples to justice.'

Doreen presses her hands together into a prayer position. 'Thank you.'

'For everything,' adds Jim, pushing his glasses back up on to the bridge of his nose. His voice is strained as he asks, 'Have you any idea why Staples killed our little girl?'

'I'm sorry, but not yet,' says Rick, shaking his head.

'Since we took him to the precinct he's refused to talk,' says Chester. 'But I'm back on duty in an hour, and as he's had a night in the cells I'm hoping that will have loosened his tongue when I re-interview him. But, I'm sorry that, as of now, his motive is the one thing we don't know.'

'Well, at least we know who did it,' says Doreen.

Beside her, Jim bows his head, clearly trying to stay composed. His fists clench around the tablecloth. 'It's not enough. That coward, staying silent when he's murdered two people? He should explain himself. Doesn't he feel any . . .' He chokes back a sob.

Doreen reaches across and takes her husband's hand.

No one else speaks. The people sitting at the surrounding tables continue on with their breakfasts, chatting, smiling, and laughing. The pool shimmers, reflecting the sunlight, and overhead seabirds soar and swoop, calling to each other. This place is everything retirees could hope for in a beachside community. Except for Jim and Doreen; it has brought them only sorrow. Moira glances at Rick, and she can see from his sad expression that he's thinking the same. They knew when they took this case it couldn't have a happy ending; that whatever they did, they couldn't bring Jessie back, but Moira just wishes they could do more.

'As and when I learn more, I'll be sure to keep you updated,' says Chester, breaking the silence.

Jim looks up. 'You think Staples will talk?'

'I'll do my very best to make that happen,' says Chester, his tone kind and reassuring. 'But even if Staples doesn't confess, I believe there's still enough evidence for a solid conviction. Moira was wearing a wire when he attacked her and we've got him admitting to the homicides on tape, plus the soundtrack of him attempting to murder Moira herself, and the photographs of the physical evidence. When we searched Staples' condo we found Jessie's cell phone and the knife he used to kill Sindee hidden in a fishing tackle box. We also have the weapon he was carrying when he attacked Moira, which is a similar type of fish-gutting knife. We've requested his cell records and I think it's highly likely there will be calls and messages that could help towards a conviction too.'

'That's good news,' says Doreen. 'We just couldn't bear it if he walked free.'

'He won't,' says Chester, his tone determined. 'We've got him, ma'am. You can be sure of that.'

Moira tries to hide it, but she worries Chester is too confident. Nothing is for certain until the verdict is handed down; smooth-talking lawyers and out-of-court deals can scupper even the most watertight of cases. Add to that the fact that Thomas Durcell – the guy who should have been the lead detective on the homicides – is angry that he was cut out of the loop and is taking it out on Chester, and there's more than enough things to cause problems.

'We're going to head back home this morning,' says Rick. 'But if you need us, you can call anytime.'

'We appreciate that,' says Jim, getting to his feet. 'Thank you for all you've done, and let me know your fee and I'll get it settled right away.'

'No, no,' says Philip, shaking his head. 'There's no charge.'

'Really?' says Jim, surprised. 'That's . . . very kind.'

'We're happy to help out,' says Rick. 'Closing the case is our reward.'

Moira nods, but she doesn't fully agree, because to her it doesn't feel as if the case is closed, not fully. Cal Staples refusing to speak – to own up to what he's done and say why he did it – leaves a bad taste in her mouth. They've got the right man, she's sure of that, but the question of why he killed Jessie and Sindee is going to bug her until she knows the answer.

'Oh, I almost forgot,' says Doreen, reaching into her handbag and pulling out a small wooden box painted a bright turquoise with the words 'Rainy Day Fund' on the top. 'You asked about the drawers of Jessie's dressing table, and whether we had a key? Well, we didn't think we did, but it turns out one of the little keys on her apartment door keychain unlocked it. We found this box inside.'

Moira takes the box. 'Have you opened it?'

Doreen glances at her husband. 'Yes, but we don't think it'll be any help to you.'

Opening the lid, Moira looks inside. There's a stack of twenty-dollar bills. Given the thickness, it must add up to around five hundred dollars.

'We always told her to keep some cash in a safe place for emergencies, just like we taught her that buying her own home was a priority,' says Jim, his voice breaking as he says the word 'emergencies'. 'She was a good girl. Listened, and worked hard. She bought that apartment of hers with the commission money she'd earned from working real estate in New York, and that box was her safety net. She was very safety conscious but . . .' He shakes his head. 'I still can't believe she's gone.'

'I'm so sorry for your loss,' says Moira, feeling the depth of the Becktons' loss like a kick in the stomach.

Rick bows his head. 'We all are.'

46

MOIRA

Back home, Moira stands in front of her walk-in closet and opens the door. The lights come on automatically and her eyes are drawn to the lowest shelf at the back of the space. It might look like it only contains a folded fake fur throw and a couple of old coats, but Moira knows what's hidden beneath: the metal lockbox that holds all the secrets from her past.

Taking a deep breath, she moves quickly across the walk-in space and kneels down in front of the shelf. She clears the throw and coats away, and then uses the smallest key on her keyring to unlock the metal box.

She lifts out the clear plastic folder on top of the rest of the contents in the box. She doesn't open it, already knowing that inside is the documentation for the three identities she has: one in her real name Emily Jane Platt – the name she can't use any more for fear of being found here in Florida; one in her current name, Moira Flynn; and one in the name of her back-up identity, Rachel Jean Baker – the identity she'll adopt if she's discovered here in Florida and has to switch to another name and another new life; creating a fresh tabula rasa. The name she really doesn't want to ever have to use.

Putting the plastic wallet to one side, Moira lifts out the two thick buff folders that were underneath it. They're held together by thick elastic bands, but still the paperwork crammed inside threatens to burst them open. Inside these folders are copies of every piece of information, of evidence, Moira had collected on Bobbie Porter and her criminal undertakings. It's the information she believes she was almost killed for, and the reason she had to abandon her career, and her old life, and start afresh here at The Homestead as Moira Flynn. But now, after the memory is clearer in her mind of what fully happened out on the balcony with McCord on that fateful night, she wonders if that's the whole truth. She puts the folders down on the floor, on top of the plastic wallet. There's only one way to find out.

In the bottom of the lockbox is another metal box. Inside it is a Glock handgun and a weapons-grade taser; she'd got a concealed-carry firearms permit and bought the weapons when she moved to the States. With the threats on her life, she felt it wise to have them as a last resort. But she doesn't need them right now, so she leaves the box where it is and instead lifts out the small cardboard carton that's wedged alongside it.

The carton is where she'd tipped the contents as she'd emptied her desk on that last day in the office. She'd not looked at any of the stuff. Leaving the job she'd loved had been hard enough without lingering over the debris of a twenty-plus-year career that was ending so abruptly. But after what she recalled following a panic attack on the eighth-floor balcony of the Surf-Sand Vista building – the repressed memory of another balcony moments after her last operation as an undercover detective had gone bad – she wonders if the memory of what McCord said to her before he jumped can really be true.

And, if it is true, can she handle the truth?

Moira looks at the box in her hands. She feels the cheap cardboard against her fingertips, and the barely there weight of its contents. She'd killed her career, and lost everyone she'd cared for in her search for the truth about Bobbie Porter. The need to know had burned hot and relentless within her belly. But now, with her new life here at The Homestead, and her friends who she enjoys solving crimes with, and Rick, and whatever is going on between them, the obsession has dampened, just a little.

But, although she isn't entirely sure what she'll find, and what she'll do about it, she does know one thing. She still wants answers, and this might be her last chance to get them.

47

RICK

Back home at Ocean Mist, Rick is feeling all kinds of nervous. Estelle sure doesn't seem happy to see him home, and they've spent the last hour tiptoeing around each other as she cooks dinner for Bibi and gets her settled to sleep for the night. Now it's just the pair of them, sitting out on the back porch, in side-by-side rattan chairs, watching the sun sinking low in the sky and turning the horizon the colour of liquid gold.

The bug chorus is as loud as it always is at this time of day, but the silence between him and his daughter feels far louder, and a hell of a lot more uncomfortable. Rick knows he has to be the one to break it. He's let his daughter down so many times. He doesn't know if it's possible to rescue things and build some kind of relationship with her and his granddaughter, but he knows for sure he has to try.

'I'm sorry.'

Estelle stays silent. She tucks her shoulder-length, curly blonde hair back behind her ears, and crosses her arms.

'I screwed up bad with your mom, I know that. Me trying to pretend things were okay – burying my head in work, and all. It was a coping mechanism, but it didn't help anything.' He exhales hard. 'Especially not for you or your mom.'

'Yeah,' says Estelle. Her voice is so quiet he can hardly make out the word.

'But I loved you both, love you still, more than anything,' he says, looking at her, although she still won't meet his gaze. 'I should've listened to you back then. I should have been there for you more. I should've—'

'We both made mistakes, Dad,' says Estelle, finally looking up and meeting his gaze. 'I was angry, really mad, and I channelled it all at you. But it wasn't you I was mad at, not really, it was the cancer. The world. The injustice of it all.'

'But, honey, I—'

'No, let me say this,' says Estelle, putting her hand on his arm. 'I need to get it out, and it's taken me a long while to do it.'

'Sure,' says Rick. Feeling tension building in his stomach as he wonders what she's going to say. Fearing it's going to be bad. Knowing he deserves it.

'I'm sorry, Dad.'

Rick's breath catches in his throat. 'You're—'

'I treated you bad, and I am sorry. That's what I wanted to say when I arrived here a few days ago. I'd psyched myself up and was going to blurt it out the minute you answered the door.'

'But I didn't answer the door,' says Rick, realising that perhaps Estelle's behaviour towards him, and Moira, when she first arrived hadn't been for the reasons he'd initially thought.

'No, you didn't. And that threw me. Made me feel all kinds of emotions . . . about you and about Mom, and I kind of clammed up and suddenly I wasn't sure if I should have tried to come here. It all just . . .' She shakes her head. 'You'd moved on and I thought you probably didn't want me arriving and screwing it all up.'

'I never thought that,' says Rick, feeling tears prick his eyes and blinking furiously to keep them at bay. 'I was so happy to see you.'

Estelle gives him a small smile. 'I'm glad. I needed to see a friendly face. After everything that's happened, I just didn't know who else to trust.'

'Can you tell me what happened with Mark?' asks Rick, gently.

Estelle blows out hard. 'He was an asshole the whole time we were together, it just took me a long while to figure out how bad of an asshole he was. By the time that I did, I was already pregnant with Bibi. I tried to make it work, truly I did, but he'd always been controlling about where I went and who I saw. Then, when Bibi came, he started complaining about not being able to live life to the full with a baby in tow. He resented her, and he resented me loving her. Pretty soon he started not coming home, and drinking a whole lot more. There were other women, I found their numbers in his pockets when I did the laundry. And, sometimes, he got violent with me.'

Rick cusses under his breath. 'That son-of-a-bitch, I'll rip his—'

'No, Dad,' says Estelle, her voice is quiet, but her tone determined. 'I've left him. I put up with his shit for a long time, but it's done now. He'd made me believe he was all I had. He never told me that you'd tried to get in touch. It was only last week that I found your postcards. We'd had a storm that'd damaged the roof and caused a leak. I was clearing out a closet in the room with the water damage when I found them. Some were ruined from the damp, but I still managed to read a lot of them, and I realised you still cared about me, you'd never given up on me even after how badly I treated you.' She shakes her head. 'Mark had controlled my life for so long. I think almost everything that man told me was a lie. And I said that to him after I'd packed Bibi into the car, and told him I was leaving.'

Rick doesn't speak for a moment. Somewhere in the distance a dog barks.

He'd hated Mark, never trusted him, but he'd almost convinced himself he'd been wrong and Estelle was happily married and living her life, even if he wasn't in it. Learning now that she'd been unhappy and locked into a relationship with a man who manipulated and lied to her, a man who was violent towards her, sickens him. 'I'm so sorry. I should have tried harder to make contact. I should've—'

'No,' says Estelle, putting her hand on his arm again. 'You did everything you could.'

They sit in silence as the last of the sun's light drops below the horizon. The porch lights flicker on, and a moment later a dozen sprinkler heads pop up from the lawn and send water arcing across the grass.

Rick stares into the spray, thinking on everything Estelle's just told him. The fury towards her asshole husband is still there, bubbling hot in his stomach, but he swallows it down. Stays calm, as she wants. For now, anyways.

He turns to look at her. Moves a stray lock of curly blonde hair that's fallen across her face back behind her ear. 'She'd have been proud of you, you know? You're a great mom to Bibi, and what you've done, getting out of a bad situation and coming here, that took real courage.'

Estelle looks down at her lap. Nodding. 'I should have done it sooner. I feel like a fool for not seeing him for what he was earlier.'

'You're not a fool, honey,' says Rick, gently.

'I treated you bad,' says Estelle, the regret heavy in her voice.

'You were real young, and you were hurting,' says Rick, clenching his fingers around the cushion on the rattan seat as the fury fires hotter inside him. 'Mark took advantage of that. But it's done now. You're here, and you're safe, and you're going to be okay. This can be your home, yours and Bibi's, for as long as you want. I've got two guest bedrooms and we can get a swing-set for the garden and whatever else you think Bibi would enjoy. I'm here for you, honey. I've always been here for you.'

Getting up, Estelle disappears inside the house, and returns a minute or so later with two bottles of beer. She hands one to Rick, and sits down beside him. He twists off the top, and looks at his daughter, unsure of what to say.

'To starting over?' says Estelle, holding up her beer in a toast.

'For sure,' says Rick, pushing thoughts of the things he'd like to do to Mark, her son-of-a-bitch husband, from his mind and smiling as he clinks his bottle against hers. 'Starting over.'

48

MOIRA

She opens the cardboard box. Inside is the debris of a life she can barely stand to think of as hers: a chipped coffee mug with a picture of a dog on it, a few battered notebooks, peppered with fading Post-its between their pages, a couple of ancient magazines and some old CPD certificates. Lifting them out, she sees gathered at the bottom of the box a collection of pencil stubs and dried-out biros, and a handful of USB sticks.

She flicks through the magazines, double-checking there are no notes or messages left for her inside, then turns her attention to the notebooks. She goes page by page, reading the notes and making sure there's nothing added. First up is her CPD journal where she'd documented her reflections on each training course she'd attended, and second is her notebook filled with 'To Do' lists. Then she reads through her meeting book – the notes from team meetings. She smiles as she skim-reads the notes and remembers the laughter and camaraderie in their team. Then sits for a moment, fighting back tears, at the thought that McCord and Riley are dead and gone.

Putting down the last notebook, Moira sorts through the old certificates but finds nothing from McCord. She frowns. Was the memory false? Did her mind fabricate McCord telling her he'd left evidence in her desk drawer?

She looks back into the box. The only things left to check are the USB sticks. There are five of them in there, but she can't remember how many she'd had of her own. Suddenly the memory seems less real, more like some strange daydream. Is it possible it wasn't actually a real memory?

There's only one way to know.

Getting to her feet, Moira carries the USB sticks downstairs to the dining table and opens her laptop. Pip, the elderly sausage dog, and Wolfie, the fluffy terrier, look up from where they're lying happily snuggled together on the sofa. Marigold, her ever-enthusiastic young Labrador, bounds over to see her, a half-chewed squirrel toy in her mouth. All three were so happy to see her when she'd collected them from the Dog-N-Pup Home-from-Home on her return from Shimmering Sands, and she's thankful that they've quickly settled back into life at home.

Smiling, Moira gives Marigold a belly rub, before turning her attention back to the laptop and plugging the first USB stick into one of the ports. With her heart hammering against her ribs, she double clicks on the new device icon, and opens the USB.

Her heart rate steadies as the files appear. She recognises them; they're old photographs. There aren't many, so she clicks on each one in turn, double-checking they are what she thinks they are: a picture of her when she graduated from the academy, and another with her class; a few pictures of her in uniform; and then a number of screenshots of online articles reporting on cases she'd worked. There's nothing from McCord.

She removes the USB and puts in the next one: it's her household budget spreadsheet and records of work expenses paid for from her own money and claimed back through the payroll; again, nothing from McCord. With her hopes starting to fade she plugs in the next USB. Files appear, but when she clicks on them they seem to be corrupted and unopenable. The next one is the same. Damn.

The last USB stick is silver with a cracked case. It looks so beaten up that Moira doubts it'll even work. Still, she needs to check it. Pushing it into the USB port, she double clicks on the icon and waits as the folder opens.

Over fifty items appear in the device folder. There are no file names, only numbers, and they're a mix of images, PDFs and spreadsheets. Moira's breath catches in her throat; this isn't her USB stick. The repressed memory *was* real. Then she tells herself not to get ahead of herself; the USB could've found its way into her drawer accidentally and could just contain some dreary old police policy documents or something else just as dull. The only way to know if what's on it is from McCord and connected to her old boss and mentor, Detective Superintendent Harry George, and criminal gang kingpin, Bobbie Porter, is to open the files.

Moira takes a breath, and clicks on the first file.

The image is a set of photographs showing bank statements in the name of H R George. As she flicks through the pages, her gaze is drawn to a regular monthly cash deposit that's been highlighted in yellow: £20,000 paid in on the fifth of the month, every month. The statements cover a two-year period, starting well before her and her team began investigating Bobbie Porter's criminal activities, and continuing up to the month that her failed, fatal operation took place.

She closes the file and clicks on the next one. It's a photo that's been taken outside the private members club, The Shelborne, in Mayfair. In it, Detective Superintendent Harry George, in a black suit, is enthusiastically greeting a younger man who looks like a wealthy city type: well-cut navy suit, brown brogues, leather briefcase.

Moira clicks on the next file. This one is another picture of the two men. They're in different suits, and seated at a restaurant table on an outdoor terrace that looks like that of the five-star hotel

Grand Central. They're laughing as they eat a meal of steak, salad and chips. There's a bottle of red wine on the table. Moira reads the label and raises her eyebrows. The bottle alone would have cost over four hundred pounds. That's a lot of money to spend on wine, even for a detective superintendent.

The next file shows a series of images of the two men at a café in Regent's Park. They're in more casual clothes – Harry George is wearing a battered old Barbour jacket and a tweed cap, and the younger man has on a beanie hat, fluffy hooded parka and jeans – and the time of year looks more like winter. The first photo shows them drinking coffee, the steam from their cups obvious in the picture. In the second picture, the younger man has a messenger bag on the table, and looks to be removing something wrapped in brown paper. In the third image, the younger man is handing a brown paper parcel tied with string to Harry George. In the fourth photo, George is tucking the parcel into a gym bag at his feet.

As Moira clicks through the files, she finds eight more of the two men together. Five of them capture the moment a parcel is handed over to Harry George. Flicking back through the images, she checks the date stamp on the corner of each picture: the fifth of the month. Whoever took these pictures – McCord she supposes, if he left her this USB stick – was purposefully watching Harry George, and creating a chain of evidence linking her old boss to this younger man and the £20,000 that appeared in his account every month.

The next image gives her the full context. It looks as if it's been taken with a long lens at dusk. It shows the younger man from the pictures with Harry George sitting on the deck of a huge super yacht. There's a woman standing with her back to the camera, who is holding a tumbler out to the man. He's smiling up at her. The next picture shows the woman sitting down, and leaning over to kiss the man. Her face is still away from the camera, but there's something distinctly familiar about her. The third image is the money shot. The woman, sitting on the chair beside the man, with his hand on her thigh, laughing.

Moira's breath catches in her throat. She'd recognise that woman's face anywhere.

Bobbie Porter.

Her auburn hair is a little longer in the pictures than it had been when Moira had seen her, and her make-up in these pictures is more dramatic – lots of mascara and red lipstick – but it's definitely her.

Moira exhales hard.

These photos show a clear line of sight between Bobbie Porter, the younger man, and her old boss, Detective Superintendent Harry George. And the younger man and Harry George share the connection of the parcels exchanged on the same day that £20,000 in cash was paid into Harry's account each month. Moira knew about Harry's connection to Bobbie, of course, after witnessing the conversation between them at his house, but if she'd reported it, it would have been her word against his. To have photographic proof is a very different situation. But one problem still remains: no one else in law enforcement knows that Bobbie Porter is a woman, or what she looks like. The only officers who did, aside from Moira, are dead.

She continues clicking through the files. There are witness statements, crime scene pictures and documentation showing the extent of Bobbie Porter's criminal activities. Moira recognises some of them from the paper case files she has in the lockbox upstairs, but some are new to her. Each details the awful things that Porter and her gang inflicted on others: drugs, prostitution, trafficking and more. There are more photos too, these ones putting Bobbie Porter at the locations of the crime scenes, and with several of the people from within the criminal organisation who've done time before.

Moira wonders why McCord never showed her this stuff. He must have been investigating Porter for a long time, months if not years. Why didn't he act on it himself and expose Harry? In her recovered memory, when she heard McCord's words clearly for the first time, he'd said Harry George had blackmailed him, forced him to betray her and kill their colleague, Jennifer Riley. He'd said that Harry had wanted him to kill Moira too. McCord had looked like a person on the brink. His usually calm, cool-in-a-crisis demeanour replaced by wild eyes and a shaking gun hand. After all these months of thinking McCord had been turned and gone dirty, now Moira is starting to believe he didn't want to do what he did. If that's true, there has to be something on this memory stick that will give her a clue to why he went from investigating Porter to helping her evade capture.

Three files later she finds her answer.

First is the video. Taken through the large bay windows of Harry George's Highgate home, it shows that there's far more about the relationship between Moira's ex-boss and the criminal, Bobbie Porter, than just the purchase of the detective superintendent's silence and ability to make police interest go away or fail. There's no sound, and the video is grainy and a little shaky – probably filmed on a phone – but it's clear enough to see what's happening. It shows Porter and Harry George clinking glasses of what looks like whisky and talking, but within less than a minute the conversation changes to an argument – angry expressions and open mouths, jabbing fingers and flushed faces. Then, the anger switches into something very different. Moira grimaces. The rest of the video shows her old boss and Bobbie Porter kissing, and then having sex; all with the curtains open. There's passion between them, and a familiarity that tells Moira this wouldn't have been the first time this happened.

She clicks on the next file. It's a voice recording; patchy but audible. There are two voices on it – McCord and Harry George. As she listens, a rising sense of horror and fury builds within her, and everything falls into place. McCord gives Harry George an ultimatum – resign or he'll take the evidence he has to Internal Affairs and his career will be over. It's a strong threat, but Harry George just laughs. Rather than agreeing, or pleading with McCord not to turn him in, his voice becomes low and filled with menace as he details all the horrific things Bobbie Porter's gang will do to McCord's mother, father and two younger sisters.

Moira's shaking as she clicks on the next file. It's a picture of McCord's youngest sister, fourteen-year-old Geraldine, her face bloody and bruised. Moira remembers McCord telling her that his sister had been mugged on her way home from school. How he'd been quiet, sullen even, whenever they were in the office after that. The date stamp on the photo is two weeks before the failed operation Moira led.

The last file is another audio file, again of McCord and Harry George. Harry tells McCord that Geraldine's mugging was a gentle warning, a taster of what would happen to his family if McCord doesn't do as Harry says. Then he sets out exactly what is to happen during the operation Moira is about to lead to capture Bobbie Porter: make sure Porter escapes, and kill any coppers in the room.

Moira feels nausea rising in her throat. She tastes sour bile on her tongue.

McCord must have planted the USB stick in her drawer before they went out on the operation. He must have doubted that he'd be able to do what Harry George had told him to do, and he knew the deadly consequences for his family if he didn't. Maybe he'd planned to end his life, or maybe putting the USB in Moira's desk drawer was an insurance policy of sorts. But she'll never know.

What she does know is the truth about Harry George. Her ex-boss is utterly corrupt. He's on the payroll of one of the most vicious criminal gangs, and has protected them for years. He has a sexual relationship with the head of the gang, and blackmailed a young, talented and principled detective into killing a colleague and taking his own life.

Moira exhales hard. She cannot let that stand.

She's stayed off the radar since she moved here to The Homestead. She cut all ties with London and, with her new name, hoped that she'd never be found. She's not even so much as googled Harry George or Bobbie Porter for fear that an IP address trace could give them her whereabouts. But McCord's last request was that she expose Detective Superintendent Harry George for what he is – a liar, a dirty copper, and a criminal.

Harry had been her boss, and her mentor, and acted like a father to her – celebrated her rise through the ranks, was there for her when her relationships went bad, and took the place of the family she'd lost on each and every birthday. Now everything he ever did or said is tarnished, ruined. Rotten deep inside, just as he must be.

She thinks of the wretched look on McCord's face as he'd said those final words to her before he leapt over the railing and was lost into the darkness.

Expose him.

End the corruption.

Please.

Moira knows what she has to do.

She can't bring Al McCord and Jennifer Riley back, but she can get justice for them and end this. She has to do something, the right thing, even if it could bring the mob after her again. She thinks of the documentation for her third identity kept safe in her lockbox – Rachel Jean Baker. She hopes doing this won't mean she has to use it, but if it does, then so be it. There's corruption deep in the heart of the Met, and she can't, she won't, sit back and let that continue.

Opening up Gmail, she creates a new email account. Searching the internet, she finds the addresses of the news editors at all the major newspapers in the UK and enters them into the 'To' field of a new email. Then she begins to type.

49

PHILIP

After receiving Chester's message first thing, they gather at the house. Philip isn't at all keen for James Golding to be inside his home but Lizzie forced the issue, saying that as Chester has come all the way from Tampa to see them, and is keen for his uncle to make up for his previous poor behaviour, they should be supportive. Philip likes Chester, he's a good, hard-working sort, and it's not the lad's fault he's got an arsehole for an uncle, so reluctantly he had to agree. He doesn't like it though.

He leads them out to the garden, while Lizzie makes iced tea and serves oatmeal and raisin cookies on their best china. Rick and Moira still seem a bit odd with each other, and Rick's making small talk with Chester, and studiously ignoring his uncle, rather than chatting to Moira, which is unusual in Philip's book. Moira herself looks a bit distant; like she's got something bothering her. Philip doesn't ask her about it though. He never likes to pry.

Instead, as Lizzie passes out the drinks and then takes a seat beside him, Philip clears his throat to interrupt Rick and Chester's conversation, and says, 'So tell us the latest.'

'He's confessed,' says James Golding, in his usual lazy drawl. He turns to glare at Rick. The purple bruising around Golding's eye is a reminder to all of the punch-up between the two men; a fight Golding instigated, of course. 'And it's a good job, considering you went charging into the penthouse before we'd gotten the motive on tape.'

'For all we knew Moira was in trouble,' says Rick, the tension in his voice clear. 'Staples damn near throttled her anyways.'

'You overreacted,' says Golding, dismissively. 'You should've—'

'Rick did the right thing,' says Chester, speaking over his uncle. 'Moira's safety was the priority.'

Golding shakes his head and mutters something about amateurs. Rick clenches his fingers around his glass of iced tea so tightly that Philip worries it'll crack. It seems the issues the two of them had at the end of the operation are still very much live and present. Philip would like nothing more than to throw James Golding out of the house, but Chester is a good, honourable man, and so as long as Rick can tolerate James Golding, Philip will also try to stomach him for a little while longer.

'I brought something,' says Chester, putting a small tablet computer on the table and turning on the screen. 'I thought you might want to see it, but you didn't get it from me, okay?'

There's a video file open on the tablet. It looks like the interior of an interview room. Philip frowns. 'Is that a police tape?'

Chester gives a small smile. 'I can't possibly comment on that.'

Philip tuts. It seems some of James Golding's dodgy methods are rubbing off on his nephew. 'Did you bootleg a copy, son? That's a serious breach of the rules.'

Chester blushes. 'I . . . I—'

'What the hell does it matter to you?' says Golding, irritation in his voice. He pushes his shades on to the top of his head. 'Do you want to watch it or not?'

Philip purses his lips. Doesn't take kindly to rule breaks or to James Golding looking at him like he needs to shut up. He has the right to his own opinions, and he's not subordinate to bloody

Golding. He's just trying to look out for Chester, although no one seems to recognise that. His new heart monitor vibrates on his wrist and starts beeping. He looks down and sees that his heart rate has gone into the red zone, *blast it.*

'Take a couple of deep breaths,' says Lizzie, putting her hand over his.

Philip does as she says, and starts to feel a bit calmer.

Lizzie smiles. 'It'd be good to see the video, right?'

'I'd like to see it,' says Rick, giving Philip a rueful look that says, *it's here now so let's go with it.*

Philip nods and keeps taking the deep breaths. The doctor has him keeping a journal of all the times his heart rate goes into the red zone. He's not supposed to be getting worked up, but he's always been quick to react to things. As he told the doc at the time, it's going to be pretty difficult to keep his heart rate in the range they'd prefer. 'Yes, yes, of course, I just don't want Chester getting into trouble.'

'He'll be fine,' says James Golding, waving away Philip's concerns.

Chester nods. 'I'm okay with it.'

'Fine,' says Philip, conceding defeat. He takes a cookie and munches through it fast. He's hungry and irritated. Very hungry.

'Alright then,' says Golding, tapping the screen to start the video. 'Here we go.'

On-screen the video starts to play. Chester is sitting at a grey, plastic table opposite Cal Staples. There's another man in the room, leaning up against the wall by the door, wearing a badly fitting suit. Philip recognises him as the man who'd attended Sindee McGillis's crime scene – Detective Thomas Durcell. It's clear from the questioning that the interview has already been going on for a while.

'Interview with Cal Staples reconvened at 19.47. Detectives Golding and Durcell are present,' says Chester Golding. He passes a piece of paper across the table to Staples. 'It's signed.'

Staples takes the paper and reads it. Nodding, he looks back at the detectives. 'Okay.'

'You've got what you want, so talk,' says Durcell, gruffly.

'Well, the thing is.' Staples looks down at the paper in front of him. 'Super-max doesn't sound so nice. How about an open facility, and a decent TV?'

'No chance,' growls Durcell. 'Keep talking or I'll rip up that agreement and have the prosecutor push for the death penalty. Your only decision will be whether you want the needle or the chair.'

Across the table from Philip, Moira frowns, unimpressed. 'You gave him a deal?'

'It was the only way to make him talk,' says Chester.

'Keep watching,' says Golding, bossily. He drops his shades back over his eyes. 'It was worth it, you'll see why.'

Philip isn't convinced, and he can tell from Moira's expression that she isn't either. He hates deals being cut. If people do the crime they should do the time, it's as simple as that. Anything less short-changes the families of the victims.

'How much time will Staples do?' asks Moira.

Chester opens his mouth to reply but his uncle beats him to it.

'I don't know what's on the paper,' says James Golding, shrugging. 'Ten years? Maybe a bit less if he plays nicely inside.'

'But first-degree murder is life without parole,' says Rick, frowning. 'He's guilty on two counts, and that's not even including the attempted murder of Moira.'

Golding shrugs again. 'Just watch it, yeah.'

Philip clenches his fists. Ten years doesn't sound much like justice to him. He feels his heart rate increasing. Tries to calm himself, and breathe deeply, but a couple of seconds later the heart monitor starts beeping.

'Oh, for God's sake,' he says, ripping off the Velcro strap and chucking the heart monitor on the table. 'Bloody thing.'

Lizzie looks at him and his discarded heart-rate monitor, worried. 'Philip? The doctor said—'

'Fine, fine,' he says, reaching across the table for the monitor and strapping it back on to his wrist. 'Just play the tape.'

Chester taps the screen and the video continues to play.

'The apartments on the eighth floor were finished almost a year ago, but the owners wanted to sell the units on the lower levels before opening up the penthouses to the market. It seemed a waste, all those fancy apartments sitting empty.' Staples grins again. 'So I figured I could put them to a good use.'

'Like what?' says Chester Golding.

'Whatever people wanted, so long as they had money. Units like that can fetch a good price by the hour or the night, you know what I mean?' says Staples, winking.

'Why don't you enlighten us,' says Durcell, scowling.

'No imagination? Well, alrighty then.' Staples leans back on his chair. 'Parties, mainly. Discreet, and exclusive. Special guests and special requests.'

Chester Golding frowns. 'Like?'

'Jeez, do you guys live under a rock? Like high-class hookers and blow.'

Over by the door, Durcell smiles.

The smile is quick, but it tells Philip that the interview with Staples is playing the way the detectives want. Good. Because the smug, boastful way the man is talking really grates on Philip. Two women are dead, and Moira still bears the bruises of her encounter with him. The man has no decency. He doesn't seem regretful one jot.

'How did it work?' asks Chester Golding. 'Didn't anyone notice?'

'I'm smart. Used my head,' says Staples, arrogantly. 'I put out-of-service signs on the elevator when I needed it for exclusive use, and I smuggled the people in through the least-used service entrance. It worked well for months.' His expression darkens. 'Until that bitch found out.'

'Who?' asks Chester Golding.

'Sindee McGillis,' says Staples, spitting out the name. 'It was a week before the broker's open was meant to happen, but she brought some people to the penthouse at sunset for an off-market viewing, and walked in as one of my special parties was just getting started.'

'That can't have been good,' says Durcell.

'True that,' says Staples. 'The bitch managed to get out of there before her clients saw what was going on, but she knew and that's when she became a real problem.'

Chester Golding nods, as if he understands.

'I tried cutting her in on the action first. It was a sweet deal I offered, but she refused. Told me to quit my job within the week or she'd tell the owners what I was doing.' Staples shakes his head. 'I couldn't let that happen. Losing my job and my side hustle wasn't an option.'

'So, you decided to kill her?' says Chester Golding.

'Before the broker's open seemed like a good time. I figured if there'd been a dead body in the penthouse no one would want to buy it anyways, so I'd be able to carry on without interruption for a while longer.'

'But it wasn't Sindee in the penthouse that evening, was it?'

Staples exhales, and for the first time in the interview his cocky demeanour fades. 'I didn't know it was Jessie. With all that platinum-blonde hair, and the way she dresses, she looked just like her boss out there on the balcony. I was really close before she turned around, and by then it was too late – she'd seen the knife.'

'But you didn't stab her?' asks Chester Golding.

Staples shakes his head. 'Didn't feel right. I figured a dive off the balcony was a kinder way to go.'

284

'A kinder way to go? This man threw an innocent young woman to her death and he thinks he was being kind?' Philip curses out loud. 'And you gave him a deal!'

Rick grimaces. Moira and Lizzie frown.

'Please keep watching,' says Chester. 'We get the right outcome, you'll see.'

'Then what happened?' asks Chester Golding.

'I got the hell out of there,' says Staples. 'I erased the video files from the cameras that'd caught my movements, and when I got called out to let the cops into the apartment, I acted like I knew nothing.'

'How did Sindee react?'

'Well, that was a bit of a bonus,' says Staples, the smug tone returning to his voice. 'She was really shaken and didn't believe Jessie killed herself, even if that's what the coroner's report said. I'd used Jessie's cell to send that "I'm sorry" message to her folks, but I wasn't sure they'd believe it – that the cops latched on to that was a real stroke of luck. So, I made up a bunch of stuff about how it was a criminal gang who bankrolled my special parties, and that they killed Jessie, thinking she was Sindee, and that me and her, we were both in danger now – if we didn't shut up, we'd both be next.' He laughs. 'It worked too, until those seniors began poking into Jessie's death, and Sindee started getting twitchy. I told her to sit tight and it'd blow over, but she wouldn't. When they called that big meeting in the penthouse, she told me she was going to tell them everything. I couldn't allow that.'

'So, you killed her?' asks Chester Golding.

'Stabbed her, as I'd originally planned to,' says Staples, with a shrug. 'She bled more than I'd figured. I had to clean myself up fast, before the seniors got fed up of waiting for her and I was summoned to the eighth floor to open the penthouse for them.'

It shouldn't shock him, the man's lack of empathy for his victims, because he'd had a lot of killers in his interview room over the years, but Philip feels sickened by Staples. The lack of remorse, and the smugness about what he did and the deal he's got. It makes him sick to his stomach.

'And what about the criminal gang?' asks Durcell.

'What gang?' says Staples. 'I told you I made that up to get Sindee to play ball. This was my operation. My smarts. My money.'

'Is that right?' says Durcell, walking over to the table and picking up the paper. He smiles at Staples, and then shakes his head. 'Then that's your deal voided.'

Staples' smug expression disappears as he realises his error. 'But, I—'

'You couldn't resist, could you? You couldn't let anyone else take credit for what you did? Not when you're so damn pleased with yourself. But your deal was conditional on you giving up the names of everyone else involved. If there wasn't anyone else, then there's no deal.' Durcell shakes his head, looking at Staples with utter contempt. 'Pride comes before a fall, and your fall is going to see you locked away for the rest of your life.'

James Golding taps the screen of the tablet and stops the video. 'There you have it, folks.'

'Was there ever a deal?' asks Moira.

Golding shrugs. 'Who's to know for sure, but if there—'

'No,' says Chester, interrupting his uncle. 'I had a hunch that Staples was trying his luck by using some bullshit "I'm just a pawn for a bigger gang" excuse to try and get his sentence reduced, and Durcell backed me up.'

Philip's impressed. Durcell might have been a lazy whatnot earlier in the case, but agreeing with Chester and the way they'd played Staples had been a good judgement call. 'A chap like Staples would never want to appear subordinate. Fraudsters and psychopaths always want to boast about what they've done in the end.'

'For sure,' says Rick. He looks at Chester. 'You did a good job.'

'I think so,' says James Golding, nodding smugly.

Rick shakes his head. 'I meant you, Chester.'

Chester looks a little embarrassed. 'Thank you.'

'What happens next?' asks Lizzie.

'Staples has been charged, and the prosecutor is keen to push for the death penalty, but whatever happens he's going to live the rest of his days in a jail cell,' says Chester.

Good, thinks Philip. They've caught the killer, and justice will be served. It's the best they could hope for. He reaches for another cookie.

'You've already had one,' says Lizzie; her tone is gentle, but firm. 'You know what the doctor said.'

Reluctantly, Philip comes away empty-handed. The doctor has put him on to a special 'healthy heart' diet and Lizzie is making sure he sticks rigidly to it. He's not allowed any of the good stuff – no cream, or full-fat milk, or treacle pudding, or bacon. His stomach rumbles. He really misses the bacon.

Lizzie gives him a smile. 'There's some carrot sticks and hummus in the fridge if you're hungry.'

Philip grimaces. He doesn't want bloody hummus and carrot. He's not a rabbit.

James Golding takes a cookie and has a big bite. 'These are delicious, Lizzie. I'll have to stop by more often.'

Philip scowls. 'Isn't it time you were going, Golding?'

'Philip,' says Lizzie, sternly. 'Don't be rude.'

'It's okay,' says James Golding, laughing. He stands up, and looks around the table. 'I've had enough of working with y'all to last a lifetime.' He gives Lizzie a smile. 'Aside from you, sweetheart, I've never met such a bunch of uptight, interfering assholes.'

We're a good team, thinks Philip, watching Golding finish the cookie. 'You're the arsehole.'

'You should go,' says Lizzie, stiffly, as she gets to her feet. 'I'll see you out.'

'Until next time,' says James Golding, winking at Philip.

'There won't be a next time,' says Rick, under his breath.

James Golding looks towards Rick and laughs. 'I reckon I'll be arresting you meddling seniors for sticking your noses into something again soon enough.'

'*You* asked for our help,' says Rick, clenching his fists.

Philip catches Rick's gaze and gives a little shake of his head. 'He's not worth it.'

James Golding laughs, and points his fingers, gun-style, at Rick. 'See you soon, champ.'

As Lizzie leads James Golding back through the house to the front door, Philip does his best to keep his breathing calm and steady.

'I'm so sorry,' says Chester, getting up to follow his uncle. 'I shouldn't have brought him, but he insisted. He told me he was going to apologise for his behaviour at the operation.'

'It's fine,' says Philip. 'You did a good job with the case. Thanks for the update.'

Chester nods. He picks up the tablet and smiles at the three retired detectives. 'Thank you, again. I really couldn't have done it without you guys.'

As Chester hurries after Lizzie and his uncle, Philip does a few more deep breaths.

'You okay?' asks Rick.

'Yes, yes. I'm fine now that awful man has gone,' says Philip. 'Let's go back inside.'

They wait in the kitchen. On the countertop are the morning papers from the UK – a couple of broadsheets and one of the more quality redtops, which Lizzie likes to order for the telly guide and soaps round-up. Today the headlines are all about the same case – the uncovering of police corruption in the London Met's most senior ranks, and the capture of a major criminal kingpin, Bobbie Porter.

Philip taps the headline of the paper on the top of the pile, *DIRTY COPPER AND HIS KINGPIN LOVER*, and looks at Moira. 'Looks like there's trouble in the Met. That's your old force, yes?'

'It was,' says Moira. She looks pensive, and from her tone it's clear she doesn't want to talk about the news.

Philip watches as Moira glances at Rick and a look passes between them. There's concern in Rick's expression, and something Philip can't quite identify in Moira's. 'You okay?' he asks her.

'Yeah,' says Moira, turning away and looking out toward the garden. 'I'm fine.'

Philip frowns.

If there's one thing he's sure of, it's that Moira isn't fine.

50

MOIRA

'You want a ride?' asks Rick.

Moira looks at his hopeful expression and into his kind eyes, and almost says yes, but instead she shakes her head. She needs to be on her own right now. 'I think I'm going to walk back. It's such a lovely day.'

Rick looks crestfallen, but quickly manages to hide it. 'Okay, sure.'

They stand next to the jeep, on the pavement outside Philip and Lizzie's place, with the silence growing awkward between them. Rick shuffles his feet from side to side, looking like he's building up to saying something.

'Well, I'd better get going,' says Moira. 'It was nice to see you.'

'You too,' says Rick, holding her gaze, an intense expression on his face.

They've still not spoken properly about Estelle – what happened between Rick and his daughter when Alisha died, or what's been going on since Estelle and Bibi showed up on his doorstep almost two weeks ago. And since they got back from Shimmering Sands, he's been fully occupied with settling them in.

The time apart has made Moira realise just how much she'd been enjoying her time with him, and how quickly he'd become an important part of her new life. And that scares her. Especially given what she's done.

She gives Rick a small smile, then turns and heads home.

As she walks along the pavement, Moira thinks of the newspapers lying on Philip and Lizzie's countertop. She didn't know the story would break today, and so she hasn't had the chance to read the articles yet, but from the headlines alone, she knows that sending the contents of the USB to several news outlets has worked. She also emailed the files to the top brass in Internal Affairs at the Met and the London mayor's office, and has had several phone conversations with investigators who have been assigned the case. She wonders how far they've got in the investigation, and whether her old boss, Detective Superintendent Harry George, has been arrested yet.

She wonders what he will say.

Moira reaches the junction at the end of the road. Rick's jeep passes her, en route to his home, and she stops. Thinking. Instead of turning left, towards her house, she heads right. The small Publix along the street stocks international newspapers and it's only a ten-minute walk from here. She can't put it off any longer; she needs to know exactly what the media are saying and she doesn't want to just read it online. She needs to see it in print. Hold the physical newspapers carrying the story in her hands. Then she'll believe that it's true.

The mid-morning sun is growing in strength, the heat reflecting back at her from the pavement. Along the road, the heat makes the air dance, hazy above the blacktop. It's going to be another gorgeous day here in Florida, but, given the time of year, the temperature is probably barely above freezing back in London.

◆ ◆ ◆

She reads the papers sitting outside on her covered patio, with the dogs sleeping at her feet in the shade. A pair of blue jays peck at the seed on the bird table, and a single squirrel works hard to get some peanuts from the hanging feeder. The newspaper headlines are all versions of the same theme:

DIRTY COPPER AND HIS KINGPIN LOVER

MET IN SLEAZE & VICE SHOCKER

CORRUPTION DEEP IN THE MET: WHEN WILL IT END?

LUST & LIES: THE DOWNFALL OF DIRTY HARRY

Moira reads each one in turn, from the broadsheets to the red tops. She looks at the pictures: the super yacht where Bobbie Porter lived when she was in London; Bobbie Porter being led into court in handcuffs, her head bowed; Detective Superintendent Harry George being escorted from the offices of New Scotland Yard in handcuffs, glowering defiantly at the camera, his fury clear from his expression; the photos from McCord's USB showing Harry and Bobbie together, intimately. A crime scene picture that literally shows Bobbie Porter holding a smoking gun. Neither of them is going to get away with what they did. The evidence is too plentiful, and too damning. Or at least Moira hopes it is.

She takes a sip of her coffee. All the papers bar one mention the evidence having been sent to them by an unnamed police source, but compiled by the talented young detective, Al McCord, before his death while working a case to bring down Bobbie Porter's organisation. Two of the papers mention another gifted young detective who lost her life in the same operation as McCord: Jennifer Riley. They also mention that the leader of the operation, Detective Chief

292

Inspector Emily Platt, was injured in the line of duty and medically retired shortly afterwards. They say they were unable to reach her for comment.

She hopes they won't try any harder to reach Emily Platt.

Moira flinches as her mobile starts buzzing on the table somewhere beneath the papers. Rummaging about, she finds it, frowning when she sees the London number on-screen.

She hesitates for a moment, then answers. 'Hello.'

'DCI Emily Platt?' says an unfamiliar male voice.

Moira says nothing. Her heart rate accelerates. Her mouth goes dry.

'Hello? Can you hear me?' says the man, his clipped British accent edged with concern. 'This is Barnaby Sedgewick, I'm calling from executive recruitment at the Met.'

Toggling to her internet browser app, Moira searches for Barnaby Sedgewick. He comes up on the Met's website as leading the team who handle top-level recruitment. There's a picture: he's mid-thirties, with a close-cropped Afro, kind eyes and a handsome face.

She toggles back to the call. 'Can you switch to video?'

'Erm, okay . . .' There's a bit of rustling at the other end, then Barnaby appears on-screen.

Moira exhales. It's him: the guy from the Met website. 'Hi. I'm DCI Platt, or at least I used to be.'

'Excellent,' says Barnaby. 'I'm glad I've managed to track you down. There's no record of your latest address on any system.'

'I know,' says Moira. Refusing to say more.

Barnaby's smile fades slightly. He looks a little confused. 'I managed to get your number from your contact in IA and I'm calling firstly to thank you, you'll have seen the media today I'm sure, and thanks to the evidence your team compiled we have strong cases against Bobbie Porter, Harry George, and a bunch of others.

Nothing is guaranteed, of course, but the prosecutor is hopeful we'll get the right result at trial.'

'Okay,' says Moira, wondering why her Internal Affairs contact didn't call if they'd simply wanted to thank her.

'Anyway, that's not actually the reason I'm calling,' says Barnaby. 'I know you took medical retirement last year, but we'd like you to come back to the force. Your record was exemplary – you closed more cases than ninety-nine per cent of our other detectives, and you've helped remove a major player, and a source of corruption in our own ranks, when you could've walked away.'

Moira starts shaking her head. 'I don't think I—'

'Wait, don't make a decision right away, but know if you do choose to return you'll get a promotion to chief superintendent, and an uplift in pay to match. More importantly, we want you to head up a new anti-corruption squad. We can't be sure that we've caught all the bad apples. Porter and George could have bullied or turned other officers, and we need them identified and exited. And there could be others like McCord who've been blackmailed into doing the criminal gang's bidding. Porter is in custody, but there are others from her organisation still out there. Until the whole network is dismantled, no one is safe.' Barnaby gives her a sincere look. 'We think you're the best person to get that job done. We can't have what happened to McCord and Riley happen to anyone else, can we?'

Moira feels his words pummel her like a one-two punch to the stomach. Al McCord, Jennifer Riley and all the other victims of Porter's empire deserve justice. She doesn't want to go back, but she wants Bobbie Porter's organisation dismantled and any other officers under their control released. She's surprised to hear herself say, 'Okay, I'll think about it.'

'Great. Take your time, and let us know in a couple of weeks,' says Barnaby, giving her a smile. 'We're really keen to have you back with us, DCI Platt.'

'Like I said, I'll think about it,' says Moira, and ends the call.

She looks at her three dogs snoozing peacefully in the shade of the patio cover. Feels the warmth of the Florida sunshine on her skin. And remembers the new-found camaraderie with her ex-law enforcement friends – Philip, Lizzie and Rick – and the fact that Rick is more than a friend, and could, maybe, be a lot more.

Then she thinks about McCord diving from the balcony back in London, and Riley bleeding out in her arms, and all the other people damaged by Harry George and Bobbie Porter. Tension builds inside her, and her stomach begins to churn.

Moira needs to make a decision.

51

LIZZIE

Two weeks later

Lizzie hears the opening notes of 'Ode to Joy' floating above the sounds of the ocean and knows it's her cue. Taking a breath, she tightens her grip around the bouquet of pale pink roses and white gardenia blooms, and steps on to the beach. Her pink polished toenails sink into the warm, sugar-white sand, and she smiles.

This is perfect.

She walks along the pathway lined by white velvet ropes, following it across the beach towards the floral archway. Her long, floaty cream chiffon dress ripples in the sea breeze and she's thankful. It's scorching hot, and the light wind gives some welcome respite from the early afternoon sun.

Up ahead, beyond the people sitting in the chairs either side of the pathway, Rick and Moira stand to the right of the flower-covered archway. David DeBoise, the officiate for the ceremony, stands to the left. In the middle, in his smart trousers and white linen shirt, looking nervous, is Philip. He smiles when he sees her, and Lizzie wonders if he'd been as worried about her not turning up today as he had been when they got married all those years ago. She meets his gaze and smiles back.

As 'Ode to Joy' continues playing, she moves across the sand to join Philip. He reaches out and takes her hand, and she kisses him on the cheek. It means a lot to her that he's here, renewing their vows on St Pete Beach – one of her favourite places in the world. He isn't a fan of beaches, but once he knew that it was her dream, he'd insisted they do it, even though he hates the sand. She'd worried he'd only agreed because he had been given more bad news about his health after his mini heart attack, and wanted to give her something nice to remember him by. But as the days have passed, and he's looked healthier and stronger with each one, she's slowly started to stop worrying. Almost.

'You look beautiful,' he says.

'So do you.'

Lizzie looks down at his white trainers and smiles again. They were the one thing he insisted on – to stop the sand getting on his skin. She wiggles her own toes in the sand, and looks back at their friends, who've travelled here from The Homestead, sitting in the horseshoe-shaped row of white wooden chairs that surrounds the archway. There's Mark and Jack, the hippie academic twins, wearing matching white suits and even more multicoloured beaded brace-lets and necklaces than usual. Next to them sits Hank, who works part-time at the CCTV hut as well as being a resident, and along from him are community patrollers Wendy-Mae with her little dog, Sweetie, in a cute baby-blue handbag, and Jayne Barnett alongside her. Lizzie knows Philip will be especially happy when he discovers Jayne has brought a celebration cake baked by her father for them to enjoy later.

On the other side of the aisle, Olivia Hamilton Ziegler sits next to her friend Betty. They're both wearing jewel-coloured maxi dresses; Betty has styled hers with her usual pearls, while Olivia wears a long, gold necklace. Betty's friend, Alfred, is resplendent in a periwinkle-blue cropped silk shirt over a rather wonderful black tweed kilt. Sandi, the landlady from The Roadhouse where they hold the patrollers' meetings, sits next to him in a simple yellow shift dress and sandals. On the end of the row are Estelle and Bibi, Rick's daughter and granddaughter. Little Bibi waves at Lizzie, and Estelle gives her a thumbs up. They might have only known Lizzie for a week, but they're already a welcome part of the group.

Lizzie stifles a sigh and smiles back at them. She wishes her kids could have flown out for the ceremony, but with their work and the grandchildren's school term, they aren't able to make it to Florida for a few more months. It doesn't matter though, she decides. They'll just have a wonderful party to celebrate once they are here.

David DeBoise clears his throat and gives Lizzie and Philip a little nod. Lizzie turns to Philip. His eyes are shining and he looks happy.

Lizzie smiles. This is everything that she'd hoped it would be.

As the waves roll on to the shore, the sea birds soar overhead, and the sun shines down on them, the ceremony to renew their vows begins.

52

MOIRA

It's a beautiful ceremony.

Moira's never been married. Never been engaged. Until just over a year ago her whole life had been her work; it had meant everything to her. Lovers had come and gone, six months here, one night there, but she'd never had the time, or the inclination, for deep, involved relationships. Never had much time for friends, even. Not until now.

She watches as Lizzie and Philip walk along the beach to have some photos taken at the shoreline as the setting sun turns the sky on the horizon a rainbow of purples, pinks and oranges, and smiles. Then she feels her phone buzzing in her bag.

Pulling it out, Moira sees that she has two missed calls and a voicemail. Dialling the answer service, she puts the handset to her ear and listens.

'Emily, hi, it's Barnaby Sedgewick, calling from the Met Police. It's been a couple of weeks and so I'm going to have to ask for your answer. We're all keen to get you back on board and up to speed on the investigation. Give me a call, please. I know you'll do the right thing.'

Moira saves the message and ends the call.

She's been putting off the decision, but it's crunch time now.

The Met want an answer.

Standing up, she walks past the wedding arch, and out towards the waves lapping the beach. She looks out across the ocean. She came to Florida to hide from her old life, and to start a new one: less stress, less pressure, and no connection to crime fighting and law enforcement. But things have turned out a little different.

It's gorgeous here, but bad things still happen in beautiful places. She thinks of the Becktons, who moved to the beach for the promise of a retirement in paradise, and lost their only daughter when she moved to be closer to them. The state prosecutor is confident they'll secure the conviction of Cal Staples, but Moira knows it can never make up for losing Jessie. All it will give the Becktons is the knowledge that the person who killed their daughter will live the rest of their life behind bars. Although, perhaps then they'll be able to start to get closure, and to heal. Perhaps.

She takes a breath, inhaling the salty sea air.

Maybe, with Bobbie Porter in custody, and the Met taking action against her ex-boss and mentor, she herself will be able to begin the healing process. She can't bring back Al McCord and Jennifer Riley, but if Porter and George are found guilty at trial and sent down, she will, finally, have got her colleagues justice. And she'll have got justice for herself too. Won't she?

Moira thinks about what Barnaby said, about dismantling the whole of Porter's criminal empire, and the size of the work that still needs to be done, and exhales hard. The offer is very attractive, she can't deny that. This moment feels like another tabula rasa. Her slate is clean now. It's up to her to write what happens next – stay here in Florida, or go back to London.

'You want to tell me about it?' says Rick, from behind her.

'Sorry, I was miles away,' says Moira, turning to face him.

He smiles. 'I know. Anything I can help with?'

She shakes her head. 'No, it's fine, really.'

'Okay then,' says Rick. He looks a little awkward; worried. Fiddling with the cuff of his linen suit jacket. 'I wanted to talk to you, if that's okay?'

'Sure.'

'I'm sorry I didn't tell you about Estelle. We'd not spoken in years, and I was embarrassed that my own daughter wanted nothing to do with me. And I was worried, that if I told you about it, you'd want nothing to do with me either.'

'I wouldn't have judged you,' says Moira, softly.

'I know,' says Rick. 'But *I* judged me. I should have behaved better when Alisha was ill, but I threw myself into the job rather than being there with her. It was only in her last few weeks that reality hit me and I took a leave of absence to nurse her. I still regret not doing it sooner.'

'And that's what drove you and Estelle apart?' asks Moira.

'Largely that, yes,' says Rick. 'And her controlling boyfriend.'

He tells her everything: the arguments between him and Estelle before Alisha died, how Estelle moved out right after the funeral, how she'd married Mark really quickly, and that Rick hadn't been invited. Then about all the times Rick had tried to make contact, and how he'd been turned away. About the letters and postcards. How Estelle had told him now that she'd never known he'd written her, and kept trying to build a bridge between them for all these years, and that her husband had abused her, manipulated her, and controlled her life, until she'd recently, finally, broken free. He tells Moira how he'd not even known he had a granddaughter, and that Estelle and Bibi are going to stay with him for a few months while they get back on their feet. He tells her that it doesn't need to change anything between the two of them. That Estelle understands. That Moira's the first woman he's felt anything for since the death of Alisha.

When he's finished talking, Moira takes him in her arms and holds him close. She feels his strong, man mountain-like body against hers, and wishes they could stay in this embrace forever, and forget the rest of the world.

But real life isn't like that.

Slowly, she pulls away. 'It's okay. I get it.'

'I'm not sure if you do,' says Rick, his expression serious. Reaching out, he takes hold of her hands. 'I love you, Moira Flynn.'

She looks into Rick's handsome face and sees the tenderness in his expression, and the hope. He loves her, the her that is Moira Flynn. Then she thinks about the message on her voicemail. The Met want her back, the her that is Emily Platt, and they'll give her a promotion, a grand title and a team to take down the entire criminal network built by Bobbie Porter.

She squeezes his hands. 'I . . .'

Rick puts a finger to her lips, and smiles. 'I don't expect you to say it back, but I wanted you to know how I feel. I've kept my feelings bottled up for way too long. I want there to be no more secrets between us.'

His words sucker punch her in the heart. There are already so many secrets between them, but he just doesn't know it. Should she stay here in Florida, living her new life as Moira Flynn with good friends around her, and see where this relationship with Rick might go? Or should she return to London as Emily Jane Platt, rejoin the Met Police, and hunt down every last element of Bobbie Porter's criminal empire?

It's time.

She can't put it off any longer.

Moira takes a deep breath, and makes her decision.

ACKNOWLEDGEMENTS

Firstly, thank you so much for reading this book – I hope you enjoyed this latest adventure of the Retired Detectives Club as much as I did writing it. It was fun to take the retired detectives away from The Homestead for a little while, and what could be a better place than the beach!

I am super lucky to work with a wonderful bunch of people. Firstly, a massive thank you goes to my fantastic agent, Oli Munson – a legend and a wise adviser – to whom I owe so much. And to all at A M Heath, for always being fabulous.

The whole Thomas & Mercer team are a dream to work with and I feel incredibly lucky to be working with you all. A gigantic thank you to my editor – the brilliant Victoria Haslam – for all your insightful words, support and guidance. And another huge thank you to the lovely Ian Pindar – you are a structural editing genius. Big thanks to Sadie Mayne and Ian Critchley for your great work in copy-editing and proofing, and to @blacksheep-uk.com for the fantastic cover design. And, as always, an enormous thank you to the lovely Nicole Wagner, and the marketing and PR teams, for all your support and enthusiasm.

As ever, a huge thank you goes out to all my family and friends for your encouragement and support. And a special shout-out to

Andy for all the book chat and cheerleading, and to Red for waiting while I write, always hopeful that it's nearly walk time.

The crime-writing and -reading community is such a lovely place and I'd like to say a huge thank you to everyone for their support, and especial thanks to my best buddies, crime writers extraordinaires Susi Holliday, Alexandra Benedict and Helen Giltrow for their continuous awesomeness. To all the readers, bloggers, reviewers, and fellow crime writers – you are all fabulous!

If you'd like to find out more about me, you can hop over to my website at www.stephbroadribb.com or get in touch via Twitter (@crimethrillgirl) or Facebook (@CrimeThrillerGirl) – it's always great to connect.

And, if it's not too cheeky to ask, if you enjoyed reading this book, I'd really love it if you'd leave a review.

Until next time . . .

Steph x

FREE *CONFESSIONS* BOX SET

Join Steph Broadribb's Readers' Club and get a free box set of short stories including 'The Empty Chair', 'Burning Dust' and 'The Lookout Game'.

You'll also receive occasional news updates and be entered into exclusive giveaways. It's all totally free and you can opt out at any time.

Join here: https://stephbroadribb.com/ and click on Join My Readers' Club.

ABOUT THE AUTHOR

Steph Broadribb was born in Birmingham and grew up in Buckinghamshire. A prolific reader, she adored crime fiction from the moment she first read Sherlock Holmes as a child. She's worked in the UK and the US, has an MA in Creative Writing (Crime Fiction) and trained as a bounty hunter in California.

Along with her other novels in the Retired Detectives Club series – *Death in the Sunshine* and *Death at Paradise Palms* – she has also written the Lori Anderson bounty hunter series and the Starke/ Bell psychological police procedural books (writing as Stephanie Marland). Her books have been shortlisted for the eDunnit eBook of the Year Award, the ITW Best First Novel Award, the Dead Good Reader Awards for Fearless Female Character and Most Exceptional Debut, and longlisted for the *Guardian* 'Not The Booker' Prize.

Along with other crime fiction authors, she provides coaching for new crime writers via www.crimefictioncoach.com.

You can find out more about Steph at www.stephbroadribb.com, and get in touch via Instagram (@CrimeThrillerGirl) and Twitter (@crimethrillgirl).

Follow the author on Amazon

If you enjoyed this book, follow Steph Broadribb on Amazon to be notified when the author releases a new book!
To do this, please follow these instructions:

Desktop:

1) Search for the author's name on Amazon or in the Amazon App.
2) Click on the author's name to arrive on their Amazon page.
3) Click the 'Follow' button.

Mobile and Tablet:

1) Search for the author's name on Amazon or in the Amazon App.
2) Click on one of the author's books.
3) Click on the author's name to arrive on their Amazon page.
4) Click the 'Follow' button.

Kindle eReader and Kindle App:

If you enjoyed this book on a Kindle eReader or in the Kindle App, you will find the author 'Follow' button after the last page.